As Max stepped across the threshold into twelve-year-old Alex Dantell's room, she froze. Wolfe  *nearly collided w*

The mattress had been and slashed open. Che science kits were dump

"Alex did this?" Max asked, wishing she believed it.

Steve's loud curse confirmed her fear as he pushed past her into the room. The P.I. turned to stare at her and Wolfe. "I was just up here not a half hour ago."

Wolfe touched Max's shoulder, turning her attention to the wall where a family portrait hung. Atchison and Yvonne Dantell stood on either side of their son. They all smiled brightly into the camera.

Glass clung in shards to the picture frame, which was cracked around the blade of a long, narrow dagger. The blade tip had struck precisely in the center of the boy's chest.

"I think," Max said, "that someone besides us is already looking for the boy. And we do *not* want that person to find him first."

Dear Reader,

From the moment I heard Silhouette was planning a line of stories about "strong, savvy, sexy heroines," I knew I wanted to write one. It only makes sense, since I grew up in a family of strong women, with parents who told me I could be anything I wanted to be.

Growing up, I wanted to be an explorer, an astronaut, a secret agent—and a writer. I haven't accomplished the first three yet, but thanks to Bombshell, I can finally let loose my inner Indiana Jones.

My heroine, Mad Max Riley, has a knack for finding trouble, and she isn't afraid to kick a little butt. She has a softer, romantic side, but any man who wants to see it is going to have to be able to keep up with her!

I hope you enjoy Max's adventures in *Missing Incorporated* as much as I've enjoyed writing them.

Tess Pendergrass

TESS PENDERGRASS

MISSING INCORPORATED

Silhouette®

BOMBSHELL™

Published by Silhouette Books

America's Publisher of Contemporary Romance

SILHOUETTE BOOKS

ISBN 0-373-51402-6

MISSING INCORPORATED

TESS PENDERGRASS

As a child, Tess dreamed of exploring the Nile, climbing Mt. Everest, or becoming an astronaut. She became a writer instead, which turned out to be an adventure of its own. And even if she has never made it to outer space (or even Egypt), she *has* climbed mountains, flown a Blackhawk helicopter (in a training simulator) and swum in an alligator-infested pond (though not on purpose). Tess grew up in the fog in Northern California, but currently lives in sunny, steamy Georgia with her husband and daughter, their sixteen-year-old cat, and Maggie, the devil dog. She has learned to love sweet tea and tries to avoid the alligators.

For my sister, Katy, the most intrepid woman I know.
Thanks, K, for everything.

Chapter 1

Max Riley adjusted the optical zoom of her digital camera. Her subject telescoped closer across the shallow river valley below. Shaggy hair and several months' growth of beard couldn't hide his arching cheekbones and thin lips, or the faint scar across his nose from a close encounter with some Class V rapids in South America three years before.

Max's pulse pumped up a notch as she clicked a rapid succession of photos from behind her screen of low-lying arctic shrubs, their autumn shades of russet and saffron providing her ample camouflage.

Her quarry knocked his boots against the rough-timbered porch of the valley's small cabin before entering with his morning's catch of rainbow trout and Dolly Varden.

Max edged backward on knees and elbows until she dropped out of the cabin's line of sight, below the ridge.

"What did you see?" Lionel, her assistant, demanded as she scrambled to where he waited with their packs in a stand of spruce trees. His blue eyes flashed with eagerness beneath unkempt black bangs. At twenty-four, he was only five years younger than Max, but sometimes his youthful enthusiasm made her feel ancient. "Did you see him? Is it Dantell?"

"It's him." Max flicked on the camera's view screen to give Lionel a look.

Lionel's breath hissed through his teeth. "I wouldn't have recognized him if I'd passed him on the street. He looks like shit."

Max took another glance at the tiny figure on her camera screen. He wasn't just shaggy, he was gaunt. Atchison Dantell's overalls sagged on his spare frame. Max guessed he was finding feeding himself off the land a lot harder than trekking the Andes with a world-class film crew or climbing Kilimanjaro with a bevy of local porters to pack his supplies.

He was sticking it out, though. She had to give him that. He'd disappeared into this Alaskan wilderness after his plane crashed nearly four months before, and, as far as she knew, had received only minimal supplies, flown in less than once a month.

"This guy's serious," Lionel said. This was his first "find," but even the excitement of success couldn't disguise the doubt in his voice. "I don't think he's going to be too happy to see us."

"Probably not." It wouldn't be the first time Max had

tracked down a missing person who didn't want to be found. She checked the knife sheath hooked to her belt. She didn't expect violence, but it was best to be prepared.

"I thought he was dead," Lionel admitted, as Max packed her camera into her daypack. "I mean, why would a guy like that run out on the life he had? One of the world's most famous adventure photographers. Heir to a fortune. Did you see that Maserati in his garage? A supermodel wife. I don't get it."

The wife hadn't gotten it, either, Max thought. Yvonne Dantell had displayed more anger than grief when she'd begged for Max's help finding her missing husband, but she'd been certain he was dead.

"Why would he walk out on all of this?" Yvonne had demanded, striding ahead of Max and Lionel through the Dantells' Pacific Heights mansion in San Francisco. Despite the airy feel of the raised ceilings, comfortable oak furniture and Ansel Adams prints, Max estimated the value of the living room's furnishings alone to be worth more than her entire condo.

"Those idiots up in Alaska couldn't find a grizzly bear if it walked up and bit them in the ass." Yvonne had gestured them impatiently toward the leather sofa. "Maybe there was no body in the plane wreckage, but it's got to be somewhere."

Yvonne had thrown herself into a matching dove gray leather recliner, but her long, slender fingers paced the chair's arms restlessly. "They're telling me that without definitive evidence that he was killed, I might have to wait seven years to have him declared dead. Seven years before Alex can inherit his father's money. Don't they understand that Atch is a man who had everything? He just inherited his father's media empire, for God's sake. He was going to be company president. Could anyone give up all of that?"

Seeing the bitterness frozen into Yvonne Dantell's stunning bone structure, listening to the story of a man about to lose his world-hopping freedom to assume leadership of a company he had by all accounts never shown any interest in, Max began to wonder if maybe someone could. And she had felt the first niggling doubt about Atchison Dantell's death.

"I don't think finding him alive is going to give Mrs. Dantell the closure she was hoping for."

Lionel's voice snapped Max back to the wilds of Alaska, to a cool breeze that filled her suddenly tight lungs with all the expanse of a thousand miles of near-empty mountains.

"I didn't take this on to get closure for Yvonne Dantell."

She had been about to turn down the search when Yvonne had called in the Dantells' son, Alex. Tall for his twelve years, blond like his mother but with his father's thin nose and wiry frame, the boy's blue eyes had filled with desperate hope when his mother had told him Max was going to look for his father.

Max had told herself the kid would survive not knowing what had happened to his dad. He would survive the wild beating of his heart at every ring of the telephone, every knock at the door, every glimpse of a familiar curve of jaw through a crowd, an expectancy that would last for agonizing years, long after any real hope had died. He would survive the sudden, choking grief that would swamp him when he least expected it—blowing out birthday candles or using his learner's permit for the first time.

Alex Dantell would survive the pity and the guilt, the anger and the bursts of gut-hollowing terror. He would survive it all.

Max had. Without so much as a plane crash for explanation.

Maybe if Alex had been a couple of years older, she could have turned her back on him. Maybe if he hadn't been so open, so eager to help.

The raw love and hope and fear that she'd seen in Alex Dantell's eyes had driven her out into this Alaskan wilderness and now it prevented her from leaving Atchison Dantell to his hardscrabble life in this breathtaking valley.

She could understand his walking away from a loveless marriage, from money, from fame, from a life he didn't want. She couldn't understand, or forgive, his walking away from a son who adored him.

"It's time for a little chat with Mr. Dantell." She led Lionel back up to the top of the ridge, crawling once more to her spot behind the bushes. Smoke curled from the cabin's stovepipe chimney.

"What are we going to do?" Lionel whispered, excitement radiating from him. "Break down his door?"

"I think I'll try knocking," Max said dryly, her own tension under tight control. "You head to the river and wait by his canoe. We don't want him skipping out on us before we get a chance to talk."

"Don't you want me to stick close?" Lionel asked. "In case he gets angry?"

Max glanced at her assistant. She hadn't hired Lionel for his physical prowess, but for his skill with computers and gadgets. With his tall, skinny frame and wide, slightly myopic gaze, Lionel looked every inch the computer geek.

She knew he ran three or four miles a day and that his minor in marine biology at UC Santa Cruz had sent him scrambling around ocean cliffs studying sea lions, so she had expected him to be able to keep up with her on this trip, trekking over rough terrain. But she had agreed to his accompanying her only because he had his pilot's license.

Normally, she preferred working alone so she would only be responsible for herself. But she'd brought Lionel with her on this search because she'd known they'd need to hire some minuscule, bone-rattling excuse for an airplane to fly them out into the wilderness, and she'd wanted a backup in case the pilot had a heart attack.

So her fear of flying wasn't completely rational—that was why they called it a phobia.

"Atchison Dantell isn't the violent type," she said. He would have a rifle—he was roughing it in the Alaskan wilderness, after all. But she doubted he would use it on another human being. He wasn't a dangerous criminal. But if things did get ugly, she wanted Lionel out of the way. "I'm more worried about him running than shooting. You've got the longest legs. Stay by the boat until I call for you."

Lionel nodded, satisfied. "Roger."

"Let's do it."

Max pushed herself to her feet and started down the

ridge toward the cabin, Lionel skidding close at her heels. She wasn't eager for the coming confrontation, but it wasn't fear of Atchison Dantell that bothered her.

The end of the chase, she thought. And regret, too. Not pity for Atchison Dantell, but nagging doubt that the answers she found would give young Alex any more peace of mind than not knowing gave her.

Or maybe it was neither of those things. Maybe it was the thought of returning to San Francisco, to her office and her solitary condo and the two travel articles she had to finish for her freelance day job for the *San Francisco Sentinel* by the end of next week.

Maybe she had found Atchison Dantell so quickly not because she was such a talented hunter, but because she understood all too well the restlessness that drove him to escape. Maybe she thought too much like her quarry—maybe all the best hunters did.

Lionel struck upriver toward the rocky beach where Dantell had left his canoe. Max strode straight for the cabin's front door.

As she neared the cabin, she braced herself for the possibility that Atchison Dantell had seen her coming and might greet her at the door with rifle in hand. Doubt, fear, second-guessing—they could only hinder her now. Focus and quick thinking were what had kept her alive through dozens of risky encounters in the past.

Her sharp rap on the door brought a crash and grunt from the cabin's interior, confirming that she'd caught Dantell by surprise.

"Hello?" she called out. "Is someone there?"

She'd hoped a feminine voice would allay his panic

that his hideaway had been discovered, but there was no answer at the door.

"Max!" Lionel's shout turned her toward the river, where Lionel was already in motion, long legs carrying him diagonally across the shrubby meadow away from her. "He's on the move!"

Max dodged around the side of the cabin. *Damn!* The window. Dantell had a hundred-yard head start on her, maybe fifty on Lionel, heading for the ridge opposite her old lookout.

Max raced after them. Despite his gaunt appearance, Dantell's lifelong conditioning kept him ahead of Lionel as they started up the ridge. Max's shorter stride put her at a disadvantage on the level ground. She hit the slope hard, her breath coming sharp from the sprint and the unfamiliar altitude, but she was used to running up stairs. As her legs pumped the incline, she outpaced the men, gaining ground.

Dantell reached the ridge top first, turning to run along it. Lionel paused at the top and shouted something before following.

Max threw herself up the last few yards of the slope, then skidded to a stop as she saw what had excited Lionel. On the other side of the ridge lay a small, narrow lake, a dark jewel set against a backdrop of spruce and birch. Tied to a rough dock at the lakeshore below her was a little Cessna floatplane.

Max swallowed a burst of fury at herself. She should have posted Lionel at the window instead of the river. She should have reconnoitered the area more thoroughly. But regrets wouldn't help her catch Dantell.

He was running toward a spot where a rockslide had smoothed the steep slope of the ridge. A path wound down to the lake and along the shore back toward the plane. He was pulling away from Lionel now. He'd have plenty of time to untie the plane and push away from the dock before pursuit reached him.

Max glanced down the slope below her. *Slope* was a generous term. It wasn't straight down, but the less steep spots were covered with scree. A broken neck waiting to happen. No wonder Dantell was heading for the path, despite his panic.

Max pulled air deep into her lungs, steadying her breath. Lionel wasn't going to catch Atchison Dantell from behind, and neither was she. She had two choices. And she sure as hell wasn't going to choose letting Dantell go.

She breathed again, centering herself, screening out the sounds of running feet, Lionel's shouts, the tension screaming at her that Dantell was getting away.

Calmly, deliberately, she plunged downward, her hiking boots sliding and skipping on the dirt and loose rocks as the barely controlled fall hurtled her toward the lakeshore.

Her right foot skidded into a rock, jolting her off balance. For a second, she lost her footing. Desperately, she bent her knees and lowered her center of gravity, dodging the ground's attack with swift footwork. Her quads screamed, her calves burned, but she hung on to her crouch, skidding down the last ten yards to the jumbled rocks at the bottom.

Her legs shuddered as she sagged to the ground,

gasping for breath. She might have pulled something in her right leg. Her hands burned. Gravel. Maybe a little blood. And her butt hurt. She must have sat down hard at one point, though all she remembered was the blur of movement.

She closed her eyes briefly, in a quick prayer of thanks for surviving. Then she returned to action. A quick glance showed Atchison Dantell scrambling down the saner path several hundred yards away, all his attention on Lionel behind him. If Max kept low, he'd never see her. Her muscles protested as she scrambled behind the piled rocks down to the dock. It was going to be one long, painful walk back to the pickup point.

Unless she could convince Dantell to give her a lift.

Swallowing a gasp of shock as frigid lake water closed around her, she edged out into the water along the dock, then heaved herself up behind the plane.

Dantell had forgotten her, probably assuming she'd given up the chase. He was slowing as he neared the dock and her hiding place. He knew Lionel panted far behind him. He had all the time in the world.

He was reaching for the line tethering the Cessna's nose to the dock when Max opened the cabin door and stepped out of the plane.

"Atchison Dantell, I presume?"

Chapter 2

"Riley. I heard you were back in town."

Max turned toward the familiar voice as she stood in the lobby of the *San Francisco Sentinel* waiting for an elevator. Given a choice, she always took the stairs, but in an attempt to discourage terrorists and disgruntled employees, the building's stairwells were designated for emergency use only.

The man beside her looked like neither terrorist nor journalist in his casual suit, gray with a hint of tweed. His sandy hair, always slightly ruffled as though he'd just come in from a pub crawl, and the fine lines around his eyes from too much time in the equatorial sun gave him an air of bluff bonhomie. But the devilishly amused glint in Davis Wolfe's hazel eyes could easily hide fanaticism or madness.

It did *not* hide the dangerous sharpness of his mind or the rather more dangerous hint of temptation in his smile.

"What brings you slumming today?" he asked, his voice a shade richer than his suit, but with the same slightly rough touch of tweed from his Welsh accent.

Max could never quite decide if the man's 007 charm was meant to seduce her or scoop her.

"Wolfe." She acknowledged him with a nod. "I thought you were off dodging bullets in Sudan or somewhere. There was a rumor you were kidnapped."

"Not successfully. Amateurish attempt. The only real danger we faced was the execrable driving of our local guide." The heat in his smile intensified. "I was almost disappointed you didn't get a chance to rescue me. The idea of being tracked down by Mad Max Riley has a certain appeal."

He probably thought that toe-curling smile was irresistible. Max firmly uncurled her toes. "Whatever makes you think I would have come looking for you?"

His smile turned positively rakish. "You couldn't have resisted the chance to show me up."

The man did have a point there.

"Or the chance to boost your career, rescuing an internationally renowned correspondent."

Max's eyebrows rose in mock surprise. "You had an internationally renowned correspondent with you?"

The elevator doors creaked open on that perfect exit line, but of course Wolfe merely followed her into the car.

"You're here to see Grant," he said.

Max shifted the strap of her briefcase. She had no intention of discussing her appointment with the *Senti-*

nel's senior news editor with Davis Wolfe. "I have a couple of travel articles to turn in."

He nodded at her tailored crimson shirt and black slacks. "You don't dress up for the travel department."

She slanted him a smile. "Maybe I was just hoping to run into you, Wolfe. You know you're irresistible."

He laughed, the humor disarmingly genuine. "Only to my creditors, I'm afraid. What does Grant want? Is he trying to get an exclusive on Atchison Dantell's recent reincarnation? Don't let him bully you. The outdoor adventure magazines will be drooling for that story."

Good advice, except she knew it already. And for all his put-on big-brother arrogance, Davis Wolfe knew she knew it. Her byline might not rival his in international affairs, but she had seriously tweaked his ego when she'd won the *Sentinel*'s Outstanding Story of the Year award that spring. Max had been as surprised as Wolfe that she'd broken his five-year streak taking home the accolade, but she'd never let him know it.

"Don't worry, your Pulitzer dream is safe for this year—there is no Atchison Dantell story," she told him, as the elevator doors opened on the sudden chaos of the newsroom. Keyboards clicked, phones rang, copiers hummed, but it was the tumble of human voices that drove the room's energy. Laughter, arguments, excitement, frustration.

Sometimes she missed it, the insanity of the in-house deadlines, the caffeine jags, the intensity, in the same way that a whiff of ramen noodles made her briefly nostalgic for her college dorm days. Today, the memory of the camaraderie, of feeling a part of something alive and humming, struck her with the force of a blow.

"No story?" Wolfe asked. "A multimillionaire adventurer who regularly appears on magazine covers as one of the world's most beautiful people crashes his plane in the Alaskan wilderness, is presumed dead for four months, then is miraculously found alive—that's a story."

"If you want to write it, be my guest." Max threaded through the aisles of cubicles toward Grant Fowler's office.

That was why she'd quit the paper to go freelance. Freedom. Freedom to follow a story or not. Freedom to pursue her own obsessions. And what had that freedom gotten her? A sporadic byline, just enough income to pay her expenses and a reputation for finding the lost: lost explorers, lost cities, lost souls.

Atchison Dantell's decision to return to civilization to face his son had convinced her the man did have a soul. It was her own she worried about.

Max shook her head, trying to scatter the gloom that had dogged her since her return from Alaska the week before. She had told herself she was just tired, but maybe it was more than that. Maybe—just maybe—the reunion between Atch and his son, Alex, had dug a knife into that empty hole where her own family ought to be.

She frowned at the man keeping pace beside her. She didn't need to fill that hole with Davis Wolfe or any of the rest of the dysfunctional family of the newspaper world.

"You can stop following me now."

Wolfe shook his head, nimbly dodging a scurrying intern. "I'm here to see Grant, too. Urgent business. It better be, or he's paying for the lunch I left behind."

Urgent. That was the message Max's secretary, Simone, had passed along to her just twenty minutes ago. Max had assumed what Wolfe had suggested—that Grant Fowler wanted to pressure her to write a piece about Dantell for the *Sentinel.* But he wouldn't invite Davis Wolfe in for that.

"Interesting," Wolfe agreed, as they arrived together at Grant's door.

A glass wall gave the senior editor's office a clear view of the newsroom. Max could see him through the door, sitting behind his desk, his thick white hair wild as Einstein's, his close-set eyes scowling through round glasses as he spoke on the phone.

He glanced up and gestured for her and Wolfe to enter.

"I don't care what Aldridge threatened," he barked into the receiver as they shut the door behind them. "Being a congressman doesn't give him or his family's company special privileges. Just make damn sure you can back your story up."

He slammed down the phone and turned his gray-eyed scowl on Max and Wolfe. "As Mark Twain put it, 'There is no distinctly American criminal class except Congress.'"

Wolfe raised an eyebrow. "I don't recall him having much good to say about editors, either."

"Or reporters," Grant growled. He pushed himself up from his desk, peering at Max over the tops of his glasses. "Look, kid, you're a good writer. You've got good instincts. But this Atchison Dantell thing—"

"I'm not writing a story about Atchison Dantell," Max said. "Not for anybody. I already told you that."

Her respect for Grant Fowler didn't mean she'd let him intimidate her. She liked writing for the *Sentinel,* and she liked the credibility it gave her in her other pursuits—most of the people who hired her to find their missing treasures—or relatives—knew her from her byline. But if Grant thought he could bully her, he'd find out she didn't need this job badly enough to compromise her principles.

But Grant didn't follow up with threats. His scowl had changed to puzzlement, mixed with relief. "I guess I'm surprised, but I'm glad to hear it. I was worried about how you'd react when I gave the story to Davis."

"To *Wolfe?*" Max turned on the other reporter in outrage at his disingenuous deceit, stealing her story. If he tried that wicked smile on her, she'd wipe it right off. But her fury flickered as she saw he looked just as surprised as she was.

"Considering the financial and sociopolitical implications, I need somebody with Davis's experience." Grant pulled off his glasses and rubbed the bridge of his nose. "I thought that given your contacts in the outdoor adventure field you might take on the human interest side of the story, the biographical stuff, especially since you met the man, but if you're dead set against it, I'll understand, Max."

"What are you talking about, Wolfe's experience?" Max demanded. So she didn't want to write the story. That didn't mean she liked having it taken away. Besides, it didn't make any sense. "I was the one who was there, up in Alaska."

Wolfe didn't look any happier about it than she did.

"I'm sorry, Grant. This touchy-feely stuff isn't my cup of tea. I do hard news, serious journalism. The European Union is struggling with infighting, the Middle East is imploding and this country's federal trade deficit is teetering on the brink. I don't have time to waste on irrelevant human interest—"

"You're saying what I write isn't relevant?" Max kept her voice dangerously low. "Since when did diplomatic maneuvering become more relevant than actual human experience?"

Wolfe grimaced at the frost in her voice, but Grant raised his hands in exasperation.

"What isn't relevant about a billion-dollar multimedia conglomerate?" he barked. "The Burkhartt-Dantell Media Group controls nearly as many radio and television markets as Clear Channel. They own newspapers in fifteen countries. Not to mention a dozen big-name periodicals, a book publisher and a movie studio. You're reporters. Hasn't it ever occurred to you that whoever controls the media controls the dissemination of information? That's power."

Grant slammed his glasses back into place, the better to scowl at them. "Who's going to wield that power now? That's the question."

Wolfe shrugged. "The Burkhartt-Dantell board of directors seemed to have everything under control while Dantell was presumed dead. My guess is he'll leave them to it now he's back. He inherited a large portion of the company when his father, Matthias Dantell, died, but it's not quite a majority interest. If he tries to fight the rest of the board for control, he'll lose."

"He never wanted his father's media empire," Max said. Her brief mention of it on the stomach-twisting flight back to Anchorage had turned Atchison's gaunt face gray. What had he called the board members? *Silver-tongued piranhas*. "But he might fight, if they pushed him to it."

"Oh, hell." Grant's scowl faded as he glanced from Max to Wolfe and back. "You haven't heard."

Max's stomach clenched involuntarily at the tone of his voice. "Haven't heard what?"

Grant ran a hand through his untamable hair. "Atchison Dantell is dead. Verifiably dead this time. He committed suicide last night."

The three-story pink-and-white Victorian gleamed like saltwater taffy between its more somber neighbors in the shocking sunshine of a San Francisco autumn day. That might have seemed appropriate for the travel consultant's business on the first floor, but that afternoon it fit neither Max's own business—Quest Research—nor her mood.

Business. As she climbed the narrow stairs to the third floor, Max scoffed at herself. Businesses offered services and made money. As far as the IRS was concerned, Quest Research was nothing more than a tax write-off. Even taking on the occasional paying client like Yvonne Dantell, Quest's inflow could barely cover the salaries she paid Lionel and Simone, much less the rent and other operating expenses.

It didn't matter. Even without her reporting income, her father had planned her inheritance well. As long as she lived simply, money wouldn't be a deterrent to Quest's continued operations. To her continued search.

Search for what? Max paused before the door at the top of the stairs, the small bronze plaque that read Quest Research, M. Riley. For a sense of purpose? For vindication? For her father?

Sheridan Riley was long dead, as dead as Atchison Dantell. The disappearance of a career diplomat in Istanbul, even the mysterious disappearance of a man as well-respected as Sheridan Riley, didn't generate the kind of media frenzy that Atch Dantell's plane crash had inspired. But it had generated an intense, if low-profile, search by both Turkish authorities and the CIA. If he were alive, he would have been found. It was time for her to accept that and move on with her life.

Her father's assistant and best friend—and Max's martial arts instructor—Tomas Gregory, had suggested as much to her more than once over the past eleven years. She hadn't listened. And now her search for the lost had ended up killing someone.

Max pushed open the door into Quest's main office. Sunlight spilled through the western windows to fill the surprisingly open space with light. Pale oak floors and vanilla walls glowed with warmth, brightened by Turkish carpets and Japanese prints of storks and koi.

The wall to Max's left, between the front door and her private office, was covered with a six-foot-tall Mercator projection of the globe. Not proportionally accurate, but she liked the sepia-toned, old-fashioned print. And, okay, maybe it made her feel a little bit like Indiana Jones.

Not today. Today she felt like Captain Ahab, and from the expressions on her two associates' faces, she looked it.

"Max!" Lionel jumped up from beside Simone's curved desk. "I have something I have to tell you—"

"I know." Max crossed the room, slinging her briefcase down beside Simone's desk. Simone's nutmeg-colored hair was pulled back in a sleek French knot above her sage green suit, and the rest of her looked equally cool and collected, but the concern darkening her eyes confirmed to Max exactly what news Lionel carried.

"It may be a bit of a shock, so you might want to sit—"

"I know," Max repeated.

"It's Atchison Dantell," Lionel burst out, flustered by her response. "He's dead. The official news reports aren't saying any more than that yet, but the rumor is he hanged himself. The SFPD investigators are calling it a suicide."

"I know." Max glared at him. "I heard it from Grant Fowler half an hour ago. I hired you to keep me up to speed on the information superhighway. I just got run off the road."

"Lionel tried to call you before your appointment with Fowler," Simone said calmly. Simone had been raised by a strict grandmother and nuns at a Catholic boarding school. She was hard to intimidate. "He couldn't get through."

Max followed Simone's gaze to her briefcase where her cell phone lay turned off and unchecked. She felt her cheeks redden.

"I don't like to be interrupted," she grumbled, digging out the offending phone and switching it on. Ten messages from Lionel. One from Simone. One from Tomas Gregory. Had he heard, too?

Max blew out the furious irritation she'd been nursing since leaving Grant Fowler's office, clearing room for the sea of guilt it had been holding back.

"I'm sorry," she told Lionel. "This was a closed case, but you were still on top of it. Thanks for trying to warn me."

She dropped into one of the wide cushioned chairs in front of Simone's desk. "Dantell must have known he'd have to return to his life eventually. I thought he was ready to face it."

"It's not your fault." Lionel hovered over her like an anxious stork checking on its chick. "You couldn't have known he was suicidal. I mean, he seemed glad to see his kid. And like you said, he couldn't have hidden out forever. Somebody was bound to stumble across him eventually."

"Maybe." Max couldn't block out the first glimpse she'd gotten of Atch Dantell's eyes when she'd stepped from his plane—the desperate eyes of a trapped animal. "But it didn't have to be me. I didn't have any business dragging a man back to a life he tried to escape."

"His wife paid you," Simone said, her voice tart. "That made it your business. You were out there to find his body, to find closure for his family. It's not your fault he was still alive, and it's not your fault he's dead."

"Of course it's not her fault." The familiar voice, cool and calm with just a hint of something foreign, prompted Max to spin around in her chair. The slender, dark-haired man standing in the office door looked as cool and calm as his voice.

"Tomas!" Max restrained herself from jumping up to

hug him. Tomas Gregory was not the huggy type. "When did you get back?"

"This morning."

She didn't ask where he'd been. He would tell her if he chose. And she didn't say how glad she was to see him. Every time he left on one of his buying trips, she half expected never to see him again. But that was her own baggage. Tomas had left the diplomatic world when her father had disappeared. Being an antiques trader didn't hold the same dangers.

"You heard about Atchison Dantell?" Lionel asked, half eager, half deferential.

Trying to see Tomas from a stranger's perspective, with his pale hazel eyes that seemed to see through a person's soul, his almost preternatural calm and his voice that held just a hint of the Eastern Mediterranean—or maybe of Dracula—Max could see why Lionel and Simone sometimes found him intimidating. Tomas's fulfilling Lionel's lifelong dream by teaching him how to fly a plane had only increased Lionel's awe of the man.

But Max couldn't remember a time when Tomas hadn't been a part of her life. He was the closest thing to a family she had left.

"I tried to call with my news, but Max had her cell phone turned off again," he said.

"We've told Max it's not her fault," Lionel assured him. "Besides, Dantell was in bad shape when we found him. He would have starved over the winter if we hadn't brought him back."

"Of course it's not Magdalena's fault," Tomas repeated, crossing to the windows to close the blinds. In the muted golden light, his eyes turned the dangerous color of whiskey. "But that doesn't mean she bears no responsibility."

Max sank into her chair. "You warned me about sticking my nose where it doesn't belong."

"The day you started this business, four years ago."

Lionel made a strangled noise in his throat. "That's not fair! Max has done a lot of good with Quest Research."

"Not to mention saved lives," Simone added, her own cool finally ruffled. "That anthropology professor in the Amazon, for instance...."

Max tuned them out. *This business.* This business of finding the lost. It had seemed like a good idea at the time, a time when she couldn't do *nothing* any longer. A creative excuse to return to the places her father had been assigned during his diplomatic career, an excuse to investigate him while she investigated other assignments for the *Sentinel* or Quest Research.

Finding a lost city in Morocco for a travel article for Grant Fowler. Investigating the legend of a vanished nineteenth-century train robber in Russia for one of his descendents. Stolen artifacts in Istanbul. A missing activist in Southeast Asia.

Foolishly dangerous, Tomas had called it. *And not only to yourself. You'll learn nothing you want to know.*

"You told me so," she said, just loudly enough to stop the arguing around her. She pushed herself to her feet and turned to Simone. "I'll be in my office, but don't put anyone through. I won't be taking any new cases for a while."

Lionel slapped a palm on the desk. "You're kidding, right? You're not going to let Atchison Dantell put Quest out of business. Just because one case went a little bad—"

"Bad?" Max asked, as sick at the idea of closing Quest down as Lionel. "A man died. How much worse can it get?"

"Worse enough." Tomas's quiet warning sent a sudden shiver down Max's spine.

"What do you mean?"

A dark expression Max couldn't identify crossed Tomas's face. "The president of the Burkhartt-Dantell Media Group has died, leaving one of the most lucrative and powerful media companies in the world without a leader. The wolves are already circling. And pity any lamb that gets in their way...."

He cut himself off. "I assume Lionel ascertained that the police believe Dantell committed suicide?"

Lionel nodded, pleased by Tomas's acknowledgment. "He hanged himself. There was a note."

Tomas glanced over the three of them, the feathery lines in his olive-toned face deepening grimly. "There's another development in this case of which even the police are not aware. The Dantells' son, Alex, is the one who found his father's body. But since telling his story to the detectives late last night, the boy has not been seen.

"Alex Dantell has disappeared."

Chapter 3

The crush of television vans and milling sound technicians blocked traffic in front of the Dantell mansion, despite the best efforts of uniformed SFPD officers. Max had found a two-hour-limit parking spot barely a block away. Apparently the TV crews weren't crazy enough to risk parallel parking on the steep streets leading up to the Pacific Heights aeries.

Max had to admit the view was worth the vertigo. The Dantells' substantial bungalow on its prime corner lot faced north toward the bay. Its neighbors, stately Victorians and Art Deco mansions, crowded close, a phalanx of wealth and privilege overlooking the city the Gold Rush built.

Tension buzzed through the waiting crowd, but it was obvious nothing worth filming was expected any time soon. Max squeezed past a long-haired kid passing out doughnuts and a blond anchor whose assistant was emptying a bottle of hairspray over her in a vain attempt to combat the afternoon breeze.

Davis Wolfe leaned beside the gate to the Dantells' front walk in his faintly disreputable suit, casually chatting with the young officer on the opposite side of the fence. Max's eyes narrowed. Nothing Wolfe ever did was casual.

"Come with me," she ordered, pitching her voice low as she caught Wolfe's elbow.

"What are you doing here?" he demanded, as she steered him down the sidewalk along the wrought-iron fence.

"Grant assigned me to the human interest side of this story, remember?" She gave him a grim smile. "I'm here to help."

"You told Grant you didn't want any part of this story," Wolfe reminded her, his hazel eyes sharp with suspicion. "And I don't need your help. That young officer was just about to spill his guts to my irresistible charm when you—"

"You were still standing on the sidewalk," Max said, guiding him into the narrow walkway between the Dantell mansion and the ornate Queen Anne Victorian next door. "Do you want me to get you inside the house or not?"

As they passed behind a spreading magnolia tree, moving out of sight of the other reporters, Wolfe dug in his heels.

"How do you propose to do that?" he demanded, glancing up at the spike-topped fence. "Breaking and entering? This isn't one of your daredevil stories, Riley. It's a suicide."

"Of a very wealthy and well-connected man," Max agreed, using every technique Tomas had taught her for staying cool under provocation. "So why are you wasting time out here with the talking heads instead of finding out what's going on behind the scenes at the Burkhartt-Dantell Media Group?"

Something between amusement and anger flashed in Wolfe's eyes. He leaned forward, his low whisper intimate against her ear. "According to Officer Williams, Toby Mittard, the vice president—or, rather, the new acting president—of the Burkhartt-Dantell board of directors is inside this house as we speak, consoling the grieving widow. I intend to gain an interview with him when he tries to leave. Highly effective without landing me in jail."

Max turned her head, her nose mere inches from his. Wolfe's eyes glittered dangerously as he smiled. So he thought he was intimidating. She was tempted to leave him to his own devices, but without him, she had no legitimate claim to be reporting on Atch Dantell's suicide.

"Tell me," she purred, straightening up into his space, the warm scent of his aftershave distracting her for only a second. "Did Officer Williams tell you *why* Mr. Mittard risked coming here and being mobbed by nosy reporters instead of making do with a telephone call?"

Wolfe's eyes narrowed. She'd never noticed the green flecks in them before. They darkened in challenge. "You're bluffing. You didn't even know he was here."

"No, I didn't." She held his gaze, hard and steady. "But I do know why he's not going to give you an interview, no matter what you learn from the police."

Wolfe pulled her farther behind the magnolia. "All right. Give."

"Come with me."

He gave a frustrated snort, but he really didn't have much to lose. "Where are we going?"

"Servants' entrance."

The "trade entrance," Yvonne Dantell had called it when she gave Max and Lionel directions for their first consultation. The entrance reserved for visitors Yvonne didn't want the neighbors to see, Max thought with a small smile as she led Wolfe up the narrow lane to an unobtrusive side gate.

"Not locked," she observed, pulling the gate open. "I wonder if Mr. Mittard had to enter this way this afternoon."

"Stop." Wolfe grabbed her arm. "I'm not going in there. *You're* not going in there. That's private property."

"There's a bell." Max pointed to the door recessed under a modest lintel. "For delivery people and reporters. If no one answers, we'll try something else."

"*We* are not doing anything until you tell me what you're doing here." Wolfe's keen eyes narrowed, his piercing scrutiny even more unsettling than his usual flirting. Max feared he saw more than she cared for anyone to see. "What happened between you and Dantell in Alaska? Why were you so determined not to write one of the most compelling stories of your career?"

It would feel good to tell him to go to hell. But the stakes were too high. And little as she liked to admit it, he deserved an answer. She might not trust Wolfe not to steal a hot lead, but she knew he'd risked jail—and, in at least one case, worse—to protect his sources. She had to trust he would protect the safety of a child.

"When Atch Dantell gave that television interview where he said how grateful he was to come home?" She shrugged. "Not so much. I told him I wouldn't lie, but I let him imply he'd been waiting for rescue out there, after bailing out when his plane malfunctioned."

"The plane crash wasn't an accident?"

"He meant to disappear."

Wolfe let out a silent whistle. "I wondered. Where was the big story about how he'd struggled to survive and had almost lost hope of ever being rescued? I thought maybe you were keeping it hush-hush so you could collaborate on a book. Your story, his photographs. *New York Times* bestseller list stuff."

Max shook her head. "No book."

"And you let him get away with that bullshit?"

His disappointment cut unexpectedly deep.

"I didn't do it for him," she snapped. "He wanted to be the one to tell his son why he'd done what he had. I thought Alex deserved that."

Wolfe's chuckle held no humor. "I would never have pictured you for the sentimental type."

"Live and learn."

"I'm always looking to learn more about you, Riley." His dangerous smile flashed as his accent sharpened. "Maybe I can melt that ice water in your veins by telling you about my poor and lonely childhood in the wild hills of northern Wales—"

"Stuff it, Wolfe."

"It's not your fault the poor bastard killed himself."

Then why did everyone keep assuming she blamed herself? "Thanks for the psychological evaluation, Doc, but—"

"Go home, Riley. Atchison Dantell was going to check out one way or the other, and you couldn't have stopped him. You don't owe him a thing."

"I'm not here for Atch Dantell."

"His son?"

Was she that transparent, or was he just that perceptive? The intensity he hid behind that bad boy smile stirred up an awareness she didn't want to acknowledge.

Wolfe's voice softened. "What that kid needs is privacy, to be left alone with his family and any high-priced therapists Yvonne Dantell decides to hire—"

"And what good are they going to do him?" Max asked. "Unless you know a therapist who consults by mental telepathy?"

"What are you talking about?"

"Alex Dantell hasn't been seen since the police questioned him about finding his father's body last night."

"That poor kid found his father's—" Wolfe's gaze snapped to Max's. "What do you mean, he hasn't been seen?"

"He's disappeared."

"Run away?" He sucked in a breath. *"Abducted?"*

"Unclear."

Wolfe was shaking his head. "I don't believe it. How could you know that, even if it were true?"

"I never reveal my sources." But Max's smart-ass

response held no humor. Tomas had given her that same answer to the same question. "You can't print this."

Wolfe's curse was short and to the point. "Bloody hell. An unreportable family bloody drama will stink up a good story faster than a politician can lie."

Max pushed through the gate to the side door. She punched the bell, the rattling buzz sounding faintly inside. Wolfe cursed again as he stormed up the walk to stand beside her.

Max didn't expect Yvonne Dantell to be opening her own door today. But even less did she expect the door to be opened by a six-foot, skinhead bodybuilder sporting a fire-breathing mermaid tattoo on his bulging right arm below his sleeveless black muscle shirt. He filled the door frame, incongruous against the background of the huge Greek revival kitchen.

"Freakin' reporters." His voice was surprisingly light for his bulk, but still menacing. "Get the hell off the property before I break your heads in."

"Charming," Wolfe murmured, but he didn't move, and neither did Max.

"We're here to see Yvonne," Max said. She offered Muscle her card. "She knows who I am. I think she'll want to see me."

"She doesn't want to see nobody," Muscle said, ignoring the card with deep satisfaction. "Send a note with your regards."

"We'll wait while you let her know we're here." Max held out the card again. "It's urgent."

Instead of slamming the door in her face, Muscle made the mistake of grabbing her wrist instead, a snake-quick strike with his left hand. He jerked her toward him, probably intending to lever her arm up behind her to walk her to the curb.

Instead of resisting, Max stepped toward him, throwing her left hand up to his shoulder and shoving. As he stumbled back, her left foot slid behind his.

He fell, pulling her with him. Adjusting quickly, she grabbed her fist with her free hand and jerked, managing to pull her arm free before he dislocated it, but not before he sent her sprawling across the black and white tiled floor.

She hit one of the fluted columns separating the cooking area from the breakfast nook. The impact bruised her ribs, but she managed to scramble behind the column, dodging Muscle's charge and winning a split second to get to her feet.

He grinned at her, his white teeth an unpleasant gash across his bullet-shaped face. He lunged, an off-balance grab for her arm that let her escape farther around the column. But he couldn't fool her again. He wasn't nearly as slow-witted or clumsy as he wanted her to believe.

He'd just maneuvered himself between her and the door. It wasn't about getting her to the curb now. He meant to hurt her.

As if.

Max edged backward. Retreat meant fear. He believed it. He grinned when her back hit the marble-top island in the center of the kitchen.

"Max?" Wolfe stood in the doorway, cell phone in hand.

She shook her head. She'd never get to Yvonne if the cops got involved.

Wolfe shrugged and leaned against the door frame with a raised brow that said he was letting her take the lead.

Muscle stepped around the column. Nice and slow.

This time, his lunge was neither off balance nor clumsy, but his hammer-fisted strike still whiffed harmlessly inches from Max's shins as she levered herself to the top of the island and danced out of his reach.

Her blow was even quicker than his, her boot connecting solidly with the side of his head. But she didn't manage to slam his skull against the marble, and he dodged back. He raised a hand to his temple.

Max raised an eyebrow. "I don't want to hurt you."

He grinned again. "Sorry I can't say the same."

Max centered her stance, ready for his next attack. *Or not.*

Tomas hadn't yet taught her a counter that would be effective against the 9mm SIG-Sauer Muscle pulled from the back of his waistband.

From the corner of her eye, Max saw Wolfe edging toward Muscle, ballpoint pen in his hand and something rather sharper in his eye. Nice thought, but she hoped he wouldn't make any sudden moves. Muscle looked like he knew what to do with a gun.

"What the hell is going on in here?" The sharp male bark from the hallway turned Muscle's head, but not Max's. She didn't intend to shift her gaze from that gun. "Spike?"

Spike? *Please.*

"Reporters," Spike drawled, still amused, still aiming his gun dead-on. "Didn't take 'get lost' for an answer."

"Put the damn gun away."

He slid the gun back into his waistband—and Wolfe pocketed his pen.

Max turned to face the man giving the orders.

He matched Spike for height and nearly for muscle, but he had hair—dark, medium length, in an expensive, casual cut—and wore a sports jacket over a bronze-colored silk shirt with no tie. He definitely had the looks to carry the outfit off. Yet there was nothing overhyped or macho about his manner, no swagger in his blue eyes. They were all business.

Despite Yvonne Dantell's long-legged-model length hanging on his arm.

"You!" Yvonne's red-rimmed eyes blazed as she stared at Max. "This is all your fault!"

Crouching on Yvonne's marble countertop, Max guessed she didn't exude the professional compassion she had hoped to convey during this interview. Wolfe moved up to the counter and offered her a hand. She dropped to the floor beside him.

"Mrs. Dantell, I'm so sorry for the terrible tragedy that—"

"Not sorry enough!" Yvonne shrieked, stepping into the kitchen. "Damn you!"

"What's this? Mr. Spencer? Yvonne?" A second man appeared in the hallway behind the widow and the suave Mr. Spencer. Toby Mittard. Max knew it without introductions, though a glance from Wolfe confirmed it. His simple, conservative suit and the gold monogrammed ring on his pudgy right hand whispered money. But it was the way the two hired security men deferred to the stout, balding, soft-voiced man that told her where the power in the room lay.

He took Yvonne's arm from the well-dressed Spencer. "Calm yourself, my dear. What is this?"

Yvonne pointed a manicured nail at Max. "She's the one who dragged that sorry bastard back here against his will. She's the one who made him do this. This is all her fault."

"I did what you paid me to do." Maybe it wasn't diplomatic, but Max had enough of her own guilt without shouldering Yvonne's. "It's what I'm good at. That's why you hired me."

"How dare you come here today?" Yvonne's voice shook with fury. "Get out of my house! Toby, I want you to tell the police. If Max Riley sets one foot on my property—"

"Max Riley?" The man called Spencer broke in. For the first time, his blue eyes warmed a notch above glacial. "*You're* Mad Max Riley? Maybe I should have guessed, but I had no idea you were as lovely as you are intrepid."

He stepped forward, his hand rising from its previous position hovering over the holster hidden under his jacket. "What an unexpected pleasure. I've followed your career since the article you wrote about finding that frozen climber in the Andes for *Wilderness Adventure Magazine*."

He didn't offer a hand to Wolfe, whom Max could feel bristling beside her.

His handshake was warm. "Steve Spencer. Spencer Investigations."

"I've heard of you." Max hoped she didn't sound as startled as she felt. Not security, after all. "Out of L.A. You have a reputation for results as an investigator."

He shrugged, not too cool to look pleased. "Look, I'm sure you'll understand, but Mrs. Dantell isn't giving any interviews today."

He nodded at Toby Mittard, who took the hint and turned Yvonne toward the hallway.

"Mrs. Dantell! Wait!" Max called around Steve's intervening chest. His broad chest. "We're not here for an interview. We're here about Alex."

Based on the sudden silence as everyone in the room turned to stare at her, she guessed Spencer Investigations was here for the same reason she was and that Toby Mittard knew all about it. Tomas's information had been accurate. Not that Max had ever doubted him.

"Mrs. Dantell, please." Wolfe's crisp, cultured voice sliced through the sudden tension in the room. "I'm Davis Wolfe with the *San Francisco Sentinel*. My colleague, Miss Riley, and I are not here to intrude on your grief. We'd like to offer our help finding your son."

"You can't have heard he's gone," Yvonne gasped, clutching Mittard's arm.

The stocky businessman had a chilling glare. "What the hell is this, Spencer? This can't leak out, dammit. *Nobody* knows."

"The board of directors knows," Max guessed, and was rewarded by Mittard's blanching.

"What do you want?" he demanded through clenched

teeth. "An exclusive? Fine. I know Wolfe's work. I'll give him an hour interview on Burkhartt-Dantell. You forget about the boy."

"We're here to offer our help," Wolfe repeated. "I have extensive contacts in law enforcement, and Miss Riley is extremely good at what she does—"

"Mad Max Riley is *flashy*," Spike corrected disdainfully, before Max could react to Wolfe's unexpected praise. "Spencer Investigations gets the job done. Discreetly."

This from a guy with a shaved head and a flaming tattoo on his arm?

"I'm not here to step on your toes." Max spoke directly to Steve Spencer. "But I met Alex. Maybe I can offer a different perspective on his disappearance. He wasn't abducted, was he?"

It was another guess, based on Mittard's annoyance level, but she could see in Steve's eyes that she was right.

"That's in our favor."

"Our favor?" Mittard barked. "A boy worth more money than Prince William out on the street where any fortune-hunting scumbag can grab him and hold a multinational company hostage? That's in our favor?"

"She means the boy may come back on his own," Steve said, unexpectedly coming to Max's defense. "Just like I told you. He's had a shock. Once he gets cold and hungry, he'll head for home."

Yvonne's green eyes blazed. "My son is not a company pawn and he's not a spoiled brat. He's a boy who's just lost his father. He's not thinking straight. He's not going to give up as long as he's got this crazy idea about Atch's death."

She pointed at Spencer. "I hired you to bring him home, not stand around in my kitchen arguing with reporters."

"Take care of them," Mittard said, jerking his head at Max and Wolfe. "I'll do that interview with you, Wolfe, but if this leaks out, your career is over. Come, Yvonne. You need to rest. Take that pill the doctor prescribed for you."

This time, Max said nothing as Mittard escorted the widow from the room. Yvonne might not have loved Atchison Dantell, but she obviously loved her son.

Max waited until she was gone to ask, "What crazy idea about Atch's death?"

Steve Spencer grimaced. "Finding his father like that freaked the boy out. He told the 911 dispatcher that his father had been murdered."

"Murder?" Wolfe asked.

Steve shook his head. "Dantell hanged himself in the garage. The widow identified the handwriting on the note as his. I'm sure the police expert will confirm it."

"But Alex wouldn't believe it," Max said.

"The note he left his mother said his father would never commit suicide and that he was going to find out who killed him."

"Can I see the note?" Max asked. "And Alex's room?"

"You can get the hell out of this house," Spike said, cracking his knuckles. "Shit, boss. We don't need these assholes screwing up our investigation. We don't have time for this crap."

"No, it's all right." Whatever Steve felt about Max's request he hid behind a smile. "I'd love to see Mad Max Riley in action. She might find something we overlooked. And if she doesn't, she might back off and let us to do our job without interference."

A challenge. Max returned Steve's smile. "She might."

Spike only grunted. "It's your call, boss. I'm gonna run a last check on the phone system."

Steve turned to Max and Wolfe. "The boy's room is upstairs."

As they followed Steve into the hallway toward the living room and the stairs, Wolfe fell into step beside Max.

"Gee, thanks for helping me out with Mr. Homicidal in there earlier," Max murmured. "Nice to know you've got my back. With your pen. What were you going to do, start writing my obituary?"

Wolfe raised a sandy brow. "A pen can be a handy weapon, but I didn't think I'd have to use it. You seemed to have things under control. I like to watch a competent woman work." His hazel eyes glinted amusement. "Don't tell me you couldn't handle a thug like Spike."

"He's got more brains than he lets on, and he outweighs me by a hundred pounds." Not to mention that although Spike obviously had martial arts training, he wasn't the kind of guy who fought by tournament rules. Then again, Tomas hadn't spent all those years teaching her to fight in tournaments, either.

Wolfe's expression told her he wasn't buying her complaint.

"Okay, yeah, in a fair fight maybe I could have taken him," she admitted, turning back on Wolfe from the curving staircase leading to the second floor mezzanine. "But in case you hadn't noticed, the guy pulled a P226 on me."

"You've just admitted Spike is no idiot," Wolfe reminded her. "I hardly think he's stupid enough to shoot an unarmed reporter in front of witnesses, not with police officers swarming around the house."

"How long have you two worked together?" Steve asked, waiting for them at the top of the stairs. The smile he shot Wolfe held humor, but no warmth. "You bicker worse than me and Spike."

Max couldn't quite decipher the look that passed between the two men.

"Alex's room?" she asked, stepping between them.

"Right down the hall." Steve led them on. "His mother's given us a list of the items she thinks are missing. Clothes, toothbrush, school backpack, cell phone."

"The phone system Spike's checking," Max said. "You're set up to find him if he calls?"

"At least a general location," Steve agreed. His steady gaze locked on Max's. "His mother and the Burkhartt-Dantell board are dead set against police involvement. They're afraid word will leak out and the wrong people might find the boy."

"They could be right," Max said, though freezing out the police cut a significant resource from the search. "Don't worry about us. I can keep a story shut down and so can Wolfe."

"Thank you." Wolfe's voice held only a trace of irony.

"I'm glad to hear it," Steve said. "Because this kid has been a potential kidnap target since the day he was born. Spike and I know what we're doing, and we're doing everything we can to find Alex Dantell. We don't want anyone out there looking for this kid except us."

He pushed open the door at the end of the hall and gestured at Max to enter. As she stepped across the threshold, she froze, nearly causing Wolfe and Steve to collide behind her.

The mattresses had been tipped from the sturdy oak bunk beds and slashed open. Chests full of video games and science kits were dumped across the floor. A bass guitar had been smashed to pieces against the wall.

"Alex did this?" Max asked, wishing she believed it.

Steve's loud curse confirmed her fear as he pushed past her into the room. He turned to stare at her and Wolfe. "We were just up here not half an hour ago."

Wolfe touched Max's shoulder, turning her attention to the wall, where a family portrait hung. Atchison and Yvonne Dantell stood on either side of their son, unmistakable love in their faces as they gazed down at the boy, who smiled brightly into the camera.

Glass clung in shards to the picture frame, cracked around the blade of a long, narrow dagger whose blade tip had struck through the photograph into the wall, pinned precisely in the center of the smiling boy's chest.

"I think," said Wolfe, his voice carefully cool, "that someone besides us is already looking for the boy. And that we very much do not want that person to find him."

Chapter 4

"And then they kicked you out?" Lionel's voice rose in indignation until it squeaked. He shot an embarrassed glance at Simone, sitting in front of Max's desk taking notes, and cleared his throat. "And they're not going to report it to the police?"

"They can't report the break-in, or they'd have to report Alex's disappearance," Max explained, though she felt as frustrated as Lionel.

The open windows of her private office at Quest let in a mild bay breeze tinged with salt and fish, but only the fading memory of afternoon sunshine. Precious time was sinking with the sun. By midnight, Alex would have a twenty-four-hour head start on Spencer Investigations, and Spencer was already behind whoever had broken into Alex's room.

"Who does this Spencer guy think he is?" Lionel demanded, as he paced between the windows and the office door. "His ego can't handle a little help from the best?"

"Spencer Investigations has a good reputation," Simone murmured, ever the pragmatist. "They're based in L.A., but they've done work in San Francisco. Steve Spencer must have some skill."

Lionel snorted. "Maybe. But Max doesn't just have skill, she has *talent*."

"Yvonne Dantell doesn't want me anywhere near this search." Max couldn't quite match Simone's cool calm. Simone's unflappable composure had convinced her to hire the young woman soon after starting Quest. Her water tempered Max's fire, a sort of personnel feng shui.

And then there was Lionel. He flung himself into the chair beside Simone, his disgust palpable. Max almost smiled. He helped balance her tendency to take herself too seriously.

"Just because no one wants us doesn't mean we're going to sit back and do nothing," she assured him. She pushed a sheet of paper across the desk.

Lionel and Simone peered at the pencil drawing she'd rendered.

"A crucifix?" Lionel asked doubtfully. "You think vampires are after Alex?"

Max snatched the drawing back. For a moment, she could hear her father's voice, imitating his own father's soft brogue. *Stop fretting, Magdalena, you don't have to be perfect at everything*.

"It's a knife," she growled, pushing it back toward them.

"The one the intruder left in Alex's room. Good quality steel, but plain, except for this design on the handle."

"It looks like…" Lionel paused, struggling with diplomacy. "A sort of tall, narrow flag on a pole?"

"Or a quill pen," Simone suggested. "Something an old-time writer might have used."

Max sighed. "Okay, it's not the guy's monogram, but it must mean something to him. Lionel, I want you to see if you can get some background on it."

"A red flag. Danger?" Lionel muttered, taking the paper as he stood. "Or maybe he's just a really big fan of Edgar Allan Poe."

He wandered out of Max's office, still mumbling.

"And me?"

Max handed a second sheet to Simone. "Here's a list of Alex's contacts. I want addresses of friends, teachers, bass guitar instructor, whatever."

"Steve Spencer gave you this list?" Simone's narrow cinnamon eyebrows rose.

"I happened to notice it when he showed us the phone-monitoring system he'd set up." Max allowed herself a self-satisfied smile. "Get some basic info on these people, our standard procedures, in case Spencer doesn't cover his bases. And see if you can find a recent photo of Alex."

"Right." Simone rose, somehow graceful even in a short sheath skirt and high heels. "Cell phone?"

"I'm turning it on now," Max grumbled, digging her briefcase out from under her desk. She made a show of clipping the phone to the waist of her slacks, smoothing the crimson silk of her shirt over it. "I'm going to do some legwork on the knife, but I'll be at home later."

Simone paused in Max's office door. "Be careful."

"You should save the warning for Alex," Max said, adjusting the strap of her bag. "He's the one in danger."

She could feel it like a spider creeping up her spine. If Simone had worn glasses, she would have been peering over them in skepticism. "Really? You're the one who's already been threatened at gunpoint."

"Misunderstandings don't count. I'm not a kid out there all alone in a world full of pedophile predators and potential kidnappers, with some knife-wielding nut after me."

"Alex Dantell isn't just a kid," Simone reminded her. "He's a walking fortune. And that knife-wielding nut isn't going to be happy if you get in the way of his finding that boy."

"I can take care of myself."

"Good," Simone replied tartly. "Then do it."

Max rolled her eyes, listening to Simone's heels click across the outer office floor. She didn't need Simone fussing over her, though sometimes it felt good to know someone cared.

She shook her head, sweeping away a sudden twisting in her chest. Like that longing she'd felt earlier at the newspaper offices. She didn't need a family, didn't need anyone else to worry about. Worrying didn't keep people from leaving. Besides, she was an adult, and she *could* take care of herself.

Alex couldn't. Not for long.

She glanced out the window at the tangled streets below, crowded with traffic and colorful passersby. Electrifying for tourists. Energizing for residents. Deeply dangerous for a frightened boy.

"Be careful," she whispered, closing the window.

* * *

Twilight had darkened the streets by the time Max arrived at the Pieces of Time Antiques warehouse on Harrison Street. Pieces of Time had a shop on Jackson Square, a showcase catering to Barbary Coast tourists and affluent browsers, but Tomas preferred to spend his time in the organized chaos of the warehouse store.

A Closed sign hung in the front window, and the lights had already been dimmed, but the barred gate had not been shut and Max found the front door unlocked. Waiting on a lingering patron, Max guessed, following the echoing sound of low voices into the half-lit gloom.

Broken up by decorative screens, towering wardrobes and jutting walls, the warehouse at night always gave Max a pleasant shiver of apprehension, as if anything or anyone might wait around the next corner, from an ancient Chinese dragon coiled on a Louis XIV writing desk to a pair of Persian slippers tucked next to a velvet-upholstered Queen Anne wing chair to the angry ghost of a Russian tsar come to reclaim a family heirloom.

Max paused as she realized what had inspired her flight of fancy about the tsar's ghost. The voices she heard around the wall ahead of her were speaking Russian.

And the man sitting on the gilt wood settee in the Italian parlor display to her right was packing a gun.

Maybe midtwenties, she thought, processing details even as she berated herself for her inattention. A young punk of a muscle man in a leather jacket, his lip curled in a pouting sneer as he slouched on the settee, one booted foot resting on a hundred-year-old marble-topped coffee table. She couldn't actually see the gun beneath his bulky jacket. She didn't need to. She saw it in his eyes.

"Store's closed," he said, as his gaze roved insolently over her figure.

She could pretend to leave. Outmaneuvering this self-satisfied thug in the warehouse maze wouldn't be a challenge. But one of the voices speaking Russian on the other side of the wall belonged to Tomas, and he wouldn't thank her for pissing this kid off.

"Thanks for keeping the rabble out," she said, giving the punk a patronizing smile as she strode past him.

Kid Gangster's hand moved to his jacket, but he let her go.

The low voices stopped as she walked past the wall into a display of Americana antiques. Tomas and his patron, a paunchy man of about sixty with a sharply trimmed beard beneath a balding, egg-shaped head, turned toward her. A decanter of amber-colored brandy stood on an antique sideboard beside them, and the Russian man held a snifter in his hand. Probably not a robbery, then.

Max offered the stranger a smile. "I'm sorry to interrupt. I can wait in Tomas's office until you're done."

"No, no." The Russian waved his hand. "I am the one who must go. I have an appointment. But tell me, what do you think of this clock here?"

He gestured to the stately tall clock against the warehouse wall. The light from a reproduction Victorian lamp shone on the warm red wood case. A hand-painted moon rolled across the top of the brass dial.

"Early nineteenth century?" Max asked, receiving a nod of approval from Tomas. "It's a beautiful piece."

"Exquisite," the Russian agreed. "And my front hall would be the perfect setting for such a clock. But is it worth the exorbitant price Mr. Gregory is attempting to extort from me?"

Max couldn't read anything from Tomas's smooth demeanor. Despite the Russian's geniality, there was something in his sharp gray eyes that warned he was not a man to cross. And then there was the thug just around the corner.

"I'm not an antiques expert." She shrugged. "If I love a piece despite the price, then it doesn't cost too much."

The Russian laughed, a blustery sound. "Then we have much in common, my dear. I will, of course, have to purchase it, even at such a ridiculous price."

He raised his snifter in salute to the clock and drained it. He turned to Max, but as he focused on her fully for the first time, whatever good-humored remark he intended to make died on his lips.

"My God." His wide eyes flicked toward Tomas. "Serafina?"

Max froze, her skin prickling as if she'd plunged unexpectedly into dark water.

"Forgive me." The Russian brushed a hand across his mouth, blinking in surprise. "For an instant, you looked so much like your mother. It is Magdalena, is it not?"

"Max Riley." Tomas's quiet voice was a lifeline. "Allow me to introduce Dimitri Antonov."

The Russian's expression held unexpected sorrow.

"You won't remember me. You were just a baby when your father was stationed in Moscow."

No, she didn't remember. She barely remembered her mother, who had died in Vienna not long after her father's transfer from Moscow. Still, she remembered enough to know that though her hair faintly echoed her mother's, Spanish thick and dark, her green eyes, snub nose and sharp elbows were all her father's. If this man saw Serafina Riley in her, the shrewdness of his gray eyes was no illusion.

"You knew my parents?" She cringed at the longing she couldn't quite hide.

The Russian's eyes warmed with sympathy. "Your mother was the most gracious of ladies, and your father was a good man. He believed in truth and justice. It was a terrible thing when he—" he faltered only slightly "—when I heard he was gone."

He turned his bluff smile on Tomas. "It is a sad day for truth and justice when they have to rely on the likes of two old scoundrels like Tomas Gregory and Dimitri Antonov, eh?"

Tomas frowned, and the Russian thumped him on the shoulder.

"There I go again. It is the cognac." Antonov bowed his head to Max. "I am glad to have met you again, my dear. If you need anything from me, ever, you have only to ask."

He set his snifter down on the sideboard and buttoned his coat. "Tomas, you old thief, I will send for the clock tomorrow. And I will set wheels in motion on that other matter we discussed. *Do svidanya.* Sacha!"

The young thug sauntered around the wall, not-so-discreetly adjusting the holster beneath his leather jacket, and the two men strode off toward the front of the warehouse.

Max hugged her arms across her chest, holding back the stabbing ache in her heart. "That mobster was a friend of my father's?"

Tomas stoppered the brandy decanter and lifted its silver tray. "Being a Russian oil capitalist is a dangerous game these days. A bodyguard is a reasonable precaution. I wouldn't vouch for Dimitri's tax statements, but your father respected him."

"He respected a Russian diplomat he met in Moscow during the Cold War?" Max asked skeptically, following Tomas to his office at the rear of the warehouse.

"Dimitri wasn't a diplomat," Tomas corrected. He flicked on the office light and set the brandy tray on his perfectly neat Victorian leather-top desk. "He was KGB."

"Well, that explains it, then."

Tomas ignored her sarcasm, gathering his coat from the rack by the door. "You have news about the Dantell boy's disappearance?"

Max knew from experience she'd get nothing more from him about Dimitri Antonov, at least not that night, so she didn't pursue it.

"Your information was correct," she said. "Alex Dantell is missing. The only good news is that he left under his own power."

As they made their way back to the front door, she filled him in on Atchison's suicide, Alex's belief that his father was murdered and the break-in of the boy's room.

Tomas frowned grimly, pausing with his hand on the

front door handle. "Someone has not been discreet about the boy's disappearance. That break-in could not have been a kidnapping attempt."

Max had said the same to Steve Spencer, though she wasn't sure she'd convinced him. "I agree. Whoever trashed Alex's room was looking for clues to where he'd gone. And if there were any, he made sure we wouldn't find them."

"A professional could have done that without anyone knowing he'd ever been there."

"He *wanted* us to know," Max said. "He left something behind, something I'm guessing he meant to frighten Yvonne, to ensure she meets his demands if he finds Alex."

She pulled a second copy of her drawing from her briefcase.

"It's a dagger," she explained hastily, as Tomas leaned in to peer at the sketch. "He stuck it into a family photograph. This symbol is figured into the handle in enamel. It looks like some kind of red flag."

Tomas straightened abruptly, pulling the paper from her hand. The light from the street lamp outside shone strangely on his face, turning his olive-tinted skin pale.

"I thought you might be able to tell me what that symbol could stand for—"

"No." He cut her off. "I can't tell you that."

He pushed through the door, the rumble of traffic from Harrison and the nearby freeway rushing in on them.

"What about where someone might buy a knife like that?" Max asked as Tomas secured the gate behind them. Tomas didn't deal in weapons, but he had a small collection of bladed antiques at home and he kept his eyes open for potential additions to it. "You know all the blade traders in town. If you asked around—"

"No," Tomas repeated, his coat swirling as he turned up the busy street toward the next block where Max had parked her Triumph Spitfire. "This intruder wouldn't be stupid enough to leave a knife that could be traced back to him."

"You're lots of help tonight," Max snapped back, her keys jingling as she jerked them from her bag before sucking down her irritation. It wasn't Tomas's fault. "I'm sorry. It's just that I don't have anything to go on. Spencer is the one with the access to the family, but he's not sharing much. How am I going to find this boy before he gets hurt?"

"You're not." Tomas's expression softened as he turned to her, hands stuffed in his coat pockets. "It's not your job to find him, Magdalena."

Max frowned. "Of course I have to find him. You're the one who told me just this afternoon that I bore some responsibility for Atchison Dantell's suicide."

Tomas's eyebrows rose. "So you're going to bring him back by finding his son?"

"Tomas! He's an innocent child. He's in terrible danger."

"Just like thousands of other runaway children." Tomas leaned forward, his voice suddenly sharp. "Alex Dantell is not your child. Yvonne Dantell is not your client. She has hired an experienced investigator to find her son. Trying to salve your conscience by getting in his way will not help the boy."

Max's breath caught hard in her throat. "I'm good at this," she said finally. "I won't get in the way."

"Asking around about this knife?" Tomas demanded. With his back to the streetlight, his eyes were dark holes. "What next? Interrogating the boy's friends? Asking about him out on the street? Why not put an advertisement in your newspaper? Let everyone know he is missing."

"Is that what you think of me?"

The hardness in his stance melted abruptly and he reached for Max's shoulder, but she jerked away and walked around to the driver's door of the Spitfire.

"Magdalena." He placed a hand on the convertible's hood as she climbed in. "It is not a question of your skill or your intentions. This boy's disappearance has nothing to do with you. I do not want you to get hurt."

The engine ground as she turned the ignition too hard. "Hurt? By a runaway *twelve-year-old?*"

"By an invisible intruder with a knife," he said harshly. "Or by what such a man might do to a twelve-year-old boy."

For a moment that image hung between them, marked in the uncharacteristic apprehension tightening Tomas's face.

"It would shatter you," he said, the words as quiet and dark as the night sky.

"Then I better not let it happen."

Max threw the Spitfire into gear, making Tomas leap back onto the curb as she gunned it into the street.

* * *

Her mood found little to soothe it in the stop-and-go city driving. By the time she reached her Russian Hill condo, righteous anger had given way to sapping doubt.

Tomas's words had hurt—damn him, he'd meant them to—but only because there was truth in them. Alex's disappearance wasn't her case, but she would be devastated if Alex wound up dead or injured.

Yet Tomas was wrong if he thought staying out of the case would protect her from being hurt. The guilt of not doing anything would haunt her forever.

She slipped the Spitfire into her tiny garage space and tugged down the recalcitrant garage door. The tang of homemade marinara sauce tugged at her from the homey Italian restaurant down the block, but she didn't have the energy to face Mrs. Molinari's cheerful mothering.

It wasn't just Alex, and it wasn't just Tomas. Her encounter with Dimitri Antonov had raised the ghost of her father's memory.

Even a decade later, there were times she half expected to turn a corner and see him there, his green eyes flashing a grin for his "little tiger girl." She could almost hear his voice, warmed by a slow glass of Irish whiskey, telling her stories of leopards and princes and devils he claimed to have met.

But as she reached the narrow stone steps of her building, the specters in her head evaporated as a chill crept down her spine. The recessed entranceway at the top of the stairs loomed black with impenetrable shadows but a hint of aftershave wafted beneath the scent of Italian food.

Max paused on the sidewalk beneath a streetlight and unclipped her cell phone from her waistband. "I'm dialing 911."

The hearty laughter coming from her entranceway didn't belong to a crack-addicted thief. The shadows along the wall shifted, and a man stepped into the street lamp's light.

"I didn't mean to startle you. I was buzzing your apartment. Now I see why you weren't answering."

"Steve Spencer." She frowned at him. "How did you find out where I live?"

He grinned, just a little too pleased with himself and all the more charming for it. "You wouldn't think much of my investigative skills if I couldn't hunt down an address."

True enough. Max climbed the stairs to where Steve leaned against the door frame. He'd changed out of his suave, high-priced investigator's suit into faded jeans, a corduroy jacket and a red polo shirt. It was a good look on him, with his dark hair slightly ruffled and the hint of stubble darkening his chin.

He smelled good, too, of real soap and a masculine fragrance that hinted of limes and tropical nights. He might not have shaved, but he'd splashed on a quality aftershave.

Okay, yes, he was hot. Max's eyes narrowed as she unlocked the front door. *Just what was he doing on her doorstep?*

"I'm guessing you want to come in?" she asked.

He grinned his approval, which annoyed her. Or maybe that was just her emotional exhaustion.

"Remote dead bolt," he noted, as she opened the door to her third-floor condo. "On a solid oak door. Good choice."

Max strode down the hall to drop her bag on the seafoam sofa and tossed her jacket across one of the chrome stools beneath the counter dividing the living room from the kitchen. Steve paused to hang his jacket on the turn-of-the-century coatrack by the door.

Max noticed him surreptitiously checking his hair in the mirror.

The bottle of chardonnay felt blessedly cool against her palm as she pulled it from the refrigerator, but she resisted the temptation to press it against her forehead.

"Wine?"

"Just a half glass. I'm still working." He touched the pager at his belt. While she poured, he wandered to the bay windows overlooking the street. The realtor had touted the "bay view." Max actually could see the bay, if she craned her neck just right.

"This is a great place. I like the minimalist decor."

Max didn't much care if he liked it or not. *She* liked it. The first time she'd walked through the door, she'd fallen in love with the warm hardwood flooring and the openness of the high ceilings. A few soft, muted throw rugs, warm cedar furnishings and her favorite pieces of her father's eclectic collection of world art warmed the rooms.

"The orchids are fantastic. They must take a lot of care."

"I stick with low-maintenance varieties. Simone, my secretary, watches them when I'm away."

From the deep rose *Phalaenopsis* spilling off the

black marble fireplace to the *Cattleyas* on their ledge by the bay windows, they infused the condo with life.

She joined Steve by the windows, handing him his glass of wine. She let the cool liquid sit on her tongue for a moment before asking. "What are you doing here?"

He raised one dark eyebrow. "I thought your first question would be about Alex."

She wasn't in the mood for dancing. "If you had a lead, you wouldn't be here. You'd be checking it out."

Steve shrugged, a thorough rolling of his shoulders. "No calls from the kid. We've checked his friends. Spike's cruising the shelters and the bus stations. Nada."

He took a deep slug of the wine, as if it were a shot of bourbon. "We've got a P.I. watching his maternal grandparents' house in Kansas City. A long shot."

"How far can he get on the money he had with him?" Max asked. "Could he have taken one of his parents' credit cards?"

Steve snorted, not quite laughter, as he sat down on her sofa. "Kid had his own credit cards. His own ATM card. Hell, he's got his own mutual funds and a college fund that would send four kids to Harvard."

"Is his mother's name on the accounts?"

"No, just the father's. I guess Yvonne didn't have control over much of Dantell's money. She's going to be pretty strapped until the estate gets settled. But she's got all of the kid's account numbers. Easy enough to track online—our only break today."

"Alex used his credit cards?" Max dropped onto the

armchair beside the sofa. "Where? Why aren't you out there—"

"No credit cards," Steve said. "Strictly cash. The kid walks into the bank as soon as it opens this morning. A place where the bank manager knows the kid, right? He tells the guy his dad's out in the car. They're shopping for ski equipment for a trip to Tahoe in December. He's needs to withdraw a bunch of cash from his account because his father wants him to learn the value of money."

Steve took another slug of his wine. "The kid has balls, I'll give him that."

"The bank manager didn't think it was odd that his father didn't come in with him?"

Steve shook his head. "Apparently the kid and the dad have gone on shopping sprees before. Spike noticed the discrepancy on the kid's bank records this afternoon. Yvonne placed a call to the bank manager and got the rest of the story."

Max set her wineglass down on the coffee table, the alcohol uneasy in her empty stomach. "He didn't see if Alex was actually with anyone, doesn't know where Alex went after he left the bank."

"You got it in one."

"How much did he withdraw?"

"A thou." Steve rolled his shoulders again, settling back into the sofa, his long legs crowding Max's. "But that's not the best part. Once the bank manager got talking, we could hardly shut him up. Seems like Alex had been by the bank a few times over the past several months. And his ATM has seen regular usage, too."

Max hadn't spent more than fifteen or twenty

minutes with Alex Dantell, but she would never have pictured him sneaking behind his parents' back for money. "What did he spend it on?"

Computer games? Hanging out with his friends? *Drugs?*

"We're just *hoping* he spent it." Steve grimaced. "You asked before how far he could get on the money he had on him? We were thinking not too far on the forty bucks his mom knew he had in his wallet."

"How much?" Max demanded, her stomach burning.

No, Alex hadn't spent that money. She knew it in her gut. He'd been planning for this for months, while his father was missing. He'd intended to go search for Atch Dantell himself.

Chapter 5

Max stalked to the kitchen to dump her wine. "Five thousand dollars? You said Spike is checking the shelters. What about the Mark Hopkins?"

Steve followed her, his empty glass clinking on the granite countertop in irritation. "How the hell is a twelve-year-old kid going to check into a fancy hotel by himself?"

Max turned on him, hand on hip. "I don't know. How about, 'My baby sister's asleep in her car seat, so Mom sent me in to register for our room'?"

"It's not that easy. Lots of hotels require a credit card number to register, even if you're paying cash."

"Alex *has* a credit card," she reminded him. "And if he paid cash, they wouldn't charge it. You'd never see the transaction."

"But he wouldn't know that. He's just a dumb, scared

kid—" Steve stopped himself, running a hand through his thick dark hair. "Not so dumb. Shit."

"Yeah." Max managed to resist his almost comic grimace of distress. And how sexy his dark hair looked rumpled like that. "Spencer, what *are* you doing here?"

It was that boyish grin that she couldn't resist.

"Scamming a free drink. And picking your brain."

"Your client made it clear she didn't want me involved in this case."

The grin deepened. "Did I mention I managed to pick the brain of one of the most innovative minds in my field without your even attempting to charge my client a fee?"

Max suspected her glare didn't hide her amusement. "Flatterer."

"Damn right." He curved his lips into a wicked smile. "And I haven't even gotten started. It is a pleasure to watch you think. I haven't been able to keep my eyes off you since we met."

Max never blushed. But she could feel more than her face warm at the appreciative candor in his eyes. Had it been so long since she'd felt attracted to a man? The blood at her hip even seemed to be fluttering—

No, that was her cell phone.

She snatched it out from under the hem of her shirt and checked the number. "Simone?"

"Lionel," Lionel said. "We're at Simone's desk. I think we might have tracked down your flag symbol."

Max kept her expression neutral. "Go ahead."

"Simone was on to something when she said it looked like a quill. The Egyptians used a stylized feather kind of like the one you drew to represent the feather of Maat."

"Which is?"

"The feather of truth and justice. Anubis, the funerary god, weighed the hearts of the dead against this feather. If a person's heart was light enough, they went on to the underworld, but if the heart tipped the scales, the demon Ammit got to destroy the person's soul."

"Thanks, Simone," Max said, tipping Lionel that she was not alone. "Why don't you call it a night. We'll go over the rest of the receipts tomorrow."

"Everything all right?" Lionel's voice rose in concern.

"No problem," she assured him. "I'll see you in the morning." She closed the phone and set it on the counter. "My secretary."

Steve nodded. "I've taken enough of your time for the evening." His grin quirked again. "A smooth way to make my exit before you kick me out."

Giving her plenty of opening to invite him to stay. And looking into those dangerously persuasive blue eyes, she was sorely tempted. But the ragged emotion of the day didn't excuse making that kind of mistake.

"I've got a deadline coming up."

He shrugged, heading down the hall to retrieve his jacket. "And I've got a few hundred phone calls to make. With a radical change in my luck, it could turn out our Sam Spade–wannabe runaway has holed up in a hotel room, after all."

"I hope so," Max said, though her instincts said it wouldn't be that easy. "Good luck."

"Thanks." He paused with his hand on the doorknob, then leaned forward to brush a soft kiss across her forehead. "I'll let you know when we find him."

Max leaned against the door as she closed it behind him, a flicker of guilt cutting through the attraction and exasperation left by the kiss. She should have shared Lionel's information with him. She doubted it would do anything to help find Alex, but Steve had told her about the bank withdrawals. Fair was fair.

Maybe she just wasn't as good a person as Steve Spencer. Maybe she was a terrible team player.

The building intercom buzzed, making her jump. He'd come back for something he'd forgotten. She'd have another chance to do the right thing. *Oh, goody.*

She punched the button to let him in, waiting until she heard his tread on the landing to open the door. A raised knuckle almost caught her on the nose. She jerked back, planting for a vicious kick before she recognized her assailant.

"Wolfe! What are you doing here?"

The man's sandy eyebrows tilted rakishly. "Knocking?" He lowered his hand, examining her door. "You would think someone with the sense to buy good locks would inquire who was at her door before buzzing him into her building."

"I thought you were—" No, she wasn't going to go there. "Someone else. What do you want?"

"To come in. I have something to ask you."

"Doesn't anybody in this city know how to work a telephone?"

"I could go downstairs and call you from my car," Wolfe said. "But before you decide, smell this."

He unrolled the top of the brown paper bag he carried

and lifted it toward her. Against her better judgment, Max leaned forward. Steamed rice. Ginger. Soy sauce.

Her stomach growled.

"Lemon chicken," Wolfe said, his accent warming the words like terms of seduction. "Shrimp fried rice. Mongolian beef. And lo mein with bean curd, in case you're a vegetarian."

"Not if there's lemon chicken." Max stepped aside to let him in. "The kitchen's just down the hall."

She followed him to the kitchen counter, trying not to drool while he unpacked the containers of Chinese food. His smile was decidedly unboyish in its satisfaction.

"All the way to the kitchen? Next time I'll have to try coq au vin."

"You have a Machiavellian mind, Wolfe. I'll get the chopsticks and put on some green tea."

"Beer?"

She had to smile at his wistful tone. "Sorry. Wine? Red or white."

He sighed. "Tea will do."

The food was good, and not just because she was starving. They ate sitting at the counter, and Max noted that Wolfe was as proficient with chopsticks as she was. More impressive, he seemed content to eat in silence, waiting to bring up business until they'd finished the food and Max had poured them each a second cup of tea.

"You have a question," Max reminded him, breaking open her fortune cookie.

"A favor," Wolfe amended.

She slanted him a smile. "Even Chinese takeout isn't going to buy you a favor."

He settled an arm on the counter as he turned to face her. The devil in his eyes glinted. "That's not all I'm offering."

Despite the outrageousness of his flirting, awareness rippled along Max's nerves. Wolfe had leaned into her personal space. A dare. She held her ground.

"No?" she asked.

"I have information. Toby Mittard kept his word. I've spoken with several members of the Burkhartt-Dantell Media Group's board of directors this afternoon."

Nobody wanted her involved in the search for Alex Dantell, yet they kept asking her for help. Max glanced at her fortune. "Your wisdom is in great demand." *No kidding.*

"Do we have a deal?" Wolfe asked.

"I never make a deal with the devil without knowing the terms."

"I want you to visit one of the board members with me tomorrow. He's offered to take us for a spin on his yacht."

"And I'd be going because…?"

"We're partners on this story."

She snorted.

"Because your name came up, and this bloke happens to be a Mad Max Riley fan."

"So I'm bait to get you into the interview?" She wanted to be offended, but it was a little too delicious to watch the "serious journalist" admit he needed a mere travel writer to round out his big story.

"In a nutshell."

She had to give him credit: he handled her amusement well. She shook her head. "I don't have time to do your job. This hard journalism stuff is all yours."

He didn't take the bait. "Spencer Investigations is doing everything that can be done to find Alex Dantell."

Max shied away from his suddenly intense gaze. Once more he'd pegged her too well.

"Every day that he's gone decreases the chances he'll be brought home safely," she said, defending herself. "There's a nut with a knife out there looking for him, remember?"

"And who do you think hired the nut?" Wolfe leaned closer, and she couldn't help a sudden awareness of his scent. No expensive aftershave obscured the hint of sweat, the salty ocean breeze that clung to his wind-blown hair. Nothing suave or smooth about it, just visceral male.

Kidnapper, she reminded her brain. *Knife-wielding psycho. Focus.*

Wolfe's implication struck her. "You think a member of the Burkhartt-Dantell board hired him?"

"Unless Alex contacted someone after he ran away, Yvonne and the board are supposed to be the only ones who know he's missing." His teeth showed in a grim smile. "Besides you, me, Spencer and his pet biker, your fresh-faced assistants…"

"Let's assume it wasn't you or me. Why would a board member want Alex kidnapped?"

"Leverage?" His eyes showed a world-weariness normally hidden by his sardonic humor. "He may be a real boy to you and his mother, but to the corporate world, he's just a monopoly piece. It turns out the board controls the boy's share of the company until he turns twenty-one. But there seems to be some question as to who will be controlling the board. There's a lot at stake in that battle."

"A lot of money," Max said.

"A lot of *power*." Wolfe's jaded gaze held hers. "If you pull Atchison Dantell out of the mix, the power shifts. Some of the board members are going to see the shifting as quicksand, some are going to see it as an opportunity."

"And any of them might be willing to use a child to make sure they don't get pulled under," Max concluded for him. "The man with the yacht?"

"Court Treybold."

"Treybold? The movie mogul?"

Wolfe nodded. "His son. Inherited his father's share in Burkhartt-Dantell five years ago. A few years older than Atchison Dantell, but still younger than most of the board members. By all accounts, the closest thing Atch had to a real friend on the board. They went snowboarding and skydiving together. I'm hoping he might be a little more forthcoming about the effect Atch's death will have on the company."

He let her fill in the hook for herself.

"And who might be desperate enough to employ dirty tactics." She crumpled the fortune she'd left on the counter and tossed it into the empty lemon chicken box. "I still think it's a waste of time."

"You have something better in mind?"

That was the kicker. "Fine, I'll go with you. Who

knows, maybe Treybold's got his yacht decorated like an Egyptian tomb."

Wolfe paused from sliding off his stool. "A what?"

"Nothing." It would hardly be fair to tell Wolfe about the feather of Maat when she hadn't told Steve. "I'm just hoping the morning won't be as boring as it is unproductive."

"Ouch. And here I can't imagine a morning with you being boring."

Max surprised herself by laughing. "Suave is not your forte, Wolfe."

But as she followed him to her door, she realized she was looking forward to the morning, to sparring with Wolfe again.

Bad idea. No, she was looking forward to meeting one of the board members to gain a better understanding of the intrigues swirling around Alex Dantell. If one of the board had hired a kidnapper, simply finding Alex might not be enough to keep him safe.

She might not have a magical scale for weighing the hearts of men, but if she found the man hunting Alex, she'd be more than happy to feed his soul to a demon.

A brisk breeze scudded wisps of clouds across a late-September sky, battering the seagulls circling above the marina. Court Treybold's trim motor yacht, the *Persephone,* rolled gently at its moorings near the red-tiled Yacht Club building.

Greco-Roman, Max noted of the boat's name, not Egyptian, but still, a goddess associated with the underworld. Maybe the morning was looking up.

"Hello, there!" A tall, tanned, blond man in a nautical polo shirt hailed them from the flybridge of the yacht.

"Remember," Wolfe murmured in her ear. "This is a million-dollar boat. Try not to break anyone's skull today."

"No one but yours," Max promised, smiling brightly as their host came up the dock to unlock the gate for them.

With the anchor on his shirt pocket and the Irish fisherman's sweater draped around his shoulders, the man should have looked ridiculous, a parody of a wealthy playboy pretending to be a sailor. But muscles sculpted his bronzed arms; his blond hair was bleached by sun, not peroxide; and the white-toothed grin on his sun-lined face had a self-deprecating arrogance George Clooney would envy.

"Court Treybold," he said, offering Wolfe a hearty handshake. "I enjoyed your series in the *Sentinel* on the global effects of the U.S. trade deficit."

"Good to know someone read it," Wolfe said, slanting a look at Max.

She matched his sly grin. *Yeah, beat me to it.*

Warning prickles ran up her arms. Wolfe was a competitor, despite their current forced partnership. He hadn't forgotten her beating him out of the Story of the Year. This easy camaraderie was dangerous.

His hazel gaze held hers a second too long, suddenly probing, and she glanced away. Definitely dangerous.

When Treybold took Max's hand, she felt calluses. "Mad Max Riley. What a pleasure. Atch said you were stunning, but I put that down to four months without female companionship. Please, come aboard."

Max preferred boats to airplanes, but she'd never understood boating for pleasure. After a tour of the *Persephone,* from the teak decking of the bridge to the marble in the en suite cabin bathrooms to the forty-two-inch plasma TV in the saloon, she realized she hadn't been on the right boats.

Treybold skippered them out of the marina, one hand on the wheel, the other holding a crystal tumbler of scotch and soda with which he pointed out the stunning views of the Golden Gate Bridge and Alcatraz. Max wondered how much he'd drunk before they arrived. He didn't seem impaired, but that could indicate habitual alcoholism as easily as sobriety. She noticed Wolfe watched as closely as she did as Treybold explained the functioning of the yacht, just in case one of them needed to step up as designated driver.

"You wanted to talk about Atch," Treybold said, taking his seat in the captain's chair on the bridge and gesturing them to the leather-upholstered bench nearby. "I can't believe he's gone. He wasn't in San Francisco much, generally off on some photographic adventure or other, but you always knew he'd be back with some great story to tell."

He shook his head, glancing up toward the expanse of blue stretched over the bay. "Even when his plane went down in Alaska, I knew he wasn't gone for good. Not Atch. I still expect him to show up with a camera slung over his shoulder and a week's worth of beard on his chin, happy with the world, at least for the moment."

"He wasn't happy here," Max said, not bothering to make it a question. "In San Francisco."

Treybold took a sip of his scotch, considering. "He

didn't have much use for civilization. I never saw him happier than screaming down a ski slope or shooting a kayak through some killer rapids. We'd go skydiving when he was in town. I keep a plane at my ranch up in Marin."

He offered a broad, white-toothed smile at Max. "If you'd like to learn, I'd be happy to take you for a flight."

Max tried not to shudder. *Over her dead body.*

"Not while we're working on a story, thanks," Wolfe interjected with thin affability. "Conflict of interest."

Which was utter bull. And even Wolfe could hardly have missed that Treybold's invitation hadn't included him. Max wanted to feel irritation at his territorial attitude. But an unexpected heat flickered over her skin instead.

Treybold shrugged. "The offer holds after the story is complete. Or we can take the *Persephone* out for a fishing trip. I'd take Atch and his son out sometimes. Atch enjoyed the sport, but he liked the quiet out on the water just as much."

"You had that in common," Max guessed.

His gaze sharpened on her. "Exactly. That and strangling inheritances that neither of us cared a damn about. I never let it bother me the way he did. But then, I didn't have to be president of Burkhartt-Dantell, either."

"Do you think that's what drove him to take his life?" Max asked.

"Being dragged back from playing Grizzly Adams?" Treybold's mockery hid an emotion Max couldn't quite decipher.

"He told you he'd been hiding out, not lost?"

"I guessed." Treybold adjusted the *Persephone*'s

position against the wind and the waves. "He confirmed it. It wasn't like Atch to dwell in a fantasy world. He knew he'd have to return eventually. It's a cliché, but whatever he learned about himself out there in the wilderness, I thought it toughened him up a little. He seemed girded for battle."

"With the board?" Wolfe asked, a notebook and pen in his hand despite the tiny tape recorder he'd placed on the gleaming mahogany dash near Treybold.

"Hmm." Treybold sipped his scotch. "Atch spent his youth disdaining his father's conservatism and the whole corporate culture, and when he found himself ensnared in it, he ran. But he came back from Alaska reenergized about his plans to invest in the development of media in the Third World and to promote public involvement in the media here in the U.S."

Wolfe raised an eyebrow. "I imagine that idea didn't hold universal appeal."

Treybold laughed. "I thought Old Man Calvin was going to have a stroke. Toby Mittard had to physically restrain Tyce Sheppard. The man's eighty-seven, but he wields a mean letter opener. Most entertaining board meeting I've ever attended."

He paused. "Come to think of it, the only entertaining board meeting I've ever attended. I expect the last, as well, now that Atch is gone."

"Could he have changed the course of the company by himself?" Max asked. "I didn't think he owned a controlling interest."

"No, but a bigger chunk than any of the rest of the individual board members," Treybold said. "A couple of us thought he had some good ideas. Enough to make it an interesting fight."

"A fight that died with Atch?" Wolfe asked, a subtle shift in his posture indicating he'd found the scent he wanted to follow.

Treybold's mouth twitched. "You've spoken to other board members. With Atch gone, Mittard's side has the numbers, but not to the extent they'd like. The board as a whole controls Atch's share of the company now, but to be comfortable, they'd prefer to get it into the hands of like-minded investors."

"They can sell Atch's portion of the company?" Max asked, surprised. "I thought that went to Alex."

Toby Mittard had said that not all of the board members had been informed that Alex was missing, and she couldn't tell from Treybold's manner if he knew or not.

Treybold waved his drink. "Until the boy turns twenty-one, he has no control over the disbursement of the company assets."

"I bet there are a few people salivating at the prospect of getting into Burkhartt-Dantell," Wolfe murmured.

"Piranhas in the waters," Treybold agreed. "Billion-aires with a taste for television. Corporate sharks. Foreign investors. Japanese money. British. Russian. The amusing part is, the board needs a two-thirds majority to make this kind of sale. The machinations have begun."

He raised his scotch in their direction and downed it with a flourish. "I had a call yesterday afternoon from Darius Constantine himself, giving his condolences on Atch's passing and assuring me that he felt strongly about preserving the Dantell legacy. Though I'm sure he meant Matthias Dantell."

Max hated to show Wolfe that the international business talk took her out of her depth, but she had to ask. "Who is Darius Constantine?"

"A reclusive billionaire," Wolfe said. "Family money, if I remember right, oil or gems or something. They fled Bucharest to Vienna after the Soviet occupation."

"Oil *and* gems and something," Treybold corrected. "And he's not so much reclusive as exclusive. Doesn't hobnob with the hoi polloi. And nearly everyone is hoi polloi in comparison. He was tight with Old Man Dantell, though. Constantine owns a whole damn lake up in Alaska, has his own private compound on one side, runs a fishing lodge on the other. Firebird Lodge. Atch took me up there one time."

But his smile was for another memory. "Atch used to talk about the hunting trips old Matthias would drag him on up there when he was growing up. Said his old man could turn even killing a moose into a cold, calculating business transaction.

"And I don't think Atch ever got over those dogs Constantine raises. Said they made him feel sorry for the bears."

Treybold leaned back in his captain's chair. "As it happens, Constantine knew your father, as well, Miss Riley."

"*Max's* father?" Wolfe's response would have to suffice for them both. Max could only swallow hard. Her father had known so many people.

"Indeed." Treybold rested his chin on intertwined

fingers, enjoying their surprise. "Sheridan Riley, the diplomat, correct? Constantine read about your finding Atch in Alaska. He said he respected your father greatly and asked if I had met you. Of course, I had not, but I could hardly neglect the opportunity when it presented itself."

In the form of Davis Wolfe. Max gave him a cool smile. "Disappointed?"

"Not at all." Treybold's gaze searched hers speculatively. "I wanted to find out for myself what your interest in Atch was. I thought you must be after something from him, but I see I might have been wrong. In which case—"

He leaned over to place a thumb on the stop button of Wolfe's tape recorder. "Do you mind?"

Wolfe flipped his notebook shut and set it aside.

"In which case," Treybold continued, clicking off the recorder, "you might be better served staying away from the question of Atch's death and why he might have died."

He might have been discussing the weather, his voice and expression so matter-of-fact.

Max glanced at Wolfe. A flicker of his hazel gaze told her he was right there with her. That didn't stop the tiny cold shiver that tickled between her shoulder blades. Because where they were was alone on a yacht in the middle of San Francisco Bay with a man with arms like jackhammers.

"Are you saying you don't think Atch's death was a suicide?"

Treybold blinked, wide-eyed innocence, as if the idea had never occurred to him. "I wouldn't suggest that. The police are convinced, aren't they?"

He stretched out his long legs, the picture of cool non-chalance. Max was pretty sure she no longer bought it.

"You said when he returned from Alaska, he seemed tougher," she reminded him. "That he meant to fight for his plans for the company. You don't paint a picture of a suicidal man."

Treybold reached for his empty scotch, the first sign of nerves Max had caught. "I don't think anyone can truly know another person's mind. I could have misjudged Atch in any number of ways. If the police say he killed himself, who am I to argue?"

He leaned toward them. "My point is that I *wouldn't* argue. It is in the best interests of Burkhartt-Dantell that Atch's suicide be put behind us as soon as possible. The mere suggestion that his death was anything other than straightforward would not be taken well by any number of powerful people."

"And they picked you to warn us?" Max asked, annoyed.

"Lord, no." Treybold laughed. "Atch said you were a good kid. I thought maybe I owed you a heads-up. And maybe…"

He smiled faintly as his fingers played with his empty glass. "Maybe I wanted to get a silly confession off my chest. When Atch got back from Alaska, he told me that when he was planning his disappearance, he'd wanted to leave a letter behind for Alex, explaining why he'd left. He'd even written it. He showed it to me. But he said he'd realized he couldn't ask Alex to keep his secret for him, so he hadn't left it for the kid."

Wolfe frowned. "What are you saying?"

Treybold's green eyes held Max's through the long pause after Wolfe's question, and she feared she knew exactly what he was saying, bringing up that goodbye letter. And that he darn sure wasn't going to spell it out any more clearly, tape recorder off or not.

She still had to ask. "That letter, he never said what he did with—"

A thundering jolt slammed her against the yacht's instrument panel, knocking the breath out of her. Wolfe's shoulder struck hers, and she heard Treybold's head strike the wheel.

For a moment, all she heard was their breathing as they braced for another impact. No crashing. No screaming.

No engines.

Treybold leapt to his feet, stark fear in his face, blood oozing from a cut on his temple as he scanned the water before them. "Good God. I didn't see anything. They must have come out of nowhere. We weren't speeding, barely holding steady—"

Max found herself on her feet, too, looking for the vessel they must have struck. She saw only choppy gray water spreading before them.

Treybold scrambled for the bridge door, she and Wolfe close on his heels. They climbed up out of the salon to the flybridge, Max running to the starboard rail and Wolfe to port while Treybold headed aft. Other than a discarded plastic soda bottle, Max saw no sign of debris.

"Nothing," she said, turning to see Wolfe shaking his head.

"Whatever we hit must have been submerged," Treybold said, his voice unsteady with relief. "Even something as small as a kayak, we'd see something. I'll radio the Coast Guard. We've lost engines. We could be taking on water."

"I'll check down below," Wolfe offered.

Treybold nodded. "If someone's left a sunken boat out here for my girl to founder on, they're going to wish they'd never been born. Nobody hurts my *Persephone*...."

His voice trailed off, and he flashed them a shadow of his cocky smile. "I hope you two know how to swim."

"Life vests?" Max asked.

"Stored in that bench behind—"

He froze. Following his gaze, Max saw a curl of black smoke leaking up the stairs from the small rear deck below.

Jolting into motion, Treybold dashed back toward the salon as Max climbed down to the engine hatch. She saw no flames, but she smelled bitter, acrid smoke and something else—

"Riley! No!" Wolfe pulled her away from the smoking hatch, yanking her up against his chest. She could feel his heart pounding.

The unexpected concern in his green-flecked eyes troubled her as much as her reaction to his touch. She pulled free, using sarcasm to cover her surprise.

"Chill, Wolfe. I wasn't planning on throwing my body down there to smother the flames."

"Extinguisher," Treybold barked, pulling up beside them with a kitchen-sized fire extinguisher. "Call the Coast Guard."

"No." Wolfe grabbed Treybold's arm. "You know the ship's information. Give me the extinguisher—"

That smell again. A big whiff of it, like passing a semi on the road. "Diesel fuel!"

Wolfe and Treybold turned toward her, ridiculously slowly, as if time had stretched in that instant of recognition, their mouths opening in a question or surprise.

No time.

Max raced toward them, pumping her legs with every scrap of power from Tomas's workouts. Wolfe grabbed Treybold's shirt, spinning him toward the side of the boat. Max plowed into them both, the impact throwing them all over the rail.

Max felt the deck shudder as her feet left it for open air, and more than gravity hit her as she slammed into the choppy waters of the bay.

Chapter 6

Blood. She tasted it in her mouth, along with salt water and gas fumes. Water burned her sinuses and roared in her ears, dragging her legs downward.

Was it down?

For a terrifying second, Max wasn't sure which way she needed to strike for oxygen, for life. White flashed above her, bubbles churned into the water by a splashing body.

Air.

The explosion and the frigid water had knocked the breath out of her. Ignoring her burning lungs, Max scissor-kicked toward the bubbles, her waterlogged slacks and deck shoes making her awkward and slow. Desperate, she pulled herself upward toward the glimmering surface.

She broke through into sunlight, sucking a gasping

breath of air, coughing out water and that faint taste of blood. She must have bit her tongue when she hit the bay.

"Riley!"

She turned to see Wolfe, his unruly hair for once all plastered down, treading water a yard away. He had an arm draped across Treybold's chest, holding the man's head up while he choked out water.

"You hurt?" Wolfe asked.

"No. Treybold?"

"M'all right," Treybold coughed out, pulling free of Wolfe's hold. *"Persephone."*

Max followed his gaze. The explosion had torn the back end of the beautiful boat apart, sucking her stern under. The front cabin remained above water, tilted at a jaunty angle, but flames licked up the sides, sending a plume of dark smoke into the sky.

A gargled sob wrenched from Treybold's throat. "My baby. Dammit. Dammit all to hell." He struck out for the wreck, but the flames kept him back a safe distance.

"You're sure you're all right?" Wolfe demanded, swimming closer. He looked ready to grab her in a rescue hold at the slightest provocation.

"I'm fine. Ice water in my veins, remember?"

He laughed. "Can't be any colder than this bloody bay. Kick off your shoes and conserve your energy. This current is going to be hell. But, much as I hate to say it, keep your clothes on. We'll be fighting hypothermia soon."

Max kicked off her deck shoes, but she doubted they'd have long to wait for help. The explosion had caught the notice of other boaters, and she could see a sailboat less than half a mile away pulling in its sails as it started up an outboard to head their direction.

"Bloody hell," Wolfe muttered, as they watched the *Persephone* sink slowly lower. "And I thought the Sudan was dicey."

Max snorted, the salty water still burning her nose. "So much for water travel. Walking is looking better and better. Good for the environment, too. What do you think we hit?"

"Hit?" Wolfe glanced at where Treybold paddled, focused solely on the burning hulk of his beloved yacht, and lowered his voice. "In the middle of the bay?"

It had seemed a logical conclusion after the first impact. But they certainly hadn't hit another boat. And looking at the empty, fathomless water surrounding them, there didn't seem to be many other options.

Max met Wolfe's gaze. "Faulty engine? Gas leak?"

Wolfe grimaced. "God, I hope so."

Max turned back toward the sinking boat. "Bloody hell."

"Hot and sour soup." Lionel set a white paper bag printed with a red dragon on Max's desk and pulled out a plastic container. "The best thing to fight off a cold."

Max glanced up from the stack of magazine articles on Court Treybold and the Burkhartt-Dantell Media Group she was forcing herself to wade through. "I thought that was chicken soup."

"If you're going to be picky, I'll eat it myself." He pulled off the lid and stuck in a spoon before passing it to her. The second man to offer her Chinese food in less than twenty-four hours.

The first spoonful burned Max's throat, searing those cold inner places that a long, hot shower hadn't been able to warm.

"Thanks." She offered her gangly assistant a smile. "I didn't even know I needed that."

"Who knows what you might have picked up in that water." Lionel shuddered. "Thank goodness you got rescued before the sharks found you."

"There aren't any sharks in the bay. Are there?"

"Well, the leopard sharks wouldn't bother you, and there haven't been any confirmed reports of sevengill cowsharks attacking humans in the wild, but they do eat young harbor seals, and—"

"Never mind." She usually found his marine lectures kind of cute, but sharks were one thing she didn't need to add to the morning's ordeal.

Lionel sat on the edge of her desk and dug an egg roll from the take-out bag. "What did the Coast Guard say?"

Max ran a hand through her still-damp hair. "The *Persephone* sank before they could reach her. If they determine she's not a shipping hazard, they'll leave it at that."

"You're kidding, right?" Egg roll muffled Lionel's outrage. "Shouldn't *somebody* investigate a boat exploding?"

"There's no evidence of foul play."

"That's because it all sank to the bottom of the bay!"

"Maybe we did hit something. Maybe the gas tank had a leak." Max snagged the second egg roll before it reached Lionel's mouth. "Treybold told the authorities he's certain it was an accident. There's nothing to justify an expensive investigation."

"Even if they did investigate, I doubt they would find enough evidence to determine a cause."

The sepulchral announcement from right beside them sent both Max and Lionel into choking spasms over their egg rolls. Tomas stared darkly down at them, arms crossed over his chest.

"Didn't you even notice me open the door?"

Max glanced at the office door, now closed once more. Her face heated, as much from leftover hurt from the evening before as from embarrassment and choking on the hot Chinese mustard. "Simone's in the outer office. She wouldn't let just anyone walk in here."

"Not unless just anyone had slit her throat."

Lionel gulped, and Max saw him glance toward the door as he suppressed the need to make sure Simone was still breathing.

Max gave Tomas his own dark look right back. "My, aren't we bloodthirsty this morning."

"Just concerned. I warned you against pursuing this Dantell business, and this morning Lionel calls to inform me you've been nearly blown up, drowned and eaten by sharks while interrogating a member of the Burkhartt-Dantell board."

Max trained her glare on Lionel. "You called Tomas?"

"I, uh, I just—" Lionel grabbed her empty soup bowl and stuffed it in the bag. "I'll just go throw these away."

He exited the office in a rustle of crinkling paper.

"Lionel shouldn't have called me?"

Max answered the question behind the question. "I don't think a boating accident is karmic retribution for disagreeing with you about searching for Alex Dantell."

"You don't actually believe it was an accident." He watched her reaction.

"Whatever it was, it's not related to Burkhartt-Dantell." She gestured at the articles scattered on her desk. "Court Treybold doesn't own enough stock to be worth killing. Atch Dantell could cause trouble, but Treybold could only be an irritation. If someone was out to hurt him, it was more likely a jilted girlfriend or jealous husband."

"You're certain that Treybold was the target?"

She spun in her chair to glare at him. "If you're trying to scare me, you're going to have to do better than that."

But the fleeting look she caught in his eye as he crossed around her desk chilled her outrage.

"You *weren't* trying to scare me. You really think I could be in danger."

Well, duh. She should have realized that last night. He'd practically panicked at the idea of her continuing her search after she'd shown him that drawing of the knife from Alex's bedroom.

"What aren't you telling me?" she demanded. "What do you know about the symbol on that knife? What's the significance of the feather of Maat?"

His gaze snapped to hers. "What?"

Score. "I can find someone else to ask."

He hesitated only a moment before placing his hands on her desk, leaning toward her. "Anubis is out of your league."

"Anubis." She'd done some research on the Internet late the night before. "The Egyptian god of embalming. Head of a jackal. Judged the hearts of the dead."

"This Anubis prefers not to wait until they're dead," Tomas said, his voice cold. "He likes to weigh hearts while they're still beating. It means working fast with a knife."

Okay. "So he's a serial killer?"

"A hired assassin. One of the best in the world."

Max's heart squeezed in her chest. "And he's after Alex? Someone hired him to kill a *child?*"

"Kill, kidnap, frighten. It doesn't matter. You see why you have to get out of this now." He paused, reclaiming his calm, but Max had seen the frustration and concern behind it. "There is a story about a Colombian drug lord who had a rival's daughter raped and killed. The rival hired Anubis, who infiltrated the drug lord's compound, cut out his heart and served it to the man's henchmen for dinner before the death was discovered."

Max rose and moved to the window, fighting a deep chill that the hot and sour soup hadn't been able to dispel, after all.

"You are good at what you do," Tomas said. "But you don't hunt killers. If this man who left the knife is really Anubis, this is no game for amateurs. No one even knows what he looks like. Leave him to the professionals."

"Professionals?" Max asked with a brittle laugh. "You mean Steve Spencer and Spike?"

She shook her head as she leaned against the windowsill, once more looking down into the busy streets of San Francisco and wondering where one determined, haunted boy might go. Haunted and hunted.

"The boy is more valuable alive than dead," Tomas said more gently. "And Anubis has been said to have a code against killing innocents."

"He's looking for Alex," she said. "Who knows what he'll do if he finds him. If this Anubis guy is as deadly as you say, I could be Alex's only chance."

Tomas growled in frustration. "This is not your world, Magdalena. I made a promise to look after you, difficult as you make it. I will not let you get yourself killed."

You're not my father. The unspoken words hung between them. She had shouted them at him more than once, when Tomas had bullied her into training or warned her against a particularly foolish course of action.

But Max didn't say them now, maybe because she could see the flicker of fear for her in Tomas's pale eyes.

"I've been making my own decisions for a long time, Tomas," she said instead. "I'll understand if you don't support me, but I can't just walk away."

She paused. "What would my father have done?"

Tomas didn't hesitate. "He would have gone after the boy." He strode to the door and paused. "Even if it meant he never came back. I just don't want to lose you, too."

Simone paused in Max's doorway as Tomas's footsteps receded through the outer office. She raised one thin red eyebrow.

"I know he's like your godfather," Lionel said, pushing into Max's office behind her, "but if *I'd* put that expression on his face, I'd be changing my identity and moving to Uruguay."

Max threw herself into her chair, blowing out a breath she hadn't realized she'd been holding. "He's overreacting."

"To what?" Simone dropped a pile of mail onto Max's desk.

"He thinks I should give up searching for Alex Dantell because a deadly international assassin might be after him."

"Oh." Simone's expression remained impressively bland. "Is that all?"

"Assassin?" Lionel obviously hoped he hadn't heard correctly.

"The feather of Maat you identified," Max explained. "Apparently this killer, Anubis, uses it as his calling card."

Lionel winced. "Maybe it was just a red flag?"

"I'll have to warn Steve," Max said. "But I'm in the best position to continue the search. No one has any reason to connect me to Alex Dantell."

"Not quite." Simone lifted a piece of mail and handed it to Max. The postcard showed the Golden Gate Bridge at sunset. "*Someone* thinks you two have a connection."

A warning? A threat? Max flipped the card over. Neat block printing was cramped into the left-hand side of the card.

Dear Miss Riley,
Everybody thinks my dad killed himself, but he didn't. Please don't let my mom hire you to find me. Dad never found what he was looking for in Alaska. He needed more time to finish his coo. I just need time to get the proof that he was killed. I'll come home then, I promise.
Sincerely,
Alex

Max set the postcard carefully down on her desk, shaken. Lionel leaned over to read it upside down.

"His 'coo'?"

"Coup d'état," Max clarified. "Court Treybold said Atch planned to shake up Burkhartt-Dantell."

"What a cute kid," Simone said, her gray eyes troubled. "He really believed in his dad."

"Whether Atch deserved it or not," Max agreed. Stilling her disrupted nerves, she examined the postcard more closely. "It was postmarked yesterday, somewhere in the city. He had to have mailed it not long after he disappeared." He'd had a plan of some kind, so soon after his father's death. *Cute.* Hell, this kid was impressive. "He must have thought Yvonne would hire me to find him since I'd found his dad."

"Is that the name of the shop?" Simone asked, pointing to a logo on the bottom of the card.

"Bay Bijoux." Max read the tiny print. "South San Francisco."

Lionel frowned. "Does Burkhartt-Dantell have offices there or something? Why would he go to South San Francisco?"

He looked up at the same time Max and Simone did.

"The airport," they chorused together.

"But where would he go?" Simone asked.

"He's got grandparents in Kansas," Lionel reminded her. "Damn. If he goes there, Spencer will catch him for sure."

Simone cuffed the back of his head with her palm. "That would be a *good* thing, dork. We *want* Alex caught, remember?"

"Yeah," Lionel grumbled, shifting away from her reach. "But I'd still rather have us do it than Steve Spencer."

"It's not a competition," Max said, her focus on the postcard. "But I don't think he's going to Kansas. I think it's time for another trip."

Lionel sat up, his pique gone. "Really? With the time crunch and all the logistics involved, you'll want someone along who can keep you connected to everything that's going on."

Max shook her head. "I'll move faster on my own."

"Did I slow you down in Alaska?" he challenged. "I got you the fastest flights, not to mention the best deals. Come on, Max, I proved I could handle it. I won't get in your way."

It had been convenient to have an assistant along on the last trip. And she recognized that need in his eyes to prove himself—especially to Simone.

"How soon can you be ready to leave?"

"Soon! I mean, now."

"Go home and pack a bag," Max told him, reaching for the phone. "And make sure you bring a heavy coat."

Chapter 7

"You want a copy of *what?*"

She had Steve Spencer's attention finally. Warning him about a lethal hired assassin hadn't done it, but ask for something that was part of his investigation...

"I'd like to see exactly what Atchison Dantell wrote in his suicide note." Max didn't think the taxi driver spoke much English, but she kept her voice low as she spoke into her cell phone. "You could just e-mail it to me."

"That's part of the police investigation," Steve said, managing to sound both apologetic and vague. "Don't worry, Max, we have everything under control."

Sure, they did. That was why she and Lionel were heading for San Francisco International Airport, and he was sitting in the Dantell mansion waiting for Alex to walk through the front door.

"I thought of another angle on this search," she said, peering around Lionel to see what had slowed traffic to such a crawl on 101 at this time of day. "If Alex really thinks his father was murdered, where would he go to find proof? I thought there might be some kind of clue in the note his father left."

That was true enough. No need to mention the paranoid suspicions Court Treybold's coy comments had raised.

"Look, Max…" Even over the phone, she could picture his sheepish, sexy grin. "I got a call from Toby Mittard about an hour ago. He was very upset that you'd gone with Davis Wolfe to talk to Court Treybold. He sort of took my head off about it. I told him you're discreet, but he's under a lot of pressure."

So *that* was what had shut down Steve's willingness to share information.

"I'm not going to do anything to endanger Alex."

"Of course not," Steve jumped in. "But Mittard has a point. You're not on the payroll for this. Leave it to us."

That was exactly what she wanted everyone to think she was doing—especially whoever had hired Anubis.

"You're right. I don't have the manpower to do the legwork you and Spike have set up, anyway," she said, glaring at Lionel when he mimed gagging at the unassuming sweetness in her voice. "I just thought I could take a look at that note without getting in your way. Toby Mittard would never have to know. You'd just be picking my brain."

"I couldn't take advantage of you like that again." Steve's voice slowed, warming with humor and something like anticipation. "Not without offering you some kind of compensation."

Despite her frustration with him, Max played along. "Is that right?"

"Say, a good dinner? Maybe some dancing."

She imagined he had some moves on the dance floor. And elsewhere. "What if I don't come up with anything helpful?"

He chuckled. "Then you can pay for dinner."

"You realize that's a challenge."

"Absolutely."

Lionel tapped impatiently on her elbow. They had finally reached the airport exit.

She nodded. "I'll let you get back to work. And Steve? Be careful."

"What?" It took him a second to change tracks. "Oh, you mean your Abumbis guy."

"Anubis."

"Right."

She could hear the smile in his voice.

"Sweetheart, nobody is going to hire a world-class assassin to go after a little boy. I don't know where this friend of yours got his information—"

"Tomas is a retired diplomat," she said, trying not to grit her teeth. "He still has high-level contacts. He knows what he's talking about."

"I'm sure he does." He was humoring her. "But a weird symbol on a knife doesn't an international intrigue make. Somebody's trying to scare Yvonne, and they're doing a damn good job. But they're sure as hell not scaring me."

He paused, and his tone warmed. "Look, it's sweet of you to worry, but Spike and I can take care of ourselves."

The roar of a landing jet rocked the taxi, cutting off Max's biting reply.

"Where *are* you?" Steve asked. "The airport?"

"It's my cell phone," Max said, rattling the phone as she spoke. "It's cutting out. I'll talk to you later."

She flicked off the phone and passed it to Lionel for safekeeping.

"Who the hell does that guy think he is?" Lionel gathered up his laptop and overnight bag as the taxi pulled into the queue to the terminal. "Blowing you off like that."

"I can't blame him," Max admitted. "Somebody hiring a professional assassin to go after a twelve-year-old? It does sound a little far-fetched."

"We'll see how far-fetched he thinks it sounds when he's got one of Anubis's daggers sticking out of his chest."

"Lionel!"

"You like him," Lionel accused as the taxi staggered to a halt at the curb.

"I don't want him to get killed," Max corrected, resolutely not blushing as she hefted her carry-on onto her shoulder and climbed out of the cab.

"You just don't want him to get killed," Lionel repeated, falling into step with her as they entered the crowded, echoing terminal. "So, why haven't you called Davis Wolfe?"

Damn. Wolfe. "Cell phone," she ordered, dragging Lionel out of the flow of harried travelers.

"He's the one who almost drowned with you this

morning," Lionel continued. "You should have invited him to stick around for lunch when he dropped you back at Quest. Jeez."

Damn, damn, damn. She dug into her carry-on for her notebook with Wolfe's cell number. Lionel snagged it from her and programmed Wolfe's number into her phone, along with Steve Spencer's. He punched Call and handed it back.

Despite Lionel's teasing, it wasn't Steve's flirting that had distracted her from worrying about her newspaper rival—er, colleague. It was Wolfe's competence.

Whatever conflicted feelings she might have about the man personally, she'd heard enough stories, read enough between the lines of his articles, to believe he could take care of himself. And she'd seen for herself just that morning how well he handled himself in a dangerous situation.

But it might help if he knew what the dangers were.

Wolfe's cell shunted her to voice mail. "Wolfe, this is Riley."

Great. Now what? Don't look now, but there might be a shadowy international assassin behind you?

"Call me. I have news." Short, sweet, impossible for a journalist to resist. "And, Wolfe. Be careful."

Wolfe can take care of himself. But she wished he'd answered his phone.

Still, even *if* a professional assassin had been hired to take Alex Dantell hostage, that assassin would be fully focused on his primary target, Alex Dantell.

The thought made her shiver. She glanced up and down the long arc of the terminal building, suddenly ex-

periencing how exposed Alex must have felt coming
here, not knowing if the police had been notified of his
running away, his mind whirring with plans and backup
plans, determined not to get caught.

If only he weren't quite so resourceful; if only
Yvonne had notified the police; if only he had been
caught by the feds or Spike or airport security.

Standing in the swirl of airport activity, Max could
almost hear the furtive, eager snuffling of the jackal-
headed monster on Alex's trail. But Alex wouldn't hear.
He was resourceful. He was playing this round of hide
and seek like a pro.

But he had no idea how deadly a game he was playing.

"You really think he's up here somewhere?" Lionel
asked for the fifth time since they'd disembarked their
Northern Lights Air flight. He glanced around the main
terminal of Anchorage International Airport, as if he
might catch Alex Dantell buying a candy bar at the
newsstand. "There's no way a lone kid walked up to a
counter in the San Francisco airport and plopped down
a wad of cash for a ticket to Anchorage."

Another frequently repeated refrain on their endless
flight in a rust bucket from San Francisco to Seattle to
Alaska. Between exploding boats and rattling planes,
bus travel was starting to look pretty darn good.

"Northern Lights doesn't require unaccompanied
minor status for anyone over thirteen," Max reminded
him. "And he could purchase the ticket over the Internet."

"He's only twelve!"

"He's tall for his age." With an e-ticket and no check-in baggage, he could easily have used the automated check-in kiosk. *Could have.* But had he?

It was too bad airline employees were so conscientious about their obligation not to discuss passenger manifests. That could have saved her this trip—and Lionel's nagging doubts.

But without a court order, Max had to do the legwork. With Yvonne's refusal to allow police involvement, even Steve Spencer would have to rely on Alex's credit card usage to alert him if Alex took a flight. Max adjusted her carry-on and picked up her pace along the terminal. "There's the way down to the car rental counter."

"You would think Steve Spencer would have noticed an airline ticket on Alex's credit card," Lionel continued, following her through the milling passengers down the hall.

What were all these people doing at an airport at eleven o'clock at night?

"Maybe the credit card charge hasn't shown up yet." Or maybe Alex had worked out some other ingenious way to pay for the ticket.

Or maybe she'd completely misread his cryptic, determined postcard, and he never intended to follow his father's footsteps to Alaska at all—a possibility that grew larger in her mind every time Lionel asked another question.

"And what does he think he's going to find up here, anyway?" Lionel's shoulder bumped hers as he dodged the outstretched claws of a towering Kodiak bear. "Sheesh! How many tourists do you think *he* ate before they stuffed him?"

Max ignored him as they turned down the hall toward the rental counters, but Lionel continued with his theme.

"The kid's dad died in San Francisco. It's not like some moose chased him down and hanged him. How's he supposed to get out to that remote cabin, anyway?"

"Hire a pilot, just like us," Max answered, ignoring the drop in her stomach at the idea of getting on another plane. "There are thousands in Alaska. I'm sure Alex has a map. He'd have wanted his dad to show him where he'd been."

Lionel shrugged. "Yeah, but he can't plan to stay out there, right? It's only the end of September, but it could hit freezing overnight tonight, according to the flight attendant."

Resolutely pushing back fantasies of wiring Lionel's jaw shut, Max went through the motions of renting their car.

Unfortunately, Lionel had a point. A number of points. What could Alex possibly hope to find here that would change how the police viewed his father's death?

Max had a healthy respect for logic, but the truth was that she often succeeded where others had failed not by logic, but by pure intuition. When she reached the limits of research and deduction, Max had to rely on her gut and that quiet, clear part of her mind that sometimes knew the answer to a puzzle without any doubt or any logically definable explanation.

But standing at the rental car desk, waiting to head into the cold Alaskan night to their hotel, her throat constricted with panic that she'd made the wrong choice.

Alaska? What had possessed her? Arrogance, perhaps, that she should be able to whisk the young truant home without access to the resources Spencer Investigations had. She'd told Lionel the search for Alex wasn't a competition, but she hadn't told Steve she was coming to Anchorage.

No reason to get his hopes up if there's nothing to be found. And no reason to embarrass herself unnecessarily.

And maybe part of her just wanted to be the one to accompany Alex up the walk to his house, to his mother, to prove herself to Yvonne and her fancy L.A. investigators, to Davis Wolfe and his "serious journalism," to Tomas. To herself.

An agenda like that could cost a lot more than embarrassment. It could cost Alex Dantell his life.

She took the rental car keys with a murmur of thanks, and drew in a slow breath, getting herself under control. Her intuition had gotten her out of more than one tight spot on searches in the past. But this search was different.

She'd only met Alex once, briefly at that. But she could picture those intense blue eyes as he told her about snow camping with his dad, about how his dad knew how to survive anything. She could hear the longing in his voice, a silent plea for her to prove him right, bring his dad home again.

The only other person she'd allowed herself to care about before beginning a search had been the only person she'd never found. Sheridan Riley.

"What did you get?" Lionel asked, as they left the rental counter. "Tell me you upgraded to a Mustang this time."

"Right. A convertible," she said. "Perfect for a scream-ing ride across the glaciers."

"Max Riley?" The soft, diffident voice belonged to a slender, almond-eyed woman of about Max's five feet seven inches, her straight black hair pulled back with dragonfly barrettes.

"Can I help you?"

"Your friend?" The woman's voice held a hesitancy that suggested English was not her primary language, though Max detected no trace of an accent. "He asked me to tell you that he would…hunt you down?…later."

"My friend?"

The woman's smile faltered. "Yes?" She gestured toward the glass doors that led to the hotel shuttles and taxis. "He said he was in a hurry and had to run on ahead."

Max met Lionel's gaze, as confused as her own.

"I'm sorry." She offered a smile to the woman, whose face was twisting in dismay. "We're traveling with a group, so I'm not sure who you mean. What did he look like?"

The woman shook her head with regret. "Medium height?" she said. "Medium age."

"Hair color?"

"He wore a hat, for the rain." The woman's troubled eyes glanced from Max to Lionel and back. "He was dressed like a businessman?"

"Of course." Max smiled again, squelching the urge to drag the woman outside and demand she point out this "friend." "Thanks for letting us know. Did he say where he'd meet us?"

The woman shook her head.

"Okay. Thanks again." Max's smile felt welded to her

face, and her voice sounded manically perky, but the un-witting messenger merely smiled back and strode away.

"A friend?" Lionel asked. "Who the heck could that be?"

"Based on her description? Half the men in North America." Calming breaths were just not cutting it.

"Could it be Tomas, trying to make a point?" Lionel winced. "How angry *was* he?"

"Tomas would be a best-case scenario. Let's get our car."

"What are the other scenarios?" Lionel demanded, glancing over his shoulder as he trotted after her down the hall.

"Steve Spencer?" Max suggested. "Maybe an airline ticket showed up on Alex's credit card, after all."

Or maybe Davis Wolfe. Tweaking her with the in-nocent bystander would be a prank he couldn't resist. But why would Wolfe be in Anchorage? Could his in-vestigation of Burkhartt-Dantell somehow have led him to Alaska? Would he try to scoop her on a story they were supposedly collaborating on?

She remembered the way they'd instinctively worked in sync questioning Court Treybold that morning, and she didn't want to believe it.

Or maybe that was just the wicked glint in his eyes when he smiled.

Neither was a reason to trust him.

Max resisted the temptation to glance behind as Lionel was doing. Whoever had sent the woman was long gone. And the truth was that if he wasn't, she might not recognize him, anyway.

Because even Steve and Wolfe were best-case scenarios.

He asked me to tell you he would hunt you down *later*. Max set her jaw and picked up her pace.

Anubis.

Chapter 8

Occasional raindrops spat fitfully against the wind-shield of their rental car as Max pulled into a spot behind the Big Bear Charters hangar at the airport the next day. Max didn't bother to grab the complimentary umbrella the rental company representative had given her earlier that morning. Her hair was still damp from the two hours they'd spent checking the hotel parking lot for that representative.

"Do you think the guy got here ahead of us?" Lionel asked as they climbed out of the car.

"Wherever he was going, he definitely got there ahead of us," Max said, glancing at her watch in disgust. Despite the fact that the clearing clouds were only now allowing the morning sky to brighten, it was nearly ten o'clock.

"I can't believe somebody slashed our tires." Lionel

glanced at their new rental car. He'd finally gotten his Mustang, the only replacement the rental company had had available on short notice. And Max could tell he was falling hard. "Should I stay here with it, just in case whoever it was tries again?"

"He got a good four hours on us. Any more sabotage would just be a waste of his time."

"I bet it was Spencer," Lionel said, as they headed for the hangar. "He wants to find Alex first."

Steve didn't strike Max as the tire-slashing type. *Spike, on the other hand...*

She'd left messages for Wolfe and Tomas from the hotel that morning, but neither had gotten back to her. Simone told her Steve had dropped by the office the day before looking for her, but Max hadn't been able to reach him.

At least whoever had sabotaged her rental hadn't left a feather-inlaid dagger sticking out of the tires.

The muffled tones of a cell phone broke into her grim thoughts. Lionel halted beside her, digging through his field coat pockets for the offending gadget.

"Hey, what's up?" Frowning, he jerked the phone from his ear to glance at it more closely. He rolled his eyes at Max, gesturing that it was her phone. "Hello. This is Max Riley's answering service. How may I help you?"

"Oh!" He straightened. "Davis, hey, this is Lionel."

Davis Wolfe. Relief rushed through Max's limbs, weakening her knees. Not that she'd been worried about Wolfe just because he hadn't returned her calls. People didn't just disappear.

Except that people she knew sometimes did.

"Sorry, I forgot to give Max's phone back last night. I mean, not that we were together last night. I mean, we were, but we were working. Not all night, I mean…"

Lionel gave up, his ears bright red as he thrust the phone at Max.

"Wolfe?"

"Riley," the dry voice drawled. "Impressive work ethic."

"Unlike yours," she shot back, irritation hiding her gladness at hearing his voice. "It took you long enough to call me back."

"Don't you ever check your messages?"

Oops. "Listen, Wolfe, you could be in danger. Before you blow me off, call my father's old friend, Tomas Gregory. You met him at the *Sentinel* awards dinner last spring—"

"I called your office this morning trying to reach you. Simone told me about Anubis."

"Oh. Good." She hadn't realized how much she didn't want anything bad to happen to him. She frowned, suddenly suspicious. "You're taking this seriously?"

"I've heard rumors about the bloke. All very urban legend. But even if he doesn't exist, somebody using that legend to intimidate a frightened mother is sick enough to take seriously."

"You'll watch your back?"

"Ingrained habit. And good as it is to know that your eager young Lionel is watching yours, where the hell are you, Riley? We've got a story to write."

"I'm following a—" No, not a hunch. *Serious jour-*

nalism. "I'm following a lead. You'll get your human interest piece. You just worry about your end."

"Following leads of my own," he assured her, with so much smugness that she knew he was scrambling for scraps as desperately as she was.

"Good luck, then."

"You, too. And, Riley—" He paused, and she could almost see his wicked grin. "It's nice to know you care."

The Big Bear Charters office was empty, so they headed around the building to the open hangar.

"Hey, they've picked up a Britten-Norman Islander," Lionel said, pointing to a long plane with a swept-up tail sitting on the tarmac. "Room for eight passengers. It's got a twin engine. That would be something to fly."

Max forced herself to look at the plane, hearing Tomas's voice. *Face your fears.* Somehow that was easier when the fears weren't designed to lift you off the ground. Even when Tomas was the pilot, she knew gravity was really in charge.

"Cool," she managed, though the only cool thing about it was that it was marginally larger than the mosquito-sized death trap beside it, the Cessna 206 that had ferried her and Lionel on their previous trip to Atchison Dantell's remote cabin.

A broad-shouldered man wearing a fur-lined hat with ear flaps and an oil-stained yellow jacket stood beneath the wing of the mosquito, draining liquid into a clear tube.

"He's siphoning from his own plane?" Max asked, horrified.

"Fuel sample," Lionel explained. "Checking for water. Standard procedure before a flight."

Great. Something new to worry about. "Mr. Scalisi!"

The man looked up at Max's hail, his stubbled jaw settling into a scowl as he flicked the fuel sample across the tarmac.

"What do you want?" he growled as Max and Lionel approached. "Here to find another long-lost brother?"

If he thought Max was going to feel guilty for the story she'd told him when she'd paid him to fly her and Lionel out to Atch's cabin, he was in for a disappointment.

"Mr. Dantell had no complaints about your helping me find him," she reminded the man. "I assume he paid you for the supplies you flew in for him."

The pilot glanced at the Britten-Norman Islander, which Atch's money must have paid for, the scowl still working his jaw. "'Course he paid me. He was an *honest* man."

Max snorted. "He told you he was a fur trapper. I have as many long-lost brothers as he ever sold furs."

Scalisi grunted. "Maybe so, but you ain't dead. As yet."

So he'd heard about Atch's suicide. No wonder he was in a foul mood.

"The vultures are already circling," Scalisi spat. "You're a reporter, right? I guess you can really cash in now."

"I'm not looking for a story." She pulled a photograph from the inside pocket of her anorak, a copy of Alex Dantell's sixth-grade school picture that Simone had tracked down. "I'm looking for another lost soul."

Scalisi took the picture reluctantly, pinching an edge between two oil-blackened fingers. "Whatcha want with this kid? He your long-lost secret love child or something?"

"His father died recently." She couldn't divulge Alex's identity directly, but she was running out of time. If she had to play a little loose with the rules, so be it. "And he idolized Atchison Dantell. He's left home. I think he may be trying to reach Atch's cabin, to attempt surviving in the wilderness as a way of getting through his grief."

She met Pete Scalisi's skeptical gaze with a fierce stare of her own. "You know what it's like out there better than I do. How long do you think a kid that age can survive on his own? That's if he's left alone. There are predators after this boy, and I'm not talking about grizzly bears."

"I bet." Scalisi handed her back the photograph. "How do I know you're not one of them?"

"Do you know who you're talking to?" Lionel asked, his voice high with outrage. "Max Riley is one of the most—"

"Lionel." Max cut him off, her eyes never leaving Scalisi's. "I came here to hire you to fly me out to that cabin so that if this boy is there, I can take him home to his mother. But if you don't trust me to do that, I will pay you to go out by yourself and just check to see if he's there."

"And bring him back to you?"

"Bring him back to the police," Max corrected. "They can make sure he gets home safely. I hope."

Scalisi glanced from her to Lionel and back. He grimaced. "Aw, hell. Come on, then."

"What?" Lionel asked as Scalisi turned away. "Come on where?"

"Come on and get in the damned plane."

Lionel's face brightened as he hurried toward the mosquito. Max followed only slightly more slowly, though she'd half hoped Scalisi would take her up on her second offer.

"You better damn well be telling the truth this time," Scalisi said as he opened the door to the plane's tiny cabin.

"I can't tell you everything," Max said. "But all I want is to see this boy safely home. I owe it to his father."

Scalisi nodded. "Then you'd better know that you're not the only one who's come around here asking about him."

Lionel's foot slipped as he climbed into the plane, and Max had to jerk backward to avoid a collision. They both stared at the pilot.

"Somebody already asked you to fly him out to Atch's cabin?" The clock in Max's head started ticking faster.

"This guy didn't say anything about Dantell or the cabin." Scalisi pulled off his hat and ran a hand through his unkempt hair. "He was asking about the boy. Had that same picture with him. Said he was a police investigator. Said the kid was running away from a custody fight."

"What did you tell him?" Lionel asked, hanging out of the plane like an awkward hawk.

Scalisi shrugged. "Not a damn thing. I never saw the kid before in my life. What was I supposed to tell him?"

"What did he look like?" Max demanded.

"Nothing special about him. Medium build, a few inches taller than you and me. Clean-shaven, wore a hat. Had a kind of shark-like quality about him. A nose like a knife."

Taller than Tomas, it sounded like. She could see Wolfe as a shark, but he had a sturdy Welsh face. Steve Spencer? His nose could be described as aquiline, if you squinted, but it wasn't as sharp as his clothes.

Scalisi pulled a card from his pocket and handed it to Max. "Left a number to call in case I saw the kid."

Not a number she recognized. She'd have Lionel try to track it down when they got back. "Are you going to call him?"

Scalisi shook his head. "I don't think so."

"Why not?"

Scalisi waved her into the plane. "A cop who doesn't leave his name? Besides, I told him the truth when I said the kid didn't look familiar, but now that you mentioned Dantell, I can't say that anymore."

He gave Max a steady look. "I recognize those eyes and that nose now. Your story is closer to the truth than that guy's. You ain't gotta tell me everything for me to know that."

"We're getting close." Scalisi's voice rang tinny and rough through the intercom system into Max's headset. "I'll come in low over the ridge, in case there's anybody we don't want to see us coming."

"Great." Max forced herself to open her eyes and look out the bulging windshield between Scalisi and Lionel ahead of her. She couldn't take the coward's way out and hide in meditation until they landed.

As the tiny Cessna swooped up behind the ridge where

she and Lionel had hidden on their first visit out here just a week and a half before, her stomach swooped down.

Forget meditation. *Ave Maria, gratia plena...*

One of Max's few clear memories of her mother was Serafina rocking her when she was hurt or frightened or couldn't sleep, singing Aves in her warm contralto.

The plane swooped again. *Sancta Maria, mater Dei...*

As they topped the narrow ridge, Max could have sworn the plane's belly skimmed the tops of the spruce trees below.

"What's that?"

"Oh, shit."

Max didn't realize she'd closed her eyes again until her companions' voices snapped them open. No mountain in the windshield. No essential pieces falling off the plane.

But her relief disappeared as she took in the view of the river valley below. Wind had stripped the golden leaves of the few aspen along the far bank of the river, and the arctic willows shivered half-bare in the damp cold. But it was Atch's cabin that caught her eye. The remains of the cabin. The rough log walls still stood, but the roof had fallen in, the door and windows blank holes through which black smoke sullenly wafted.

"Somebody beat us out here," the pilot said, passing the cabin and sweeping back around. "I don't see another plane."

"Check over that south ridge," Max said, her voice edged with tension. "There's a lake where Atch kept his floatplane."

"Yeah, I'd see it when I dropped his supplies."

Scalisi brought them up above the ridge, but the small lake spread empty below them, ruffled and gray under the high clouds.

"Can you land?" Max asked.

Scalisi hissed through his teeth as he swept them around to the head of the valley. "Maybe. There's a good stretch of gravel bank by the cabin. I'll take a look at it."

"Maybe the cabin got hit by lightning or something," Lionel said. "It's right out in the open."

Max prayed it had been lightning. That it hadn't been a young boy trying to stay warm through a freezing rain, falling asleep and never noticing a stray spark flying from an open woodstove.

A sickening jolt jerked her back to the plane. Scalisi had brought them down on the gravel beach beside the river. Max opened the plane's door as the Cessna bounced to a stop. She hit the ground running.

She spared a glance at Atchison Dantell's battered green canoe. Water from the recent rains shimmered nearly to its gunwales. If Alex Dantell had been here, he hadn't touched the canoe.

She heard the men hit the beach behind her, but she'd found her stride and she reached the cabin first, the acrid scent of damp, smoldering wood searing her nostrils. The front door tilted inward, hanging from one hinge, its rough-hewn planks warped with heat.

The residue of that heat pulsed against Max's face as she reached the threshold, but the same rains that had filled the canoe had dampened the cabin's walls, and the fire that had blazed inside had burned itself out against them. The roof had burned off, but the beams still crossed against the sky. Inside, Max could make out the blackened wreck of an army cot, a melted camp chair, a couple of cans of beans that had exploded off rough wooden shelves and lay like burst mortar shells on the charred floor.

She pressed the sleeve of her anorak across her nose and mouth as she leaned forward to look around the dangling door.

A heavy hand grabbed her shoulder.

"Don't be a fool," Scalisi growled. "If the roof beams don't fall on you, you'll go through the floor. If there was anybody in there while this place was burning, you ain't going to help them now."

"If there was anybody in there, there wouldn't be anything left," Lionel called. His pale face, already smudged with soot, peered into the cabin through the empty back window.

"There would be something left," Max said, shaking off Scalisi's hand. "This fire burned hot, but fast. There's no sign of a body by the bed or under the table. Lionel, can you see behind the door?"

"Nothing." Lionel's voice carried loudly with relief. "Nobody by the stove or the shelves, either. No body at all."

He laughed a little frenetically at his own pun as he returned to the front of the cabin. "Whoever was here got out. If anybody *was* here. Maybe it was just lightning, after all."

Max stepped back from the threshold. "It wasn't lightning."

"It could have been," Lionel argued, glancing up at the sky. "If the conditions were right—"

"Get closer and tell me what you smell."

Lionel and Scalisi both leaned forward, wrinkling their noses against the smoke. Lionel's face paled. "Gasoline."

Scalisi's dour features turned positively grim. "You think the kid did this?"

Max gestured at the crack in the plank nearest to the drop bar that had held the door closed. "I don't know who did it. But there's no way a kid Alex's size kicked in that door."

"There's no lock," Scalisi said, squinting for a closer look. "And there was a lever to work the bar from the outside. Why the hell would anyone kick it in?"

"Maybe he was pissed." Max turned back toward the plane.

"You think that guy who was asking around about the kid came out here and got mad when he didn't find him?" Scalisi's voice came out in a pant as he hurried to keep up with her.

"I sure hope he didn't find him," Lionel said, voicing her own reply. "But we didn't find him, either. If he's really in Alaska, where else could he have gone?"

"I don't know," Max admitted, climbing into the plane. And how had he found the cabin? As she'd told Lionel, Alex would have a map. But anyone else would have had to do an awful lot of research and guesswork, unless... *Damn.* Unless Atch had shared the cabin's location with one of the Burkhartt-Dantell board members after his return. "But whoever set that fire had to get out here somehow. We'll go back to the airport and find out who brought him."

"It wasn't anybody at the charter remotes," Scalisi said, settling into the pilot's seat. "Nobody headed out this way this morning."

Desperation pooled bitterly in Max's throat. "He can't have walked out here."

The plane's engine rattled to life, and Scalisi raised his voice to a shout. "You need to check Lake Hood Seaplane Base. That's where Dantell rented that little floatplane he had."

Max fumbled her headset on. "He *rented* that plane?"

She had assumed it belonged to him. To rent a floatplane, Atch must have had contact with someone besides Scalisi after the plane crash that had supposedly killed him.

"Who would rent a guy an airplane for four months?" she asked. Especially a guy who would have been paying cash and wouldn't show a valid ID?

"A friend," she said, answering her own question. "Maybe someone he knew from his photography assignments. Someone he trusted not to betray him."

"Jim Kirygin," Scalisi said, his voice unfazed as the Cessna bucked in the currents over the valley's ridge. "Bastard barged into my office Wednesday morning to tell me Dantell killed himself and it was my fault for bringing you out here."

"*I'm* the one who convinced him to return to San Francisco."

"Dantell is the one who hanged himself." Lionel's hands waved in outrage. "Maybe we could just say it was his fault?"

"I told Kirygin to screw himself," Scalisi said dryly. "When he hired me to drop supplies at that cabin, he said the guy living there was a trapper, not some suicidal fugitive millionaire. If he wanted Special Ops secrecy, he should have said something."

He flicked at a gauge in front of him with his index finger and made an adjustment to the rudder. "Can't blame Jim for taking it hard, though. I guess they'd known each other since they were kids. Old Man Kirygin used to fly Old Man Dantell and his buddies on their hunting trips out of Firebird Lodge."

It fit. A childhood friend. A man raised on the edge of wilderness. A perfect ally for Atch in his desperate bid to disappear. A perfect refuge for a distraught boy.

Court Treybold had said Atch used to tell him stories about Matthias Dantell's Alaskan hunting trips with his friend Darius Constantine. Surely Atch had told some of those same youthful adventure stories to his son. He'd probably brought Alex on his own fishing trips up here in Alaska, flown him around in his old friend's plane.

Max settled into her seat, her muscles relaxing, flexing, settling into the ready stillness of a hunter. Her intuition hadn't misled her. Alex had come to Alaska, all right. She was only one step behind him now—she could feel it. Find Jim Kirygin and her quest would be over.

She only hoped she found him before the other hunter on Alex's trail tracked him down.

"Jim? Naw, haven't seen him for a couple of days. Took his plane. Don't know when he'll be back. Could be closed up 'til the lake freezes."

The wiry, straw-haired man squinting at Max from behind his well-chewed cigarette seemed unconcerned about Jim Kirygin's whereabouts as he hefted battered crates from the gravel ramp housing his floatplane into an even more battered Toyota truck. Behind him, Lake Hood lapped against the dried grasses of its verge, reflecting the deep blue of a clearing sky. Snow-streaked mountains massed in the distance.

The scene could have come straight from a postcard. But Max's message would read, "Wish you were here freezing your butt off instead of me."

She jerked the zipper of her anorak up to her chin. When Pete Scalisi had dropped her and Lionel off at Lake Hood, he'd told them this was the busiest seaplane base in the world. Even in the winter, planes traded floats for skis and landed here.

Tracking down the one pilot who had flown the arsonist out to Atch's cabin would be next to impossible. Still, she hadn't expected it to take so long to track down Jim Kirygin's floatplane slip with its tiny kiosk office. His slip with its empty gravel floatplane ramp and closed-up office.

"Maybe I could fly you somewheres."

She turned back to Kirygin's neighbor, repressing a shudder at the idea of getting back on any airplane, much less one that landed on water. "No, thanks. I don't suppose you flew anyone out to a remote fishing cabin today? Quick round trip?"

A medium-build man with a knifelike nose, maybe? Or a knife-wielding guy with an Egyptian alias?

"Nope." The man tossed his cigarette onto the gravel

and ground it out. "Had a rental this morning. Don't always do that, but couldn't turn down the cash."

Max's head snapped up. "Cash? What did he look like?"

"He was a she." The man's lip pursed in a silent whistle. "Sweet-looking girl. Quiet type. Told her she was too pretty to be a pilot, and she blushed like a baby, but she could sure fly. I don't suppose you've got a license—"

"I don't suppose you know Mr. Kirygin's home address?" Max cut him off, swallowing her disappointment.

The man's sun-weathered face wrinkled in thought. "Naw, can't say I do. But he wouldn't be there, anyhow."

"Do you have any idea where he might be?"

He shrugged, slamming the tailgate of his truck. "Like I said, he took his Piper. Probably went on out to Firebird Lake. He flies fishermen and hunters from the lodge up there out to remote camps. Might be up there a couple of weeks. Guides are taking folks after grizzlies this time of year."

Firebird Lake. Darius Constantine's lake, according to Court Treybold. Definitely worth a visit....

Max sighed. "Don't tell me. The only way to get to this lake is by plane, right?"

The man laughed. "Naw, them folks out at Firebird like their creature comforts, you might say. Hot tubs and God knows what else. No floatplane is going to carry all their damn luggage."

A road. In Alaska. Wonders would never cease. "Could you give us directions?"

"Sure." He glanced toward the sky, the long afternoon rays of sunshine once more obscured by clouds.

"But you might want to wait until tomorrow. The road gets a bit dicey after dark."

The deadly countdown ticking in Max's head said waiting was not an option. But as much as she hated flying, she *loved* driving.

Chapter 9

"Oh, God," Lionel whimpered as Max accelerated the Mustang out of a curve, adjusting smoothly around a pothole that pooled abruptly from the darkness. "Dicey? This road is a death trap. Watch out!"

"For heaven's sake," Max said, skimming the broken edge of the road. "It's not that bad."

"Ha!" Lionel barked. "It's not a road. It's a ribbon of Swiss cheese. It doesn't even have a yellow line down the middle! Which makes sense, I guess, since it's barely wide enough for one car, much less two."

"We've got plenty of room if we need it." Max pulled the Mustang wide around the next turn to prove it, but Lionel gasped, shooting out a hand to clutch at the dashboard.

"You're just getting back at me for that plane ride today!"

Max cut the next curve too close and felt the rear tires slide an inch. She eased up on the accelerator. "What are you talking about?"

"It's not my fault you're afraid of flying," Lionel said.

"I am not afraid of flying!" At least, she'd thought she'd hidden it well.

"You practically turned green just taxiing out on the runway this morning."

"I had concerns about the safety of Scalisi's plane." She had to ease her foot off the Mustang's accelerator again. "We don't know anything about how he maintains his aircraft. That plane only has one engine. Weather, wind currents, any little thing could have sent us plowing into a mountain.

"And since you insisted on coming along on this trip, I'm responsible for you, too. How would I explain it to your mother if anything happened to you?"

She kept her eyes fixed on the road, but she could hear the condescending smile in Lionel's voice. "Scalisi's aircraft maintenance is monitored by the FAA. Air travel is much safer than riding in a car. How many airplanes do you hear of crashing into a tree or getting nailed by a drunk driver?"

"How many people do you hear about walking away from a plane crash because they wore their seat belt?"

"You might like it if you'd open your eyes occasionally," Lionel said. "You don't get views like that from the ground. It's like you're finally free from all the garbage down below, like you can really breathe."

"Breathing airplane fuel and other people's sweat doesn't do it for me. If I needed that to feel free, I'd get myself some therapy."

Max snapped her mouth shut, shaken by her unkindness. She knew how to control her temper better than that. Tomas never allowed outbursts during their martial arts training—they always ended up with her flat on her back on the mat, so she'd learned how to keep her focus even when provoked.

"I'm sorry," she muttered, slowing the car in apology. "So, I'm not crazy about airplanes."

"Tell me about it." Lionel dropped his hand from the dash. "And I don't like winding mountain roads."

Max shot him a look. "This isn't true confessions, okay? I can handle air travel. It's no big deal."

"C'mon." Lionel's grin transformed his long face. "We're having a bonding experience here."

"We are not."

"Are, too."

Max guided the Mustang through a wide curve beneath a dark corridor of evergreens. As they pulled back out into the moonlight, the world opened up before them. A gravel offshoot peeled off to their left, toward Darius Constantine's private lodge, according to the directions they'd gotten from the pilot at Lake Hood.

Max took the main road, which curved over a bridge to the right, continuing along the bank of an oval mountain lake toward the welcoming lights of a large faux-rustic lodge. She bypassed the lodge, taking a gravel drive through another corridor of trees and parking in front of a small log cabin on a rise beside the lake.

Rugged mountains rose up behind the silver-frosted water, patches of snow gleaming against night-shrouded crags. Cold, sweet air—air tasting of fresh water and evergreens and thousands of miles of wilderness—filled Max's lungs as she climbed from the car.

"Okay," Lionel murmured, staring up into the night. "Maybe you can get some good scenery standing on the ground."

"And maybe I'll open my eyes next time we fly," Max said. Such cold, hard beauty was probably deadlier than any plane crash, anyway.

"You're bonding."

She snorted. "Am not."

Lionel grinned. "Looks like somebody's home."

Lights shone through the cabin's drawn curtains, and a curl of smoke rose from the chimney.

"It's only nine o'clock. Not too late for a social call." Max took a deep breath of the mountain air, searing her lungs. "He must have heard us drive up. Let's say hello."

Max knocked hard on the thick pine door. Someone must indeed have heard their arrival, because it only took a moment for the door to open.

"The lodge office is back at the main building." Light backlit the man in the doorway, shadowing his face, but it couldn't hide his native Athabascan features, his dark eyes catching the minimal light as he eyed them warily.

"I'm sorry to bother you," Max said. "We're looking for Jim Kirygin."

The man's neat black eyebrows rose. "And if I say you found him?"

"Then we'd like to talk with you for a couple of minutes. About Atchison Dantell."

"You reporters? You can go to hell."

But he didn't slam the door on them. Max fought down a surge of excitement. A man with nothing to hide would have backed up his words with conviction.

"My name is Max Riley. This is my assistant, Lionel Horn. We—"

"You've got some nerve, coming here." Kirygin's voice held a dangerous edge. "Atch Dantell was one of the best friends I ever had. I'm sure as hell not going to help the person who dragged him back to his death. What gave you the right to force him away from the life he chose? A good story? Money? Fame? Go crawl back under your rock, and leave me alone."

This time he did try to slam the door, but Max's foot was faster. For the first time since hearing of Atch's suicide, anger overrode Max's guilt.

"You want to know why I agreed to look for Atchison Dantell?" She matched Kirygin's bitter glare. "Because I thought his son deserved to know whether he was dead or alive."

"A real altruist." Kirygin's voice burned. "You don't know what leaving his son did to Atch. You have no right to judge him."

"Maybe not," Max acknowledged. "But I do know what Atch's disappearance did to Alex."

"You're psychic."

"My father disappeared without a trace when I was eighteen. That was eleven years ago. Not a day goes by when I don't wonder what happened to him, but at least

I don't get sick to my stomach every time the telephone rings anymore."

Kirygin's smooth, hard face creased with involuntary sympathy, but he didn't step back. "If you think your little sob story is going to make me talk—"

"I don't want your pity," Max snapped. She was running out of patience as quickly as time. "I want you to understand that I didn't have a lot of sympathy for Atch Dantell leaving his son the first time, and I've got even less for his leaving his son to find his body the second time. Atch Dantell isn't why I'm here. Alex is."

"Alex?" He missed innocent by only half a beat. "I haven't seen Alex in three years. Why would you come here to look for him?"

For a second, Max almost felt sorry for the guy.

"Lionel and I are not the only people who are going to come looking for Alex. If you give us five minutes, I'll explain why you're glad we got here first."

"I don't know what the hell you're talking about." He glanced behind her, scanning the dark trees. "But you've got a long drive back to Anchorage. I can offer you a cup of coffee before you go."

He stepped back to let them in. A futon and chairs covered with bright turquoise cushions circled a wood-stove in the open living area. Kirygin led Max and Lionel to the kitchen table, its scarred surface gleaming beneath a bare bulb.

The cabin's decor might have seemed cliché for a pilot at a fishing lodge—a rifle above the hearth, snow-shoes hung crossed on the wall, Native Alaskan animal print patterns worked into the curtains across the windows—but the snowshoes were dinged from use, the curtains hand-embroidered, and Max bet the rifle was clean and loaded.

She half expected Kirygin to throw an old-fashioned aluminum percolator on the kitchen stove to boil their coffee, but he went straight to a gleaming Braun coffee-maker on the counter and flicked a switch.

"Only take a minute," he muttered, grabbing mugs from the drain board by the sink. "Have it set up for the morning."

Max sat at the table next to Lionel, tension humming through her as her gaze swept the cabin for evidence of Alex's presence. The door off the kitchen undoubtedly led to the bathroom. A wooden stair rose to a loft above the main room, where Max could just glimpse the black-and-red fringe of Kirygin's bed throw.

If Alex was hiding up there, he would be able to hear everything they said. So much the better.

"I don't know you." Kirygin remained beside the coffeepot, his arms crossed over his broad chest. "I don't trust you. I don't have anything to say to you. But I will listen to what you have to say to me."

"I don't know you, either," Max said. "But I know that Atch Dantell trusted you with his life. I hope he knew what he was doing, because I don't have much choice except to trust that you would protect his son just as fiercely."

She set her palms on the tabletop. "Let me tell you what you already know. Wednesday night, Alex Dantell found his father's hanged body. Determined to prove his father was murdered, he ran away from home. Two days ago, Alex Dantell flew to Anchorage, where you met him at the airport."

"That's ridiculous." Kirygin might not have any guile in him, but he was stoically stubborn.

"You flew him out to Atch's cabin," Max continued. "Probably yesterday morning. I don't know why. But you didn't leave him there. You brought him back here with you."

"I told you I haven't seen Alex in three years." Still no obvious crack in his facade, but Max's intuition told her she'd guessed right. Relief rippled through her. Alex hadn't been out at the cabin when the arsonist had arrived.

"Now I'll tell you what you don't know. Lionel and I are not the only ones who followed Alex's trail to his father's cabin. Someone else has been asking around about him. Someone else got to the cabin before we did this morning—"

"Only because he slashed our tires!" Lionel said hotly.

"And someone else kicked in the cabin door, doused the floor with gasoline and set the place on fire."

"Burned the cabin?" Kirygin's chest expanded in outrage. "Who would— Why should I listen to you? You probably did it yourselves!"

"Us! Are you *nuts?*" Lionel started to spring to his feet, but Max held him back with a hand on his arm.

"You can call Pete Scalisi," she said. "He flew us out there. Someone set that fire just hours before we arrived."

"It could have been a squatter," Kirygin said.

"It could have been," Max agreed. "Or it could have been the man who stopped by Big Bear Charters earlier this morning waving a picture of Alex Dantell under

Scalisi's nose, saying he was a police investigator looking for a boy in a custody case."

Kirygin's brows drew together, but his dark eyes
didn't shift, didn't give Max a clue as to where Alex
might be hiding.

"Or it could have been the guy who broke into Alex's
bedroom to try to kidnap him," Lionel said, practically
bouncing in his seat in frustration. "The guy who just
might be an international assassin."

"Lionel," Max muttered.

He threw up his hands. "Or it might not. Who knows?
Just in case, you might want to lock your door tonight.
Some friendly advice."

Kirygin reached over and flicked off the coffeepot.
"Get out of my house. I don't want to hear any more of
your bullshit. Just get the hell out of my house."

Lionel sputtered an objection, but Max rose smoothly
to her feet. She couldn't be sure Alex was in the cabin,
but she was sure Kirygin knew where he was. He'd
reacted in all the wrong places for an innocent man.
What she and Lionel had said had frightened him. If
Alex wasn't hiding right above their heads, Kirygin
would contact him. And when he did—

A muted thudding at the front door turned all their
heads.

"Are you expecting visitors?" Max asked.

Kirygin shook his head.

"Jim Kirygin!" The muffled voice was harsh. "Open
up! You're obstructing an ongoing investigation."

Kirygin sent Max a look halfway between desperation and fury. She jerked her head toward the door.

"We'll get your back."

He rolled his eyes, obviously not thrilled at the idea of having them anywhere near his back, but he strode to the door as Max gestured Lionel to hide behind it. She pressed herself against the wall on the other side.

Kirygin cracked the door open. "What do you want?"

"Jim Kirygin?" The nasal voice cut like a serrated knife. "You're in big trouble, buddy. Hiding a fugitive minor. Could look like kidnapping to the wrong investigator. How about you let me in, and we figure out how to get you out of this mess."

"Who the hell are you?" Kirygin demanded, shifting his breadth to block the narrow opening in the door.

"Your worst nightmare." The voice quipped the cliché without any obvious sense of irony. "Name's Butch Bailey, and if you give me any more lip, I'll haul your ass into town faster than you can spit."

Max couldn't take any more. If this guy was an internationally feared assassin, she'd rather have him shoot her than be forced to hear any more of his drivel.

She moved to stand shoulder to shoulder with Kirygin. The man on Kirygin's doorstep, his hands dug deep into trench coat pockets, looked like he'd just stepped off the set of a second-rate knockoff of *Law & Order.* He held himself as if he were six foot two instead of five foot ten, his jaw set in a sneer that would have been more intimidating without the ketchup smear at the corner of his lip. But it was his long, narrow nose that grabbed her attention.

"Well." Max smiled. "If it isn't Knife Nose. We meet at last. Allow me to introduce myself. Max Riley.

I'm sure you recognize my name. You slashed my tires this morning."

"Your tires?" Butch Bailey's lips twitched, and Max could almost see the thoughts running through his mind as he gauged whether he could bluff his way through this.

She widened her smile to show a little teeth. "Why don't you come on in, Butch, so we can decide how you're going to make it up to me?"

"Speaking of having some questions to answer," Lionel added from behind the door. "I want to know about the fire."

Kirygin kneaded his hands together in front of his broad chest. "And I'm real interested in what you said about a runaway minor. If anything were to happen to that boy—"

His knuckles cracked like pistol shots.

Bailey spun on his heels and bolted, pelting back up the gravel drive toward the lodge.

Max sprinted after him. Bailey ran hard, passing Max's rental Mustang, plunging up the drive into the shadows under the trees. He'd gotten a good jump on her, but Max was only fifteen feet behind him by the time she reached the trees.

Farther up the drive, she caught a glimpse of moonlight gleaming off a blackness deeper than shadow. A Jeep parked far enough from Kirygin's cabin not to be heard. Bailey wasn't a complete idiot, after all.

That realization struck Max just before the blow to her shoulder sent her slamming toward the ground.

Chapter 10

Gravel ripped at her coat as Max hit and rolled, barely avoiding the heavy body falling after her.

Bailey's grip found her sleeve as she tried to scramble away, jerking her off balance, back to the ground. His knee struck her ribs, and air gasped from her lungs as his free hand grabbed at her hair.

He was bigger, heavier, and he'd gotten control of her head. But he made the mistake of standing, dragging her up with him. And he had both hands engaged while Max had hers free.

When he shifted his right leg back to try a stronger kick, Max hooked an elbow around his left knee and jerked. They thudded hard to the ground, but this time Max was on top, her elbow jammed solidly into his gut.

Bailey grunted, but he held on to her hair, jerking her

head to the side as he reached for her throat. Max ignored his fumbling at her windpipe, reaching downward instead. His jeans offered him some protection, but when she found her grip and clenched, his hands dropped away, reaching for the pain.

The heel of Max's free hand found his chin, and she threw his head back against the ground, her own face coming down mere inches from his.

"Get away from her!" Lionel's shout didn't affect the agonized rage twisting Bailey's face, but a sudden glint in the moonlight near Max's ear widened his eyes, and he froze, allowing Max to push herself off to crouch beside him.

Kirygin crouched on Bailey's other side, holding a gleaming curved blade to his neck.

An ulu knife. She remembered seeing the signs in the airport, "No ulu knives past this point." Apparently tourists bought the Inuit-designed knives—the crescent-shaped blade connecting at both ends to its short handle—as souvenirs without considering the consequences at airport security.

Seeing the icy sharpness of Kirygin's blade and his confident grip on the bone handle, Max felt fairly sure Bailey wasn't mistaking it for a souvenir.

"Thanks," Max managed, rubbing her throat. Bailey's thumb was going to leave a bruise.

"Are you all right?" Lionel asked, dropping down beside her. Max saw that he, too, had a blade—a steak knife from Kirygin's kitchen. Even in the moonlight, she could see him flush as he followed her gaze. "It was all I could find."

"It could come in handy," she said, looking down into Bailey's sharp face. "We don't want to kill him. Just encourage him to share."

"I'm for killing him," Kirygin said with brutal evenness. "Then he can't go after Alex anymore."

"How about the police?" Lionel's voice squeaked, obviously as uncertain as Max whether Kirygin was bluffing.

"Good point," Max agreed. "The cops don't take kindly to people who impersonate police officers."

"I didn't impersonate anyone!" Bailey objected, his eyes still riveted on Kirygin's knife. "I never said I was a police officer. I said I was an *investigator.* I am. I can show you my license."

He lifted a hand toward the front of his trench coat, but Kirygin shook his head.

"Don't."

Max opened Bailey's coat for him, digging a billfold from the inner pocket. Along with the Alaska P.I.'s license, forty-three dollars and a stick of chewing gum, she found a grainy copy of the same photograph she carried of Alex Dantell.

"You implied you were a police investigator," Max said, taking the photo before returning his billfold. "To Mr. Kirygin here and to Pete Scalisi. You slashed my tires—"

"You can't prove that!"

"Why'd you set fire to the cabin?" Lionel asked. "I don't get that."

"I didn't set fire to anything!" Bailey's eyes flared. "I don't know what you're talking about. What cabin? You were the ones who were making threats. All I'm trying to do is get a kid back to his legally appointed guardian."

His injured tone sounded almost genuine. Max sat back on her heels. Bailey might be a sleazy P.I. and a dirty fighter, but he wasn't a lethal assassin.

"Why did you attack me?"

"You were chasing me! I thought if I scared you a little, you'd crumble and give up the kid."

Dumb, but believable. "How about my tires?"

He glared mutinously, but she didn't need an answer. A cheap trick by a cheap P.I. to slow her down.

"Who hired you?"

"I told you. The boy's legal guardian. His grandfather."

Max snorted. "The boy's mother is his legal guardian. Try again."

Kirygin glanced at Max, doubt in his eyes. "Atch said his father-in-law could be imperious. If he knew Alex was missing, he might take matters into his own hands."

Max looked back to Bailey. "Maybe you better give us the guy's name."

"Matthias Dantell."

"Hoo-boy," Lionel whispered, and a shiver ran up the back of Max's spine.

"Wrong answer," she said, her voice soft and cold.

"Look, that's what he said!" Bailey started to rise, eyed Kirygin's knife and stopped. "I didn't ask for a DNA check before I took the job. If the guy's not the grandfather—"

"Matthias Dantell is the boy's grandfather." Kirygin eased his blade away from Bailey's neck. "But he's not hiring private investigators. Not unless they have a good banking system in hell."

Bailey blinked.

"Matthias Dantell is dead," Max clarified. "What did your client look like?"

Bailey blinked again. "I shouldn't be telling you any of this. That's privileged informa—"

"He hired you over the Internet, didn't he?" Lionel said.

Bailey clamped his mouth shut.

"Good enough for me," Max said. "Explains why he'd hire a slob like Bailey. I guess you take what you can get if you don't want anyone to know your name or what you look like."

Kirygin grunted a curse. "You weren't making that up? About the assassin? You think this guy's boss could be him?"

Max hoped she was wrong. "I don't know. But whoever hired Bailey, I wouldn't want him to find Alex before I do."

"How did you find me?" Kirygin asked her, running a broad hand over his face.

"Pete Scalisi said you rented that floatplane to Atch."

He turned to Bailey. "And you?"

"Can I sit up?" Bailey hitched himself up, swiping at the gravel embedded in his trench coat. "A little Web surfing. You were listed as a pilot and guide in a book of Atchison Dantell's photographs of Alaska. Seemed worth the drive up here."

Max raised an eyebrow at Kirygin. "It's not a difficult trail to follow, even if Bailey doesn't report to his boss."

"Hey!" Bailey's narrow face paled. "I'm just doing a job here. If I disappear—"

Max grimaced. "I didn't mean it that way."

"People will know where to look for me. I left records in my files. And I sent an e-mail to Matthias Dantell before I drove up here. Ghost or not, he's gonna want to know what happened to me."

Max echoed Kirygin's curse as she glanced around, noting the depth of the shadows under the trees, the hush of a night breeze across the lake that would cover any footfalls through the forest duff.

Ridiculous. Even if an infamous assassin hired a weasel like Butch Bailey to do his legwork, that didn't mean Anubis would follow Bailey to Jim Kirygin's cabin. Whoever "Matthias Dantell" really was, he was probably holed up somewhere in San Francisco, waiting to hear Bailey's report.

Still, unease prickled eerily at Max's spine.

She stood. "Mr. Kirygin, Alex has been in danger since the minute he left home, but I'm afraid it's only gotten worse. We have to get him back to safety before it's too late."

Kirygin rose, shaking his head. "I can't—"

"I know you have no reason to trust me." She clenched her fists in frustration, but she had no other choice. "But if you won't let me help him, I have to trust you. You have to get him back to San Francisco before anyone else finds him."

"Ms. Riley, I think I believe you about the danger."

"Do you? If Alex is still on your property when Bailey's employer comes looking for him…"

"He's not here. He's gone."

"Gone where?"

Kirygin took a deep breath, still struggling with trusting her. "I put him on a plane this afternoon. He should be back in San Francisco any minute."

Another search, she would have been disappointed. To have been so close and yet not be the one to deliver Alex securely to Yvonne's door... But all Max could feel was relief.

Alex on a plane was not the same as Alex in his mother's waiting arms, but it was a hell of a lot better than being trapped in a lonely, remote cabin with a killer coming after him and only a handful of nervous amateurs to protect him.

Because even though she had only some sore ribs and a couple of scratches to show after having just taken down a man who outweighed her by thirty pounds, she had begun to fear that Tomas was right. Going up against Anubis, she was a rank amateur.

And her companions, now crowded into Kirygin's little cabin, barely qualified as obstacles.

Of course, she *wasn't* going up against Anubis. Anubis was a thousand miles away, if he existed at all. All Max had to worry about now was Alex reaching his mother.

Her cell phone couldn't hold the weak signal it picked up, but she managed to dig Steve Spencer's cell number out of the address list without even requiring Lionel's help.

"You trust this guy?" Kirygin demanded as she dialed his telephone.

"Yvonne's paying him a lot of money to get Alex

home safely." Did knowing his self-interest qualify as
trust? "Might as well let him earn some of it."

"Oh, for God's sake," Bailey groaned, rising from
his seat at Kirygin's table. "The kid's not here. I'm going home."

"Not yet, you're not." Lionel and Kirygin both
stepped toward him, and Bailey sank back into his chair
with a sigh.

"As soon as we know Alex is safe, you're free to go,"
Max said, turning her attention back to the phone, where
she could hear ringing that sounded every inch of a
thousand miles away.

"Hello?" She heard Steve Spencer's voice, pitched
low and sounding wary.

"Steve? It's Max Riley. Has Alex contacted you yet?"

"Max?" The tenor of his voice changed, though he
didn't speak up. "Look, right now's not a good time—"

"Just tell me, has Alex called you?"

"No, but we… Max? I'm handling this search, remember? I know you're worried, but we're following a
good lead. Look, this signal is terrible. Let me get back
to you later—"

"I called to tell you where he is."

"What?" The word crackled across the line.

"A friend of his put him on a plane from Anchorage to San Francisco this afternoon. He should get in
about eleven your time. He promised to call Yvonne
from the airport, but I thought if I gave you a heads-
up you could—"

"*Shit.* You sure about this? How reliable is this information?"

"I've been in contact with Alex's friend. He's reliable. You might even be able to meet the plane if you hur—"

"Dammit, Max, I'm not exactly in a position to rush out and meet a plane at the San Francisco airport right now. *Shit.*" His voice sharpened, laced with suspicion. "Why aren't you going out there to meet him? He knows you."

"I'm not even in California." It was wicked to say it, but she couldn't resist. "This isn't my case, remember?"

Steve muttered something she guessed wasn't complimentary. "Give me the flight number, and I'll get somebody out there to keep an eye on him until Yvonne can pick him up."

"Flight number?" Max glanced at Kirygin, who grimaced. "I don't have it right now. I'll call you back."

She hung up before Steve could object. "He said he'd get somebody out there, but it would help to have the flight number."

"Alex made the reservation," Kirygin said. "I let him use my credit card. I didn't pay that much attention to the flight number. It was a Northern Lights flight, left at three."

"I've got my laptop out in the car," Lionel said. "If I can use your phone line, it shouldn't take a minute to get the schedule."

Max nodded. "Once we call Steve with the flight, we'll head back to Anchorage."

"Me, too?" Bailey asked, resting his sharp chin in his hands. "Or am I going to be sleeping with the fishes?"

"I'll ride back with you," Max said, disliking the idea even more than Bailey obviously did. Still, she disliked the idea of him e-mailing his mysterious employer with Alex's itinerary even less.

She turned to Kirygin. "It would probably be best if you came back to Anchorage tonight, too. If Bailey here didn't set fire to Atch's cabin, somebody else did."

"Nobody is going to burn my place." Kirygin moved to the mantel over his wood-burning stove and pulled down the rifle.

Max *really* did not want Kirygin's death on her conscience. "You don't seem to understand how dangerous this guy is. He's not going to come knocking on your front door."

"And I'm not going to be sleeping when he gets here," Kirygin said. "I've tracked every predator in these woods, from wolverines to grizzly bears. I'm not scared of one more."

Max doubted he'd had any experience *being* tracked by those predators, but she took a seat at the table near Bailey and watched Kirygin settle into a chair by the stove to check over his rifle.

"Why did Alex come up here to Alaska?" she asked.

"I guess that's Alex's business."

So much for their newfound rapport.

"He sent me a postcard." She watched Kirygin for a reaction. "Said he was looking for something. I just wondered if he found it."

Kirygin's dark eyes were unreadable. "His father's dead. What that boy's looking for is peace of mind. I don't think he's going to find it anytime soon."

He bent back over the rifle, but his hands remained still. "Alex wants to believe his father was murdered. He wants to be able to do something about it. He needs time to accept what happened."

Max had to ask. "You don't think Alex could be right?"

Kirygin looked up. "Atch couldn't resist a grand gesture. That's what made his photographs so spectacular. He crashed a plane in the Alaskan wilderness so he could live like a wild man. He wasn't afraid of death. Just of being trapped in his father's life."

She didn't want to aggravate his pain, but the question wouldn't let her go. "Court Treybold didn't seem to believe Atch was suicidal."

"Treybold." Kirygin's lip curled. "I wouldn't put much stock in anything that man said. He's a squawking raven, a troublemaker."

"You've met him?"

"Atch brought him up here once, trying to sell the guy on his vision for Burkhartt-Dantell. Treybold was more interested in drinking and stirring up trouble than business—or fishing. The type who enjoys setting people at each other's throats."

If that was Treybold's modus operandi, it had worked on her. His implied doubts and significant pauses had fueled all kinds of suspicions.

"Whatever Alex found at Atch's cabin, you think it will help him to accept his father's death?"

Kirygin rubbed his brow and sighed, relenting. "Atch told Alex he'd written a journal of his adventures over this past summer. Told him they'd go back up there together to get it sometime. I figured there was no harm helping Alex get out to that cabin to look for it."

Max's throat tightened. She could see Alex, hunched

at this very table, poring over the cramped handwriting of a man he had loved and yet could hardly have understood.

As a diplomat, her own father had left so much written material, but so little of it personal. Nothing to explain why he'd chosen the paths he'd followed, the risks he'd taken. Nothing to say whether he resented raising a willful girl alone or regretted the times a crisis prevented him from being there for a birthday or finishing a bedtime story.

"Did he find it? The journal?"

Kirygin nodded. "Right where Atch told him it would be, in a fishing box under the floorboards. I don't know if it will give him the answers he wants, but he had a right to it."

Considering Alex hoped to prove that his father's death hadn't been a suicide, Max doubted very much he would find the answers he wanted. But maybe something in Atch's journal would start to give him the answers he needed.

Bailey's chair scraped back over the wood floor. "You nut jobs gonna sit around shooting the breeze all night? Because I got better things to do than listening to some brat's sob story. Unless you're planning to shoot me, I'm outta here."

Max stood up. "Don't tempt me, Bailey."

"What are you going to do? Tie me up?" His grin looked sharklike under that sharp nose. "Nice thought, but I'll have to pass this time. Maybe we can hook up later."

"Bailey." Max growled a warning as she crossed the cabin to intercept him.

He laughed as he threw open the door. "I've even got a pair of handcuffs you can bor—"

Light flashed, and a shock wave of sound knocked him back into Max. She pushed past him to the doorway as the sound rolled past again, echoing back from the mountains surrounding the lake.

Up the drive, the shadows of the trees danced, pulsing to the flare of a twisted ball of flames.

"Holy crap!" Bailey's voice sounded tinny in her ears. "What was that? Your generator blow, Kirygin?"

Max saw a semblance of form beneath the flames. Strange place to have a generator, that far from the cabin. She should have noticed it when she'd parked the—

"The Mustang!" She darted down Kirygin's front stairs. The rental company was going to be royally pissed off. No question the car was a total loss. It would break Lionel's heart—

"Oh, God. *Lionel!*"

She was running then, her suddenly shaky legs barely responding to her urgency. She could see nothing inside the car except flame. If Lionel had somehow been blown free…but the doors, buckled from the explosion, were both still closed.

Horror bubbled deep in Max's throat as she stumbled toward the burning wreck.

A shadow detached from the trees to her left, came at her around the flames. Max howled and turned, ready in the ferocity of her anguish to take on even a grizzly bear.

"Jeez, what happened to the car?" Lionel asked, his

face painted red by flames. "Are you all right?
Max? *Max?*"

Max saw with detachment that her hand trembled as
she reached out to touch his shoulder. Solid. Bony,
warm. Definitely real.

"Are you hurt?" he asked, peering at her anxiously.

"I thought you were dead." Something choked her
words, anger or laughter. "What the hell did you do
to the car?"

"I didn't touch it!" Lionel said, as Kirygin and Bailey
ran up beside them. "I mean, I got my computer
out—" he patted the laptop case at his side "—but I
didn't even start the engine."

"Where *were* you?"

The red dancing in Lionel's cheeks deepened as he
mumbled, "Just out in the woods for a second."

"Out in the *woods?*" Max noted Kirygin's and
Bailey's expressions, and understanding dawned.
Laughter snorted through her nose, but she resisted re-
minding Lionel that Kirygin had grizzly-bear-free facil-
ities right in his cabin.

"So," Lionel said, self-consciously shifting the shoulder
strap of his computer case. "What happened to the car?"

The obvious question, but Max's brain seemed stuck
on the fact that Lionel was alive and not being burned
to charcoal before her eyes.

"You didn't see anything?"

Lionel shook his head. "Lightning?" He glanced
doubtfully at the clear sky.

Bailey dropped to the gravel, squinting against the
heat as he peered under the mangled Mustang. "I don't

suppose you're in the habit of driving around with a gas can strapped to the undercarriage of your car?"

Max dropped beside him, following his pointing finger. The twisted metal object just below the car's engine could once have been a gas can.

"Nothing fancy," Bailey said. "Just stick a rag in the gas can, light it under the fuel tank. Might not blow, but it sure did in your case."

"You blew up our car?" Lionel cried.

"How far ahead of time could you set something like this up?" Max demanded, scrambling to her feet to hold him back as the private investigator rose and brushed off his pants.

"A couple of minutes, maximum. Whoever did this must have been within a few yards of your observant friend here."

Lionel stopped struggling against Max's grip. "That's not possible. I would have noticed something."

"With what, your spidey senses?" Bailey laughed, turning to Max. "What do you keep him around for, comic relief?"

"Hey!" Lionel surged forward again, but Max pushed between the two men.

"You think maybe the two of you could give it a rest for a minute? I'm sure whoever blew up this car is finding us all pretty comic right now."

Lionel and Bailey both stilled. All four of them slowly turned, their backs forming a circle as they stared out at the darkness around them. Somewhere an owl hooted.

"Why don't we all head on up to the lodge," Max suggested.

"You think he'll attack us?" Lionel asked. His fists balled as he continued to watch the shadows.

"I think if he wanted to hurt us, he wouldn't have set fire to an empty car."

"Then why did he blow it up in the first—"

As one, they all turned toward Kirygin's cabin.

"A distraction?" Lionel asked.

"Sure as hell distracted me," Bailey said, sounding amused.

"Son of a bitch." Kirygin stepped forward.

Max grabbed his arm. "Alex is gone," she reminded him. "Take Lionel up to the lodge and call—"

"Like hell." He shook free of her grip, his strides quickening with anger. "Nobody breaks into my place."

"Mr. Kirygin! Jim!" She sucked in a breath as Lionel brushed past her. "Don't you dare, Lionel."

He shot her a defiant glance. "I can take care of myself. I took karate in college. I'm not as worthless as you think."

"I don't think you're worthless," she said. "But this guy throws *knives,* remember?"

Lionel ignored her. She turned toward Bailey, but he was following the others.

He gave her a cynical grin. "I gotta see this."

Macho idiots. So much for her plan to send them to safety while she crept quietly around the cabin and waited for the perpetrator to show himself.

"I'll go around back," Kirygin barked. "Bailey, you check the floatplane down at the lake. Horn, watch the front door in case he's inside and tries to make a break for it."

No orders for her. *Macho idiot.* Kirygin had effec-

The Silhouette Reader Service™—Here's How It Works:

Accepting your 2 free books and mystery gift places you under no obligation to buy anything. You may keep the books and gift and return the shipping statement marked "cancel." If you do not cancel, about a month later we'll send you 4 additional books and bill you just $3.99 each in the U.S., or $4.47 each in Canada, plus 25¢ shipping & handling per book and applicable taxes if any.* That's the complete price and – compared to cover prices of $4.99 each in the U.S., and $5.99 each in Canada – it's quite a bargain! You may cancel at any time, but if you choose to continue, every month we'll send you 4 more books which you may either purchase at the discount price or return to us and cancel your subscription.

*Terms and prices subject to change without notice. Sales tax applicable in N.Y. Canadian residents will be charged applicable provincial taxes and GST.

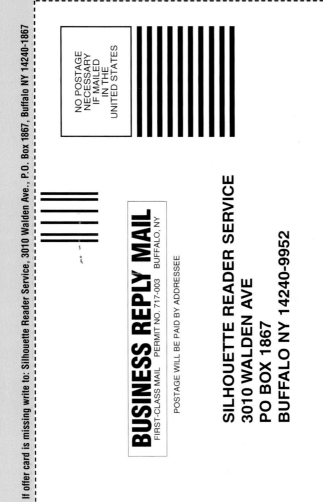

If offer card is missing write to: Silhouette Reader Service, 3010 Walden Ave., P.O. Box 1867, Buffalo NY 14240-1867

NO POSTAGE
NECESSARY
IF MAILED
IN THE
UNITED STATES

BUSINESS REPLY MAIL

FIRST-CLASS MAIL   PERMIT NO. 717-003   BUFFALO, NY

POSTAGE WILL BE PAID BY ADDRESSEE

SILHOUETTE READER SERVICE
3010 WALDEN AVE
PO BOX 1867
BUFFALO NY 14240-9952

OFFICIAL OPINION POLL

ANSWER 3 QUESTIONS AND WE'LL SEND YOU
2 FREE BOOKS AND A FREE GIFT!

0074823 IIIIIIIIIIII IIIIIIII IIIIIIII **FREE GIFT CLAIM #** 3953

YOUR OPINION COUNTS!

Please check TRUE or FALSE below to express your opinion about the following statements:

Q1 Do you believe in "true love"?

"TRUE LOVE HAPPENS ONLY ONCE IN A LIFETIME."
○ TRUE
○ FALSE

Q2 Do you think marriage has any value in today's world?

"YOU CAN BE TOTALLY COMMITTED TO SOMEONE WITHOUT BEING MARRIED."
○ TRUE
○ FALSE

Q3 What kind of books do you enjoy?

"A GREAT NOVEL MUST HAVE A HAPPY ENDING."
○ TRUE
○ FALSE

YES, I have scratched the area below.

Please send me the 2 **FREE BOOKS** and **FREE GIFT** for which I qualify. I understand I am under no obligation to purchase any books, as explained on the back of this card.

DETACH AND MAIL CARD TODAY!

300 SDL EFVK   200 SDL EFZK

FIRST NAME   LAST NAME

(STF-B-04/06)

ADDRESS

APT.#   CITY

STATE/PROV.   ZIP/POSTAL CODE

www.eHarlequin.com

Offer limited to one per household and not valid to current Silhouette Bombshell® subscribers. All orders subject to approval. Credit or debit balances in a customer's account(s) may be offset by any other outstanding balance owed by or to the customer. Please allow 4 to 6 weeks for delivery.

tively announced his plan to any intruder with halfway decent hearing. Max grinned. She could revert back to her initial plan to slip into the woods and see what she could see. Maybe the men would be enough of a distraction to give her a fighting chance.

Simple enough to slide into the shadows. Max slowed. Slowed her step, her breathing, her pounding heartbeat, until she could hear the whisper of the wind in the treetops above her, the lapping of water along the lakeshore, the heavy footsteps of the men charging around the cabin.

The arsonist must have come from somewhere. The map she'd bought at the gas station in Anchorage showed the road she and Lionel had driven in on as the only one for dozens of miles in any direction. The intruder must have a vehicle somewhere, somewhere far enough from the cabin not to have aroused their attention when it had arrived, but not too far for quick access.

In fact, if she were an audacious, self-assured international assassin, Max might drive right up to the Firebird Lodge and park in the guest parking area, bold as you please.

Max glanced toward the cabin. She could hear Bailey shouting from the floatplane dock. He'd found nothing. She couldn't see Kirygin, probably checking the back windows.

Lionel had gone through the front door. She could see him crossing the small living room to lift the rifle from where Kirygin had left it leaning against his chair.

Dammit, Lionel. The words hissed silently through her teeth. She couldn't just run up to the lodge and leave Lionel to shoot Kirygin or Bailey by accident.

Even as she started forward, she heard Lionel shout, heard the explosive report of the rifle. Kirygin's and Bailey's shouts echoed the gunshot. Max breathed a prayer of thanks. Lionel hadn't hit them. Hadn't killed them, anyway.

But Lionel yelled again, more frantically. Max saw figures in the cabin doorway. Lionel's black hair flew about his pale face as he tripped to the living room floor.

A second figure, anonymous in a knit balaclava, lithe even in black fatigues and a heavy-duty black leather jacket, struck the side of Lionel's head with the butt of Kirygin's rifle, then sprinted out the door. He leapt like a cat across the front stairs and hit the ground running.

Chapter 11

Max had an angle on the running figure, but only a desperate burst of speed brought her into position to intercept him as he ran up the drive. He spun as she neared, dropped and rolled as she grabbed for him. Max skidded precariously on the gravel, but kept her footing, spinning to follow the intruder.

The man rolled nimbly to his feet, but he'd lost his momentum. As she charged him, he tried to dodge, faltering on the treacherous gravel.

No, he hadn't slipped, only feinted. His swift kick caught Max viciously on the shins, sending her flying. She landed badly, jarring her sore ribs. She rolled, but not fast enough to avoid a second booted kick that glanced across her temple.

The third kick caught her shoulder, throwing her hard on her back.

She saw a flash of white from the killer's eyes behind his balaclava as he stood over her, then another flash as a silver blade appeared in his gloved hand. He tilted the knife, watching her eyes to see her reaction to the mark on the grip.

Like blood, it showed black in the moonlight, but Max picked out the shape of the feather of Maat.

She stilled. She heard shouts from the cabin, but she knew no one could reach her before he struck.

She could hear Tomas's voice, coaxing, badgering, commanding. *Focus, Magdalena. You must learn how to protect yourself.*

Funny, she'd never once asked him *from what.* Looking up into the black holes of Anubis's eyes, she finally knew. And knew she'd failed Tomas. She could take down a man twice the size of this one without breaking a sweat, and she'd let it make her overconfident. She'd charged in on adrenaline and anger, and they had put her right where Tomas had promised they would, on her butt and dead.

Focus, Max.

The assassin's blow was fast and as subtle as a striking snake. Max could not have followed the knife's arc with her eye. But it was years of training, not sight, that guided her hand, barely tapping the elbow as he slashed, knocking the blade inches off course, turning to follow the flow of the striking arm until she caught the wrist and jerked.

The assassin's body twisted after his hand, tumbling

away from Max. She followed, striking at the back of the killer's head with her fist. But she struck only air.

She rolled to her feet, sending a brutal kick toward the coiling shadow. The side of a hand struck her heel, the same blow she had just used on him, sending her foot toward the sky, her butt once more toward the ground.

But instead of pressing the attack, the assassin darted away. White showed again against the black of his balaclava. His teeth. He was *laughing* at her.

Max scrambled to her feet, but the pounding footsteps behind her caught her before she could give chase.

"Are you all right?" It was Butch Bailey, panting hard at her side, Kirygin's rifle in his hand.

"Why didn't you use that thing?"

"I didn't want to hit you." He grinned at her tone. "Besides, if that was the guy who hired me, I want him to live long enough to pay the second half of my fee."

Max bit back a reply, saving her breath for refilling her aching chest. "Lionel?"

"Kirygin's got him. Dazed, but not bleeding."

"Give me your keys."

"What?"

"The keys. To your Jeep."

"You gotta be out of your mind."

She straightened, and whatever he saw in her eyes convinced him. He shrugged, digging into his jeans pocket and pulling out a Budweiser key chain. "Anything happens to my baby—"

Max jerked the keys from his hand and took off up the drive. Her ribs burned, her temple throbbed and her tailbone ached, but the memory of Anubis's silent laughter drove her on. Remembering Bailey's ambush, she slowed as she hit the shadow of the trees, her senses tuned for the slightest movement.

But the sound that struck her ears had no subtlety at all. The cough and growl of a bare engine purred to life ahead of her. A single headlight flared through the trees, and a motorcycle spurted out onto the drive, spraying gravel as its black-clad rider accelerated into the darkness.

An MZ Baghira Black Panther, Max thought, noting the spare, racy lines of the dual sport bike as she ran. *Nice ride.* A vehicle you could push down a road in silence and hide behind a tree. A good alternative to parking in plain sight at a brightly lit lodge in a balaclava.

In a last burst of speed, she reached Bailey's Jeep. The quick response of the engine overrode her concern at the rust and dents. She sprayed some gravel of her own as she whirled the vehicle around and pressed the accelerator.

A massive Land Rover sporting a firebird logo loomed out of the night toward her, someone from the Firebird Lodge finally showing some interest in the noises from Kirygin's cabin. Max pulled to the side, bouncing in the ruts, and rolled down her window to hear the driver's shouts.

"What's going on down there?"

"Car caught on fire," she shouted back. "They could use your help."

And then she was past and shifting gears as she tore along the drive. Lights streamed from the lodge windows as she sped by, but none of the high-paying guests had braved the cold to check out the smoldering Mustang down by the lake.

As Max hit the straightaway to the bridge, she caught the red flash of the MZ's taillight. Anubis must have lost some time pulling off the drive to hide from the Land Rover.

The red beacon disappeared as the bike took a curve, but as Max passed over the bridge, she glimpsed it through the trees. The bike had a maneuvering advantage on the twisting mountain road, but the assassin couldn't plow through the loose rocks and potholes like the Jeep.

Max smiled grimly. She'd catch the bike long before it reached the highway down below.

Apparently the assassin reached the same conclusion. Up ahead, the motorbike's lights suddenly grew brighter as it slowed, then turned abruptly to the right and went out.

Max hit the brakes, urgently scanning the edge of the road ahead. The assassin must have turned off onto the side road leading to Darius Constantine's private hunting lodge.

Max followed, though she saw no sign of the MZ's lights ahead. Anubis must have cut them off, sacrificing speed for concealment. The paved road quickly gave way to gravel, winding deeper into the trees.

Max slowed, peering off to either side. In Anubis's position, she would pull off the road and wait for the Jeep to roar past before whistling her way back to Anchorage. Then again, she wasn't Anubis. He had a reputation to uphold, and a twelve-year-old boy had so far proven to be too wily for him. He might have decided Darius Constantine's lodge, a place Alex surely must have visited with his father, would be the next logical place to search for the boy.

And the fact that he was being pursued by an angry journalist in a borrowed Jeep? *Bet he's not exactly running scared.*

Fifty yards from the main road, the Jeep's headlights picked out a gate across the drive. A gold-painted eagle-like bird was carved into the arched wooden beam across the top. The sign beneath read Firebird's Nest.

Seeing the closed gate, Max feared she'd guessed wrong. Anubis must have hidden in the woods behind her, taking his chance to escape to the city. But though the gate between the tree-trunk-sized posts was wrought iron, it served for show, not security. No fence attached to the gate. The gap between the right gatepost and the nearest tree was easily large enough to ride a motorcycle through.

Max stopped the Jeep and cut the engine. As she made her way to the gate, the hush of the Alaskan night surrounded her. She couldn't hear the buzz of the MZ's engine, but she could see the scuffs of its tracks in the duff by the gatepost. The assassin wasn't headed back to Anchorage.

She checked the gate. A padlock dangled from a chain looped through one side, but it was unclasped. She could swing the gates open and drive through. Instead, she walked back to the Jeep and killed the headlights. Darkness joined the silence as the night pooled around her.

Driving up to Darius Constantine's front door and demanding to see the reclusive billionaire, spouting a wild story about exploding cars and motorcycle-riding assassins, wouldn't put a crimp in Anubis's plans, whatever they were.

She didn't love the idea of following a hired killer unarmed into the unknown—hadn't Court Treybold mentioned Constantine's dogs?—but the darkness was a comfortable friend. Enough moonlight filtered through the tall spruce that she could make out the gravel road to her left as she slipped into the forest. Rough trunks beneath her fingertips, soft needles beneath her feet, the tug of tree limbs at her clothes, all steadied her, oriented her as she slipped along beside the road.

She could hear the water nearby, hear the rustle of small creatures in the forest, thought she could even hear the sound of voices from the Firebird Lodge across the lake. Where she'd left Lionel.

The memory of Anubis striking him down shivered through her.

Bailey had said Lionel was only stunned, not stabbed. But a concussion could worsen. He might have bruising in his brain, a hemorrhage.

He's fine. He's not dead. But only through luck. Luck he hadn't reached the Mustang just as it exploded. Luck Anubis hadn't wasted a moment to slit his throat. Hell, luck he hadn't shot himself.

And if anything had happened to him because she'd brought him on this dangerous chase…

Max forced the thought from her mind. She'd have time for guilt trips once she got him safely back to San Francisco. Right now, she had to focus. If Anubis caught her unaware, she'd be the one needing a hospital. If she were lucky.

The road moved away from the lake, widening as it curved up a shoulder of hill. Pulled over to the side of a gravel turnout was a late-model Ford Explorer, a dark bulk against the paler stones.

Max slipped from the trees to the vehicle. The hood felt warm beneath her fingers, but not hot. Her breathing quickened. The Firebird Lodge was a long, cold drive from Anchorage on a dual-purpose motorcycle. Bringing the MZ in a larger vehicle would be more comfortable and less conspicuous.

Max crouched closer to the SUV, straining her ears and eyes into the night. If this was Anubis's vehicle, he obviously hadn't returned to it yet. Which meant he planned to hit Darius Constantine's lodge first.

She could wait for him to come to her. But that would leave Constantine to Anubis's mercy. She could—

Movement at the side of the road froze her in place. A dark figure strode down the hill toward the SUV, head bowed, hands shoved into a black coat. He wore no black hood.

A new fear stabbed into Max's lungs. An SUV parked by the side of Constantine's drive where anyone driving past would see it? Court Treybold had said Darius Constantine was pushing hard to purchase Atchison Dantell's share of the Burkhartt-Dantell Media Group. What if Anubis hadn't been hired by a member of the Burkhartt-Dantell board?

Max pressed herself against the vehicle, out of sight. What if Constantine's Firebird's Nest was a nest of vipers?

The odds weren't in favor of her taking on Anubis alone—he'd kicked her butt once already that night. But if she let him drive away, he would find her abandoned Jeep and sic Constantine's security staff on her trail.

Great.

Not much of a choice. Besides, she wasn't going to turn down the chance for a little payback.

She edged forward for one more glance around the hood at the approaching figure. He stepped out of the shadows of the trees to cross the road, and moonlight fell across his face, illuminating his profile.

Max choked back her cry of surprise, but his head snapped up, his whole body suddenly focused on the SUV.

"Who's there?" The clear, controlled voice matched the face. It was Steve Spencer.

Max's heart pounded so loudly in her ears she thought Steve must hear it, too. But even as her muscles automatically tightened for action, her knees weakened in relief.

In the shifting shadows, she might have mistaken Steve for Anubis, but she'd been up close and personal with the killer, and he barely topped Max for height. Steve had at least three inches on him. Not to mention that now that he'd stepped into the moonlight she could see he wore jeans, not fatigues, and his coat was less bulky, more tailored to show off his lean form.

"Is someone there?" He sounded less sure as he halted in the road. Maybe even a little nervous. Probably trying to convince himself she was a raccoon, not a grizzly bear.

She could slip away into the woods, and he'd never even know she'd been there. But although he wasn't the man she'd been hunting, she discovered she still had a strong desire to wring his neck.

She rose, leaning on the Explorer's hood, her chin in

her hand as she appraised Steve across the car. "I see why you'd have trouble rushing to the San Francisco airport from here."

"*Max?*" He froze in the process of reaching under his jacket. "What…?"

"What am I doing here?" she supplied for him. "Isn't *that* the question of the evening."

"How did you—" He stepped forward, stopped. "Have you been *following* me?"

Max jerked upright, his outrage setting fire to her own. "Don't flatter yourself. If I'd been following you, I'd be even farther behind Alex than I already am."

"You—" He stepped up to the SUV's hood, his face contorted with indignation. "You never told me you were coming to Alaska."

"I was following a hunch. I didn't want to say anything until I knew I was on the right track." She paused, cocking her head at him. "What's your excuse?"

His palms slapped down on the SUV's hood. "My excuse? It's my case! Not yours."

Right. He might even have a point there. Time to move on. "You've seen Darius Constantine? He's here at his lodge?"

"What?" His hands slid off the hood, and he ran one through his hair, ruffling its perfect cut. "Constantine? Yeah. I talked with him."

"How'd you figure out Alex was in Alaska? His credit card?"

Steve nodded. "Spike found the charges last night. We flew up today. And you're here on a hunch?"

"Alex sent me a postcard, asking me not to let his

mother hire me to find him. He mentioned his father's time in Alaska. I guessed he might come up here looking for closure."

"And you didn't tell me."

"So we're even." Max leaned against the grille beside him. "You thought Alex might come to Constantine, since he and Alex's grandfather were so close?"

Steve evaded her gaze. "Alex hasn't been here."

"You're sure?" Even knowing what Kirygin had told her, she couldn't shake the feeling of danger converging on Alex Dantell. "Darius Constantine has a reputation as a ruthless businessman. According to Court Treybold, he's shown a lot of interest in buying out Atch Dantell's share of the Burkhartt-Dantell Group."

Steve turned on her. "He's looking to shore up an old friend's business, so now he's a kidnapper?"

Max frowned at him. "I'm not saying he'd kidnap anyone, but if Alex Dantell just showed up on his doorstep, he might not come right out and tell you. Did you take a look around?"

Steve pushed himself to his feet. "You called while I was in there talking to the man and told me Alex was on a plane to San Francisco. Was that just a lie to throw me off?"

Max straightened to face him. "As far as I know, Alex should be in San Francisco. But until I hear he's safely in his own room at home, I'm not taking anything for granted."

"And that's why you've decided to drop in on one of the most powerful men in the world looking like a refugee from a pro wrestling summer camp?"

Max's hand flew involuntarily to her hair, half of it pulled from the barrette at the nape of her neck during her tussles with Bailey and Anubis. White synthetic stuffing poked from a tear in her coat sleeve. She touched her temple, felt the tacky ooze of drying blood.

"You're something else." The ghost of his boyish smile played around Steve's mouth as he reached out to tuck a strand of hair behind her ear. His fingers lingered on her cheekbone, a warm touch against her chilled skin. "I don't think I've ever met anyone with as much determination. As much focus."

Focus? Someone with focus would not have been distracted by the touch of his hand, the warm burring of his voice. Not when there was a killer wandering loose in the woods.

Max grabbed his wrist and jerked his hand away, turning to scan the trees around them, the moonlight-silvered road.

"I'm not here to ask Constantine about Alex," she said. "I'm here to warn him that Anubis might be coming to look for Alex here."

"Anu—" Steve pulled his arm away, amusement filling his voice. "You mean your international assassin?"

Max gritted her teeth. "International assassin or not, somebody blew up my rental car and knocked my assistant Lionel over the head with a rifle butt. And that same somebody just drove his motorcycle past Constantine's gate and is lurking somewhere on his property."

Steve's dark brows edged together, but there was still more laughter than concern in his voice. "Blew up your car?"

"I don't think he'd balk at killing a powerful businessman if he doesn't get the answers he wants."

Steve shook his head, grunting a laugh. "Your phantom car bomber wouldn't have a chance of reaching Constantine."

Max stared at him. "Constantine doesn't even have a fence around his property."

"He says he doesn't want to spend his whole life in walled compounds. Doesn't think he needs that much security here in Alaska. But that doesn't mean he's not protected."

He grinned at her again. "Anyone coming near that gate is photographed. Regular digital and infrared. He's got a state-of-the-art alarm system, not to mention his security staff, who undoubtedly have their eyes on us as we speak. And then there are the dogs. Your Anubis would have to be crazy to try to get to Constantine."

Max remembered the black-clad figure's silent laughter. "I don't think sanity is going to slow him down."

"Max, you—" Steve paused. He lifted his hand to her chin, turned her face. "You're hurt."

She flinched as he felt her temple, but his touch was too light to hurt.

"Let me drive you back to Anchorage. Spike will call my cell as soon as there's any news from our guy at SFO. We'll get you a good hot meal, and I'll take you for a soak in the hot tub at the hotel. Work the kinks out." His smile might have been a dare. "Trust me, Constantine can take care of himself."

Max could feel the weakness all the way down into

her toes. The hot tub was what tempted her. Sure. That was her story, and she was sticking to it.

"I can't leave without warning Constantine. If his men are that good, maybe they can catch Anubis and deliver him to the police. And then I have to get back to Lionel."

Steve gave a rueful smile. "What did I say? Determination and focus. I'm going to take a rain check on that hot tub, then. I'll be in touch when this Dantell case is wrapped up."

Before she could evade him—if she had wanted to— Steve leaned in to brush her lips with his. The citrus scent of his aftershave filled her nostrils. Even his breath smelled fresh, as if he would always be prepared for a stolen kiss under a moonlit Alaskan sky.

Steve paused, his lips a whisper from hers. "You sure I can't give you a lift?"

Not at all. "Hold on to that rain check."

She felt his smile against her mouth as much as saw it in his eyes. He backed away, pulling a rental company key ring from his pocket.

"I'll see you in San Francisco, sweetheart." He added a Bogey growl to the words as he climbed into the SUV.

Max started up the drive toward Darius Constantine's lodge, hearing the vehicle rumble to life behind her. Headlights swept past her, and gravel crunched as the Explorer turned and headed down the hill toward the gate.

As the noise faded into the woods, once again Max found herself alone in the huge Alaskan night. Colder now. Darker, as the moon eased behind the trees.

Irritation edged out the warmth from Steve's kiss. She'd allowed herself to be sidetracked, making targets of both herself and Steve. Just because Anubis hadn't used a gun at Kirygin's cabin didn't mean he didn't carry one.

And irritation at Steve. Maybe she should be pleased that he seemed so confident of her ability to look after herself. But the more she thought about it, the more she thought he simply hadn't taken her warnings about Anubis seriously.

And that kiss. He'd never made a secret of his attraction to her, but if he'd been seriously trying to get her into his hot tub, he would have been more persistent. He'd been distracting her. From the fact that he hadn't informed her about Alex's credit card charges? Or from why he'd come to Constantine's lodge? Had he discovered something about the businessman that he didn't want to share?

Or was that just her own guilty conscience talking? She hadn't exactly kept Steve apprised of her activities the past couple of days.

Using different methods, they'd both arrived at the same place, not far behind their quarry. Maybe if they'd been working together, they'd have found Alex by now. Maybe they could make a good team.

Max breathed deeply of the chilling air. She thought of Lionel, back in Kirygin's cabin with a possible concussion. Her fault. Maybe she just wasn't a good team player.

Ahead, the drive leveled out into a clearing. Firebird's Nest sat back against the woods, its rough timbers blending into its surroundings. Through the tall glass windows along its jutting deck Max glimpsed crystal chandeliers and a marble fireplace, but it wasn't the lodge that commanded attention.

Even at night, the view of the lake took her breath away. Starlight shimmered on its surface, playing with onyx depths. Mountains ringed the narrow valley, the snow at their peaks hinting at cold fire.

Max stepped into the clearing, her heart pounding as much from the terrible beauty as from the knowledge that Anubis might be somewhere nearby.

A door slid open, sounding loud in the quiet, turning Max toward the lodge. A man stood on the deck, his hand resting on the head of a black and white dog. The dog's attention focused on Max with as much intensity as its handler, erect ears swiveled toward her, curled tail quivering over its haunches.

Max remembered what Court Treybold had said about Constantine's dogs facing down bears. Based on the look in this dog's eye, she had no doubt it was true.

"Stunning view, isn't it?" The man's slight accent seemed as enigmatic as the mountains. "But cold. Please, join me."

As she crossed the clearing, Max reminded herself that Steve Spencer had managed to visit this lodge and return without getting eaten alive. But looking up into the intent gazes of the dog and the man, she felt unsure which was more likely to attempt to devour her.

Reaching the deck, she saw that Darius Constantine—surely this could only be Constantine himself—stood several inches taller than she, though his slender frame would never be imposing. It was the force of personality radiating from him that gave him presence.

As a friend of Matthias Dantell's, she had assumed he would be an old man, but he appeared to be in his late fifties. His hair gleamed bronze against fair skin that creased around his eyes and mouth and held a healthy color along his cheekbones.

He smiled, a faint curve to his lips, as his dog bristled by his side, warning her not to come too close.

"It is a pleasure to meet you, Magdalena. May I offer you a drink?"

Chapter 12

A whisper of a chill crept down Max's spine. "You know who I am, Mr. Constantine."

"I hope you will forgive the familiarity." He bent his head in apology. "The security cameras mounted at my gate got quite a clear look at your face. Do you realize how much you favor your father?"

"Court Treybold said you knew my father."

He gestured her toward the open sliding glass door. "I did. I have heard your name on several lips in the past two weeks. It seems as though I have been waiting for you."

"I don't remember my father ever mentioning you."

"We met only once or twice. But Sheridan Riley was a man who made a lasting impression. I did not always agree with his convictions, but I admired him for them."

Max preceded him into the lodge, the warmth a shock

after the cold of the night. A fire blazed in the marble hearth, indirect lighting giving the illusion that it illuminated the entire room. The ceiling vaulted above them, but the soft light created an almost intimate atmosphere. It would have felt welcoming, if not for the grizzly bear head snarling above the fireplace mantel. And the stuffed wolf crouching in the corner. Steve had mentioned a staff, security men, but Max neither saw nor heard a sign of them.

She hoped they were as effective as they were discreet. The broad, high windows left her feeling uncomfortably exposed. The memory of Anubis's knife sliced a shiver down her back.

The dog's claws ticked on the wood floor as Constantine followed her inside.

"A drink?" Constantine repeated, moving toward a portable wet bar.

"I'm driving."

"Coffee, then. Would you prefer decaffeinated?"

"I can't stay long."

"I can see you are in a hurry."

Max managed to keep her hands from flying to her hair, but she felt an unfamiliar warmth tinge her cheeks.

"I will not press you to stay. But please, have a seat while you tell me the reason for your call. Heikki?"

The dog at his side focused on Constantine's face, the blaze on his chest a bright splash of snow against his sharp black face.

"This is Magdalena. She is our guest. You may say hello."

Max wasn't sure if he meant her or the dog. Perhaps

both. The dog moved toward the butter-colored leather chair where she perched, looking almost as apprehensive as she was. But when she held out her hand, he sniffed it gently, then turned his head, allowing her to scratch his chest, his tail waving gently over his back. His short dense hair felt good under her fingers, and he smelled like the night.

"He's a beautiful dog." She could have sworn he grinned at her, his tail moving faster.

"Heikki is a Karelian bear dog." Constantine poured himself a glass of amber liquid, which he swirled beneath his nose as he watched the dog. "Bred in Finland. He is a gentleman, as well as a warrior, but I had the others put up in the kennel when I heard we were to have visitors tonight."

"Steve Spencer."

He smiled his slight smile again.

Heikki edged closer, to give her better access to the area below his ears.

"You've made a friend," Constantine said.

"I'm glad I didn't have to meet a pack of his friends out in the woods," she admitted.

"Karelian bear dogs don't hunt well in packs. They are too independent." Constantine seemed to approve of that. "But they make good watchdogs. They will corner a bear with unparalleled courage. And they have a well-developed sense of humor."

He sipped his drink, resting his free arm on the back of the chair opposite hers. "I'm sure Mr. Spencer told you that I have heard nothing from our young adventurer."

"How did you hear he was missing?" The question

sounded almost rude in this secluded retreat, but for all his genteel eccentricity, Darius Constantine was no mild-mannered hermit.

He seemed to take no offense. "Yvonne called me to ask my advice." He frowned down at his drink. "I only wish I could have done more. I said she must call Toby Mittard and by no means involve the police. I hope I was right in that."

He glanced at Max. "I had heard of your miraculous discovery of Atchison here in Alaska, of course, and I suggested your name, but Yvonne…would not consider it rationally."

"Yvonne doesn't know I have been helping Spencer Investigations with their search." She didn't need to add that Steve Spencer hadn't necessarily known, either.

"I will not enlighten her. My only wish is that she get her son back safely. I am afraid, however, that I am not sure how I may help you with that task."

"That's not why I'm here." Max rose to her feet, Heikki leaping up beside her, picking up on her agitation. "Mr. Constantine, I only entered your property because I followed an extremely dangerous man here from the Firebird Lodge."

"The man on the motorbike who bypassed my gate?"

Good. The infrared camera Steve had mentioned *had* caught Anubis's entrance. And the security staff had noticed.

"He blew up my car and injured my assistant. I have reason to believe he's searching for Alex, too, and I'm afraid he won't stop at arson or murder to get what he wants."

Constantine's brows rose. "And you followed him here by yourself?"

"I doubt I could stop him myself." She remembered the flash of the blade in his hand. She'd knocked it away. Maybe. Or maybe he'd only been playing with her, a cat showing its claws.

Maybe it was only the cumulative result of the long day, the violence, the dark and the cold. Maybe it was the mention of her father, maybe Constantine's detached amusement. But she suddenly felt very alone and very out of her element.

"I just came to warn you," she said. Weariness dragged at her shoulders, but she kept them taut. "I don't know if he's carrying a firearm, but he's good with a knife."

"I thank you." Constantine bent to set his drink on a glass end table. "It was thoughtful of you. You needn't be concerned. If anyone approaches this house, he will be dealt with, but I have little expectation of receiving any more visitors tonight. I suspect our friend on the motorbike has already left my property to return whence he came."

Remembering the open clearing around the house, Max guessed he was probably right about seeing anyone approaching. In any event, she could do nothing more here. At least he had taken her seriously. "I'd better get back to check on my assistant."

"I will have someone drive you back to your Jeep."

"That's not necessary."

But he was already moving to the wall, pushing an inconspicuous button beside the fireplace. "Even if I could guarantee no danger from this intruder, I would insist on seeing you safely to your car. Humans are not always the most dangerous predators in the far north."

A black-suited man with a crew cut and a discreet receiver tucked into one ear appeared in the doorway to the hall.

"Escort Ms. Riley to the front gate. And inspect her Jeep. You will start the engine for her."

The man didn't even blink at the request. "Should I lock the gate behind her, sir?"

"After Ms. Riley safely reaches the road. Tell Jan he can let the dogs out."

"Understood, sir."

Constantine took Max's hand. His was cool and smooth. "It has been a pleasure to meet you, Magdalena. Please give my regards to your friend, Tomas Gregory. I hope we will have the chance to speak again."

"Thank you." Max reached down for one last scratch behind Heikki's ear. She'd been right. The dog was easier to fathom than the man. Then she followed her unnamed escort from the lodge.

He didn't speak to her on the drive to the front gate. Even after he'd checked Bailey's Jeep inside and out and turned the key in the ignition, he merely held the door for her while she got in.

"Thank you," she told him, too tired to come up with anything better. He nodded and closed the door.

Max started the Jeep toward the Firebird Lodge, forcing herself to focus on the drive. She should have taken Constantine up on his offer of coffee. But there was something about the silent, rarified world he inhabited that would have made her nervous about tasting anything he offered. As if it might poison her, not in body, but in soul.

As it was, her soul felt as though it hung heavily in her bones. She reminded herself that Alex Dantell should be safely home by the time she and Lionel returned to Anchorage. But she hadn't found him. She hadn't protected Lionel. She'd been beaten by Anubis, manipulated by Steve Spencer and made to feel like a scab-kneed child by Darius Constantine.

For once, she would welcome the end of a search, the chance to return home and lick her wounds.

"You two look like plane crash victims. The ones who didn't survive." Simone glanced from Lionel beside her to Max in the rearview mirror.

Simone had insisted on picking them up from the airport. Max had hoped her presence might cheer Lionel, but he sat slouched in the front seat of Simone's coupe, head resting on the side window. A white bandage peeked from beneath his shaggy hair. He'd needed eight stitches, but the doctor at Providence Hospital in Anchorage had pronounced him fit for travel.

Max thought his self-confidence had sustained a greater injury than his head.

"You found out where Alex was," Simone reminded them. "You only missed him by a few hours. You got there ahead of Anubis, and you almost caught him, too. But you look like the world came to an end."

The optimistic words skirted the crucial point; Max made it. "Alex still isn't home."

Steve had called her at her Anchorage hotel at two

that morning to inform her that Alex had never contacted Yvonne and the man he'd sent to the San Francisco airport had seen no sign of him.

Lionel had tracked down the flight number, and the plane had landed at SFO on time. Either something had happened to Alex on arrival, or he had lied to Kirygin about going home.

Having learned to respect Alex's ingenuity and determination, Max put her money on the latter. But it didn't make her feel any better.

Butch Bailey, much to Max's surprise, had supplied them with his mysterious employer's e-mail address, but even Lionel hadn't been able to track down its point of origin.

"We don't have any leads," Lionel said, his voice heavy. "We're back where we started, except we know for sure Anubis is right behind us. Maybe even ahead of us. Thanks to me."

"He kicked both our butts," Max reminded him.

"You didn't have a gun. I should have been able to handle the situation."

"If I'd known we were going to run into a killer, I wouldn't even have taken you along."

"I'm not a four-year-old!" Lionel glared back at her. "Stop acting like I can't take care of myself. I contribute a lot to Quest Research. You and Simone should recognize that."

"You're both acting like four-year-olds," Simone scolded, scooting around a MUNI bus in her little Saturn like Jeff Gordon at Daytona. "What happened in Alaska is the past. We have to focus on the future."

Which pretty much led to dead silence. Which was fine with Max. The only thing more discouraging than thinking about her failure was talking about it.

"We'll start fresh in the morning," Simone said, pulling up in front of Max's condo. It sounded more like an order than a pep talk.

"Maybe I can hack into the account Alex used to book his tickets," Lionel said. "Kirygin saw his log-in ID. All I need is a password. I can make sure he really booked the flight he told Kirygin he was taking."

Great. Alex could be halfway around the world, and they'd never know it. Max decided to keep her negativity to herself.

"Good thought, Lionel. See you both tomorrow." Her carry-on felt twenty pounds heavier than it had two days before as she wrestled it up the two flights of stairs to her place.

A soft light glowed in her living room. Simone must have forgotten to turn it off after misting the orchids the day before. The citrusy scent of the golden chain orchid in the hall niche gently welcomed her home.

She paused, her eyes closing at an intense, tactile memory of Constantine's Karelian bear dog's thick fur beneath her fingers. She didn't have time to devote to a dog. She was gone too often.

But sometimes it would be nice to come home to a fellow creature that was glad to see her.

"Did you miss me?" she murmured, pausing to hook a finger under the delicate chain of the orchid's flowers.

"You've only been gone two days."

She nearly knocked the plant off its perch. Her carry-on bag thudded to the floor as she jumped forward to peer into the living room.

Tomas sat on the bench in her bay window, eyeing her skeptically. So much for the money she'd spent on her remote dead bolt.

"Are you trying to give me a heart attack?" She retrieved her bag from the hall and tossed it onto the sofa, not sure if she was still angry with him or just glad to see him.

"You should have known someone was here."

Angry, definitely angry. But she couldn't help laughing. "You'd never get over it if you couldn't surprise me anymore."

"I'm not the one you should be worried about. If you're going to insist on playing cat and mouse with Anubis, you'd better stop thinking you're the cat."

Simone.

"If Anubis wanted me dead that badly, I wouldn't be here for you to badger." She dropped onto the sofa beside her bag. She didn't like being made to feel like a snotty thirteen-year-old. Even if she was acting like one.

She sighed. "I know you're worried about me. Up in Alaska, I was frightened, too. But I can't just walk away. I wish you would understand that."

After a long moment, his posture relaxed slightly. "Where will you look for the boy next? Do you have any leads?"

"No," she admitted, stuck in the bog of helplessness that had dragged at her all day.

"The Burkhartt-Dantell board of directors plans to schedule a vote on the sale of Atchison Dantell's share of the company in the next day or two." Tomas said. "Perhaps after that, the danger to Alex will lessen."

"Or perhaps someone already has him and will find him expendable after the vote," she said. "Who are they going to sell it to? Darius Constantine?"

Tomas's face darkened. "There are other possibilities, if the board will only consider them."

"You don't think they should sell to Constantine? By all accounts, he and Matthias Dantell were close friends."

"I doubt Matthias Dantell had any more understanding of the concept of friendship than Darius Constantine."

The acid comment almost qualified as an outburst. Max narrowed her eyes. "You do know him, then. He said he knew Dad and to give you his regards."

"You *spoke* with Darius Constantine?"

Apparently Simone hadn't told Tomas every detail of her Alaskan adventure. "I tailed Anubis as far as Constantine's lodge. I thought Constantine could be in danger, so I went in to warn him."

"You *what?*" Tomas's thigh knocked a *Cattleya* over on the windowsill as he rose to his feet. His olive-toned skin had paled. "You went in…. And you told him who you were?"

"He recognized me."

"*Christe eleison.*" Tomas sank to the chair beside Max's sofa.

The hairs on the backs of Max's arms rose, even as she shrugged. "He was perfectly polite, even though I looked like a car wreck. He had his security man check the Jeep I was driving for any more of Anubis's explosives."

"He would enjoy that. He styles himself a gentleman."

"Why wouldn't he?" Max demanded, too unsettled to tolerate Tomas's enigmas. "So he's a ruthless businessman. He could have had his men toss me off his property. But—"

"He could have had them shoot you."

Max gave him a look. "Please."

"You were trespassing on the property of one of the wealthiest men in the world. A man with so much wealth, it is never seen. So much power, it is never felt. A man who has crushed powerful enemies. Who has undoubtedly survived more than one attempt on his life."

Max remembered the soft hush of security surrounding Firebird's Nest. The infrared camera at the gate. Mistakes could have been made in the name of protection.

She suppressed a shudder. "I guess it's a good thing he thought I looked like Dad."

"It's a good thing he didn't think you were worth the inconvenience of killing."

Max crossed her arms, hoping Tomas couldn't see the goose bumps. "Are you going to tell me why you don't like the man? Because if you're just going to sit around being spooky, I've got to go unpack. Just what has Constantine done?"

"I can't tell you."

"Great." Max stood and grabbed her bag. "When you think I'm finally mature enough for your pearls of wisdom, you—"

"I can't tell you, because I don't know." The rough honesty in Tomas's voice stopped her. "I have only whispers and conjectures and half-told stories."

"About his business practices?"

"I know little, even of those. Please." Tomas gestured her back to the sofa. "It is said his money came originally from gold and gems and has risen with investments in oil. It is said his money now flows in northern Africa and Iran and throughout the Middle East. Not just in oil and natural resources, but in arms and anything else of value. But since his name appears nowhere, how can I say that for sure?"

Max frowned. "His operations are illegal? Are you saying he's some kind of international criminal?"

"No." Tomas dismissed the label. "I'm saying Constantine has enough power and works far enough behind the scenes that there is very little he could do that could be prosecuted as illegal. *If* any current government cared to take him on."

It was Max's turn to shake her head. "I don't get it. Why would a man like that be interested in Burkhartt-Dantell?"

"Constantine and a few others with similar power and ambitions have discovered that controlling the sources of their wealth no longer depends so heavily on might, on armies and governments and wars. It is more efficient to control the distribution of fuel, food, labor and information."

"You're saying Constantine and his friends are buying things like media conglomerates in order to… what? Take over the world?" She snorted. "Like some James Bond villain? Sounds like a late-night talk show conspiracy theory."

Tomas shrugged. "Yes."

Max rose again. She was too tired for this. "All I care about is getting Alex Dantell home safely. If it will make you feel better, I promise to stay out of Constantine's way. If he is bent on world domination, I'm sure he's got more important things to worry about than me."

Tomas rose, too, more slowly, and the lamplight caught on the lines in his face, deepening them. "A spider is concerned with everything that touches his web. I don't want you to get caught in Constantine's. Neither would your father."

"Dad wouldn't have approved of arms dealing and exploiting political instability." She remembered Constantine saying he and her father had different convictions. "He wouldn't have backed down from doing what was right, just because it might upset some untouchable power broker."

"He wouldn't," Tomas agreed.

"You would have helped him." The hurt sounded in her voice, and she didn't care.

He took a deep breath. "I'm not saying I won't help you, Magdalena. I'm saying I can't. I couldn't help your father against that kind of danger."

Maybe it was exhaustion or the strange dislocation of the day before, but Max felt as if she were sinking in quicksand, the muddy grains clogging her brain as well as her lungs.

"Are you saying Darius Constantine had something to do with my father's disappearance?"

"No. I'm saying men like Constantine don't tolerate interference. And they fear very little. Police, politicians, the press don't frighten them. They can buy verdicts, regulations, favorable coverage."

She stepped toward him, her shin knocking against

the coffee table. She hardly recognized her own voice. "Can they buy a man's disappearance?"

"If I had any information about your father, I would have told you. I know nothing."

Nothing but whispers and conjectures and half-told stories. She found she was shaking. "But you guess something. Was my father interfering in Constantine's business?"

"No." Tomas's voice was sharp. "The projects your father was working on, his reasons for going to the market that day, had nothing to do with Darius Constantine."

"You said Constantine hides behind the scenes. How can you be so sure Dad wasn't 'interfering' in one of his schemes?"

Tomas's only answer was grim silence.

Chapter 13

It might have been hours after Tomas left when Max finally pushed herself up from the sofa. Her ribs ached from the struggles of the night before. Her eyes felt puffy and her joints loose as if she had been crying, though she had only sat in silence, memories of her father crowding around her.

The brisk scent of his cologne. The way his clipped speech revealed traces of his Boston childhood when he got excited. The calm way he stood up to bullies, whether a dishonest cabdriver in Istanbul or a genocidal warlord in North Africa.

She remembered being five or six, riding out to see the Great Pyramid at Giza by moonlight on a bad-tempered camel, leaning back against her father's chest, bundled into his overcoat.

Her eighth birthday, in Thailand, her father had promised to teach her to play baseball. It had been raining for a week, but he took her and a grumbling Tomas out into the garden. The three of them had played catch, chased pop flies and practiced bunting, barely able to breathe from the rain and laughter.

She'd heard people talk. Some grown-ups thought children were deaf. *You know the wife died when she was just a toddler. Who can blame her if she's a little wild? She needs a woman's influence in her life. Poor motherless child.*

But she hadn't thought she was a poor motherless child. She had her father and Tomas and all the marvelous people they knew. Foreign ambassadors and poets, princesses and activists, Nobel scientists and street urchins.

She shook herself, trying to shed the past. She wished she had a bottle of her father's favorite whiskey. Chardonnay just wasn't going to cut it.

She paused at the kitchen counter. The light on her answering machine was blinking. Unexpectedly, the tears she hadn't shed swelled under her lashes. A wrong number. Hers was unlisted.

Tomas had a habit of appearing when he wanted to talk with her. Simone and Lionel always used her cell phone, even when she'd forgotten to turn it on.

It wasn't that she didn't have any friends. There were all those friends of her father's from her childhood who kept up with her through Tomas. And friends from her years at San Francisco State. She kept in touch with some of them. Through Christmas and birthday cards.

Friends? When was the last time she'd even had a date?

Okay. So you're a pitiful little orphan. Get over it. She walked over and punched the button on the machine.

"Riley?" Wolfe's bluff voice filled the quiet kitchen. Max's spirits lifted. Not because Wolfe had called her. Not because someone besides a wrong number had called her. Only because… Hell, she refused to psycho-analyze herself any more that evening. "Simone told me you'd be back in town today. Meet me for lunch tomorrow. Lincoln Park. Land's End. I want to talk to you about something."

Max rolled her eyes as the message clicked off. She was going to have a chat with Simone about discussing her schedule—and giving out her unlisted number. But trust Wolfe to think no one could have anything better to do than conform to his plans.

Still, a smile tugged at her mouth as she lugged her carry-on toward her bedroom. Wolfe probably didn't have any more friends than she did.

I don't know how to explain that this is something I have to do. It's so hard for me to leave you. You are the best thing I've done in my life. Be strong for me. That may be a hard thing to ask, when you may think I haven't been strong for you. But this is the next adventure I have to take. I may not know where it will lead, but wherever I am, I will always be loving you. Don't ever forget that.

A breeze fresh from the Pacific rustled the printout in Max's hand as she read it one more time. Steve had finally faxed Simone a copy of Atchison Dantell's suicide note. Either he was getting frustrated enough to try anything or he just hoped the distraction would keep Max out of his way.

She wished he'd kept the damn thing to himself. She brushed a strand of hair out of her eyes, ignoring the dampness there as she stared out at the view of the Golden Gate.

If she'd been Alex...

She grimly interrupted that train of thought. Damn Atchison Dantell. And damn Court Treybold, too. She didn't know anything about typical suicide notes. Was there such a thing?

The police had determined the note was written in Atchison Dantell's hand. It was clearly a goodbye, and a weighty one, at that. Maybe it wasn't so strange that the note was not addressed to anyone. Atch could have expected Yvonne and Alex to know he meant the note for them. And maybe it wasn't so strange that he hadn't signed it. Maybe he'd been overcome with emotion, unable to write any more.

Maybe if Court Treybold hadn't mentioned another note, a note Atch had written while planning to fake his own death in Alaska, the omissions wouldn't bother her so much.

But since Treybold *had* put the idea into her head, the note seemed almost glaringly incomplete. The way it started right at the top of the page, as if it were the second page of a longer letter. A letter that he had decided not to send, which would explain why he had never signed it.

A letter never intended as a suicide note.

"Love letter?"

Max jerked her head up, nearly knocking her skull against Wolfe's as he leaned over the concrete bench behind her. Her heart pounded a little faster than it needed to as she turned to meet his amused hazel gaze.

"From a dead man." She passed the fax to him as he came around the bench to sit beside her.

"Atchison Dantell?" His brow furrowed as he scanned the neat lines. He shot her a sideways glance. "Don't even tell me what you're thinking."

"The same thing you are." The same thing no one else had even considered. That Alex might be right.

"I'm *not* thinking it." He passed the paper back to her.

"Treybold needs to talk to the police."

Wolfe raised a sandy eyebrow as he settled the white paper bag he carried onto his lap. "You think that's going to happen?"

She remembered Treybold's coyness about the note. "Atch was his friend."

"Not his best friend," Wolfe said, digging a paper-wrapped sub out of the bag. "I got the distinct impression that honor is reserved for Mr. Court Treybold himself. And Court Treybold's best friend just had his million-dollar yacht blown out from under his feet."

She wished she didn't know what he meant. "You think that might have been a warning, to keep his mouth shut?"

"I'm saying Mr. Treybold hasn't been eager to return my phone calls since Thursday last."

Max tucked the copy of the note into her briefcase beside her, her stomach knotting. Maybe she'd been hoping Wolfe would tell her she was way off base on this one. Maybe they both were.

"Maybe he'll see me."

Wolfe's scrutiny made her wish she'd chosen something more stylish than jeans and a yoga halter to throw on before coming to the park.

"Maybe. I've always prided myself on my charm, but he still thought you were cuter. His secretary had better taste. She told me he's gone to his vacation house in Marin. I'll give you the phone number." His tone held as much pity as cynicism. "Maybe you can take him up on that skydiving offer."

Max's eyes narrowed. Wolfe didn't give information away for free. But she'd take it.

The smell of hot pastrami wafted from Wolfe's hands as he unwrapped the sandwich he held.

Max found herself almost drooling, despite the tension in her gut. "How did you know I love pastrami?"

Wolfe glanced down at the sandwich. "This is my pastrami."

"What's mine?"

His left eyebrow tilted rakishly as it rose. "Yours?"

She refused to laugh. "You invited me out to lunch."

"A working lunch." He took a large bite of the sandwich, shreds of lettuce dancing at the corner of his mouth. "All journalists know a working lunch means bring your own brown bag. What did you think, this was some kind of date?"

He grinned, possibilities humming between them. The electricity raised the hairs on Max's arms. *Damn.* She didn't need the distraction. Especially not with this man. But it was hard not to respond to that grin.

"Wolfe," she growled.

He jerked the sandwich out of her reach as she grabbed for it. "All right. All right. If you're that desperate, you can have my other sandwich."

He dug into the white bag, pulling out a second pastrami sub. "And my other drink." He passed her the sandwich and a can of cola.

"And your other bag of chips?" she prompted.

"Greedy blighter."

"Sun Chips!"

"The French onion are mine."

The pastrami tasted even better than it smelled, and it had almost enough mustard to suit her. For the first time in days, Max was enjoying herself. Enjoying the taste of the food, the smell of the sea, the warm touch of the sun dappling her face through the branches of the eucalyptus trees.

She was enjoying Wolfe's company as he lounged beside her, the breeze ruffling his chronically unkempt hair. She drowned her smile in a sip of Coke. At least she could enjoy his company as long as his mouth was full of pastrami.

"You said you wanted to talk with me about something," she blurted when she realized it wasn't just his silence she was enjoying. This was *Wolfe*, for goodness' sake.

Wolfe shaded his eyes as he stared out over the water. "Business goes on. Come suicide or high water. I'm glad my father wasn't a media mogul."

"I heard the board is going to vote on the sale of Atch's share of the company soon. Will it go to Darius Constantine?"

Wolfe shrugged. "The group of investors he's representing is the top contender. The only serious competition is a group financed by an expat Russian, chap named Antonov."

"Dimitri Antonov." It wasn't even a question. The Russian had not been meeting Tomas after hours at Pieces of Time merely to buy a tall clock.

"You've heard of him? I did an article on his oil dealings a couple of years back. A real capitalist. Not a popular fellow with the current Russian administration."

Max hardly heard him. Tomas had said he couldn't do anything about men like Constantine, but he'd obviously urged Antonov to buy Burkhartt-Dantell out from under the man. Maybe Tomas figured an ex-KGB agent could protect himself against threats like Anubis. But he hadn't trusted her enough to tell her.

"Your turn." Wolfe turned on the bench, facing her. "What happened in Alaska?"

She didn't want to talk about it, but his green-flecked eyes fixed on hers with such intensity that she found herself describing the terror-inducing plane ride to Atch's cabin, the smell of the shrub willows at Lake Hood Seaplane Base, the overwhelming wildness of the mountains above Firebird Lake.

Wolfe's disbelieving amusement at the demise of the Mustang made her laugh, too. And somehow even her fight with Anubis seemed more embarrassing than deadly by the light of day.

"No wonder Grant Fowler considers you one of his best freelance assets," Wolfe said when she was done. "You probably couldn't do a travel article about surfing in Santa Cruz without getting attacked by a shark and discovering a sunken Spanish galleon filled with gold doubloons."

She wanted to respond with appropriately biting sarcasm, but her mind stuck on his comment that Grant Fowler considered her an asset. She knew that. But it was nice to have someone say so.

Even if he did have an ulterior motive.

"What are you buttering me up for, Wolfe?"

But his next statement took an entirely unexpected direction. "I didn't know about your father."

Max stilled.

"Grant said something once about your not having much family, but until I saw your face when Court Treybold mentioned your father, it didn't occur to me you might have lost him. I'm sorry."

Max shrugged. This was not ground she wanted to tread. "I don't know anything about your father, either."

"He wasn't a diplomat." Wolfe gave a short laugh. "I can't say diplomacy was one of his fortes. Probably would have helped him advance more quickly through the ranks. Career military. An officer in the Royal Engineers. He took up fishing after retirement. Drowned when his boat capsized in a sudden squall."

"I'm so sorry."

He looked startled by the sentiment, as if he'd told the story often enough it no longer connected to the event. "Yes."

She might have imagined the pain flickering in his eyes.

"I still miss the old man. Even his knack of always

telling me when I bloody well botched something." His eyes squinted against the sun. "Can't imagine how much worse it would have been, especially for my mother, if they'd never retrieved the body for us to bury."

If that was as close as he got to sympathy, she could manage. "You'd have dealt with it."

"I only found a couple of short newspaper accounts." His gaze held hers. "Your father told his staff he was going to visit the Grand Bazaar in Istanbul. A colleague saw him there. But he never returned to the embassy."

He left it open-ended, but she didn't answer.

"After that interview with Treybold, I wondered if you had some connection to Constantine that I didn't know about. That's why I looked up your father. I didn't intend to pry."

Max's mouth twisted. "You just couldn't help yourself?"

His back stiffened. "I just thought… I thought I should say something instead of pretending I didn't know. Maybe I understand better now why you want to help Alex Dantell."

"I don't think you can really understand unless you've been through it." Her fists tightened on the strap of her bag. "Maybe not even then."

Even now, the memories had the capacity to blot out the present, to take her back to those terrible first days, the long weeks of blackness, the wild hope and gut-wrenching despair.

"Men like my father don't just disappear." It was almost a relief to speak of it. "He wasn't an ambassador. He wasn't a political big shot. He spent his career working behind the scenes, arranging compromises, convincing people to do the right thing. He could be tough. Not everyone liked him. But…"

"But his job was to win over enemies, not make them."

"Yes." She shook her head. "He wasn't a kidnap target. Some people suggested he ran away. You can go almost anywhere from Istanbul. But he would never have done that. He wasn't Atchison Dantell. He loved his work. And if he hadn't, he had too strong a sense of duty to desert it."

She glanced at Wolfe to see his reaction, but he only nodded. "Somebody started a rumor there was a woman involved. But no one ever found anything to back that up."

"You've looked."

"The authorities suggested thieves, drug traffickers, a random sociopath." The strap twisted in Max's hands. "It's harder than you'd think to make an entire body disappear for good. That's why Jimmy Hoffa and D. B. Cooper still make such good stories. But he was my dad, not a story."

She forced her fists to unclench and met Wolfe's gaze. "So, is that what you invited me here for?"

"I think it was to apologize, actually." His hand rested on hers where she'd pressed her palm flat on the bench. "I was wrong about you."

"Oh?" She felt flushed from the memories, Wolfe's hand too warm and steady on hers to bear.

"I thought the only remaining idealists were all either naive or stupid."

Her mouth twitched, and she managed to breathe. "Which category did you fit me into?"

"I never thought you were a fool."

She snorted. "So what am I, if I'm not a naive idiot?"

"I don't know." His eyes remained serious. "Maybe someone who actually believes she can make a difference in the world, even though she knows the odds are against her."

Max shrugged off the description. "Don't get all gooey on me, Wolfe. You can't tell me your reporting isn't about trying to make a difference in the world."

"I gave up trying to change the world a long time ago."

"Reporting on poverty and genocide in far-off places isn't for someone looking for fame and fortune."

His smile was dark. "I don't see any change. There's always going to be poverty and war and famine and greed."

"And generosity and unexpected abundance and hope." Max stopped, hearing her own words. "It sounds naive."

"Right."

"You don't get over pain," she said, not sure how to explain. "It changes you. But you can make a choice about how you live afterward. I decided I'd rather live in a world where one person could make a difference. That's how my father lived. I don't stop wars or get hostages released, but maybe sometimes I help someone who's lost find their way home."

Max blew out a long breath. "Maybe I can be part of making sure my dad didn't…" She still couldn't say it. "Live in vain. That's the world I choose to live in."

Wolfe made a noise that might have been a grunt or a laugh. "I'm not sure whether I needed to hear that or I just wish you'd kept the bloody homily to yourself."

Max grinned. "Up yours, Wolfe."

"That's my girl." He smiled wryly. "I've got another appointment this afternoon, but maybe later if you find you need help, even just somebody to bounce ideas off—" He shrugged. "You know my number."

"Thanks." She glanced away so he wouldn't see how deeply she meant it. To be offered help, instead of warnings and advice… She made herself smile. "You're getting soft in your old age."

"Don't tell anyone." He gathered up their lunch wrappers and crunched them into his paper bag. He tossed the bag toward a nearby garbage can. "Nothing but net."

"So you were *aiming* for that patch of grass."

Max rose as Wolfe strode over to retrieve the trash. She couldn't help noticing how his shoulders filled his dark green shirt, his tanned arms showing muscles she hadn't noticed before. And his chinos fit all right, too.

Pitiful, she mocked herself, but she couldn't help smiling. So she noticed he looked good. He'd taken a good look at her earlier. Include Steve Spencer's kiss, and she'd gotten more ego-stroking in the past couple of days than she had in months.

Someone's cell phone rang, a jarring sound. Some people didn't have any idea how to enjoy the simple pleasures of a quiet Sunday.

Max muttered an impolite word as she realized the ringing was coming from behind the bench she'd just been sitting on. *She* was one of those people. Her phone must have fallen out of her briefcase when she put back Atchison Dantell's suicide note.

By the time she dug the phone out of the weeds, the ringing had stopped, the caller switched to voice mail.

She didn't recognize the number. Probably Steve Spencer calling to make sure she'd received the faxed note.

He'd called the night before and twice already that morning, his charm on high octane. He'd found a place near Half Moon Bay that offered private hot tubs overlooking the Pacific. It would have been even more flattering if she hadn't suspected his calls were as much to keep track of her as to flirt.

She wasn't sure she was ready to tell him what she thought of Atch's note. Of course, she'd told Wolfe. Maybe Wolfe was just easier because he didn't have a personal stake in the Dantell mess.

She had to get over her competitiveness, or whatever her hang-up was with this case. Alaska might have turned out differently if she'd told Steve she was going, treated him as if they were on the same side.

She clicked on voice mail.

"Mr. Wolfe." The accent added a faint *V* to the name. "I regret to say I am forced to be late to our meeting at the Legion of Honor. I hope this will not inconvenience you. Perhaps you will not think it inconvenient to trade my company for a few moments more with our lovely mutual friend.

"Do keep a close eye on her. Her enthusiasm is infectious, but perhaps not wise. We would not want anything unfortunate to happen to her. You may expect me soon after one o'clock."

The caller hung up without identifying himself, but Max didn't need any help recognizing his smooth, cultured voice. She could still feel the sun warm against her skin, but ice spread through her bones.

Men like Darius Constantine can buy police, politicians, the press....

How much would a man like Davis Wolfe cost?

Chapter 14

For once Max appreciated every moment of Tomas's training in self-control. Her body remained relaxed, her apologetic smile felt natural on her face as she clicked the phone shut. She passed it to Wolfe as he strode back to her, his brows raised in question.

"I didn't realize you had such good taste. We have the same phone."

His hand dropped to the holder at his waist. The clasp flapped open. "Not again. I'm going to lose the bloody thing one of these days."

"I heard it ringing, but I didn't catch it. When I didn't recognize the number, I realized the phone wasn't mine."

She watched his eyes glance at the missed number. *He* recognized it, all right.

"Speak of the devil." His wry smile might have been

genuine, but she couldn't see his eyes as he tucked his phone away, closing the case's clasp securely. "My next appointment."

"Really?" She widened her eyes to take the smart-ass out of her question.

"Darius Constantine, actually. He's in town to do some last-minute lobbying before the board's final vote, and he actually agreed to a short interview." Wolfe's expression was almost as impish as Steve's grin, a little boy caught slipping a frog into a pretty girl's desk. "I guess I have to 'fess up that I'd heard a little bit about your visit with him before you told me. He was quite charmed—obviously hasn't known you long."

She wanted to believe him, to return to the moment she'd actually considered his offer of help. Which meant her ability to trust her instincts where Wolfe was concerned had been too seriously compromised.

"My illusions are shattered." She kept her tone light, her sarcasm high. "Sneaking behind my back to get a coup of an interview like Constantine. My faith in humanity is dead."

He cleared his throat in I'm-too-cute-to-kill guilt. "After what Treybold said about Constantine knowing your father, I may have sort of used your name to get him to talk to me."

Max rolled her eyes. "Damn reporters. Can't trust 'em as far as you can throw them. So, go. You don't want to keep a man like Constantine waiting."

"I'll give him your best."

"I hope his dogs eat you."

"I'll call you," he threatened, before flashing her

that wicked grin and heading off up the path toward the art museum.

Max sucked in a breath, turning her face toward the sea as her bravado evaporated, leaving her shaken. Wolfe and Constantine. He'd confessed to meeting with the man. Admitting to a guilty conscience made him sound innocent.

Her mind spun as she tried to remember exactly what she'd said to Wolfe that morning that he might report to Constantine. If he *were* a spy.

Max groaned. Maybe she should be grateful that she *didn't* have any leads.

The bright autumn sunshine did nothing to disperse the shadows gathering around Max's heart as she hurried up the street toward Quest Research. Tomas said he couldn't help her. Wolfe might be in league with the devil. The quicksand was back, sucking away her trust.

Sure, she could rely on Lionel and Simone. But she'd already almost gotten Lionel killed.

She couldn't give up on Alex Dantell, but neither could she trade Lionel's and Simone's safety for his. She had to pull them off the case.

She was so focused on protecting her assistants from the evil intent of strangers that she almost knocked Simone to the ground as they collided rounding the corner of Quest's cotton-candy-colored Victorian.

"Max!" A tendril of red hair had escaped Simone's smooth ponytail and her normally cat-quiet gray eyes were wide. "Are you all right?"

"Yes, what's wrong?"

Simone drew a deep breath, obviously trying to collect herself. "I just got a telephone call. A man said you were in trouble at Lincoln Park and needed me right away."

Max glanced around as she pulled Simone farther into the narrow walkway between the Quest building and its slate blue neighbor. "You didn't recognize the voice? Why didn't you call me?"

Simone raised an ironic eyebrow.

Max slapped at the pocket of her soft-sided case and pulled out her cell phone. She turned it on without comment and returned it to the briefcase. "Where's Lionel?"

"I don't know." Simone's voice was troubled. "He came rushing out of his office a couple of hours ago saying he might have some kind of lead. He said he was going to check it out."

"Lionel went to check it out?" She remembered his mood the day before, feeling that she and Simone didn't appreciate him. She'd have to let him know just how much she did appreciate him—after she killed him. "He didn't say where he was going?"

"I think it had something to do with Alex's airline flights."

Max nodded, setting aside her worry about Lionel for the moment. Even he couldn't get into too much trouble at the airport. Her mind wavered on that. Okay, maybe he could. But if he got himself taken into custody by airport security, at least he'd be safe from Anubis for a few hours.

She started back up the walkway toward the tiny cement square behind the building where the Quest employees parked their cars.

"Where are we going?" Simone asked, her heels clicking on the pavement as she trotted to keep up.

"Whoever called you either wanted me out of the park or wanted you out of the building," Max said.

She paused at the edge of the building. Nothing moved in the back alley. Good. At least if she was going to look like an idiot, only Simone had to see.

She crossed to the rear door of the travel agency on the first floor of their building. It was closed on Sundays. The heavy plastic garbage cans beside the door were nearly full, which should make them steady. Again, good. Unless the lids collapsed and she plunged into the garbage.

"Stay here," she whispered to Simone, shifting the cans over a few feet. "If you see anything suspicious, call the police."

"Suspicious?" Simone muttered back. "You mean like a crazy woman climbing up the fire escape?"

But she braced the garbage cans while Max climbed on top and launched herself to the bottom rung of the ladder.

With a short prayer of thanks that the whole structure didn't collapse to the street, Max climbed to the third floor. The landing hung below the back window to Lionel's office. Lionel never remembered to shut and lock his window, but Simone always did when she left for the day.

Max smiled as she edged up to the half-open window, hearing the blinds clack in the breeze. Whoever had placed the call to frighten Simone had flustered her too much for his own good.

She risked a peek through the window. Empty. Door closed. She glanced down to send Simone a thumbs-up signal.

The window didn't make a sound as Max slid it up another three inches and climbed through. For an anal-retentive technogeek, Lionel had a high tolerance for chaos. Despite Simone's best efforts, papers spilled across Lionel's desk and filing cabinets. He'd left an open can of Coke sitting on the UCSC Banana Slug mouse pad Simone had given him for last Christmas and an empty chip bag on his printer.

There was nothing to suggest the office had been disturbed since Lionel had left it. Except… A smell tickled the back of Max's nose. So faint she couldn't place it. Tropical? Not unfamiliar, but not Lionel.

A faint sound from the outer office froze her beside the desk. Clicking? A quiet little mouse running across Simone's keyboard. So, they did have a visitor.

She padded back to Lionel's desk and slid open his top drawer. There. The sea lion letter opener *she'd* gotten him for his birthday.

It wasn't much, but she was counting on surprise, not weaponry. And on Simone calling 911 if anything loud happened.

The doorknob turned without a sound. She breathed deeply, adjusted her stance. And exploded through the doorway, barreling halfway across the outer office before the intruder even had a chance to look up from Simone's computer monitor.

He was surprised, all right. Max saw it in his eyes as he threw himself back in the chair. But the surprise cut both ways, and Max skidded to a halt three feet from Simone's desk.

"Max." Steve's grin had a hard time taking hold of his mouth. "We've got to quit meeting like this."

"You broke into my office."

Surprise must have masked the fury in her voice, because his sheepish grin settled in. "I wanted to ask you to join me for dinner later, to talk about the case, but I couldn't reach you. Simone wouldn't tell me where you were."

"You thought I might be hiding from you in Simone's computer?"

She must have hit the right tone that time, because his grin faltered briefly.

"I was afraid you'd gotten another lead on the Dantell boy's whereabouts and you'd run off to find him without me."

He was good. Just the right amount of hurt behind the guilty confession.

"And what did you find out?"

He shrugged, gesturing at the monitor. "Your computer geek knows what he's doing. I couldn't get into any of the files."

Max made a mental note never to complain about Lionel's arcane password systems again.

The front door to the office banged open, spinning her halfway around, letter opener slipping into position. But the newcomer was Simone, the loose hair flying in her eyes detracting not at all from the chilling stare she leveled at Steve Spencer as she trained a palm-sized pistol at his head.

"What are you doing at my desk?"

Steve's grin turned a little desperate. "Max and I were just having a friendly chat. It's all cool. Here, you can have your chair back."

He stood, hands held nonthreateningly out to his sides.

"It's all right," Max said. She didn't mind watching Steve squirm, but it annoyed her that her entrance hadn't had such a dramatic effect on him. She could probably be as deadly at close range with a collectible letter opener as Simone could with a .22. "I thought I told you to stay downstairs. Where did you get that gun?"

"A single girl can't be too careful." Simone lowered it reluctantly.

"Do you have a concealed weapons permit?" Steve asked.

Simone raised an eyebrow. "Does it look concealed to you?" She turned to Max. "Should I call the police now?"

Tempting as it was, Alex couldn't afford that wasted time. "I don't want to hang around that long. I'll escort Mr. Spencer outside. You call the locksmith and get our front door security improved, then call it a day."

She gestured toward the main office door, and Steve took the hint to escape. He paused to hold the door for her, but Max waved him through. She didn't trust him behind her, and she didn't really care if he knew it.

"I don't blame you for being pissed," he said, preceding her down the stairs. "It was a stupid move. I acted like an idiot, and you have every right to hate me."

He paused at the landing, his blue eyes serious. "You held out on me about Alaska. I was afraid you were doing it again."

And maybe she deserved that. "You didn't trust me, so you felt free to break my trust?"

He waited until they'd exited the building into the early afternoon sunshine before responding. "I don't think you understand how huge this case is to me. It could make or break Spencer Investigations. I'm not trying to steal your thunder. But this isn't a game for me. It's my living."

It's a young boy's life. But she held her tongue. "I hope you earn your living on this one. I really do."

"Max." His expression was rueful, rather than boyish, and even more appealing for it. "Give me a chance to apologize properly. I really would like to take you out to dinner tonight. To ask for your help instead of stealing it."

She hadn't developed an immunity to temptation, but betrayal provided powerful inoculation. "Sorry, I have plans. Dinner plans," she expanded, as suspicion flashed in his eyes. She wouldn't put it past him to put a tail on her. Might as well throw him off the scent with a partial truth. "With Court Treybold."

"You think he might know where Alex is?"

She gave him a shark's smile. "I think he has a French chef and a swimming pool. You don't want me getting in your way. Don't worry. The Dantell case is all yours. I'm officially on vacation."

"With Treybold?" Steve's temper flared before he reined it in. "I thought you were smarter than that. The man's a player, Max. He came by the Dantell house to pay his respects, and he was all over Yvonne like a fly on honey. His best friend's widow."

"At least I know exactly what I'm getting into." She

brushed past him, stalking up the walkway to the parking pad.

Yeah, right. She fumbled briefly with the keys, her heart pounding as she started the Spitfire's engine. She had no idea what she was getting into anymore.

Steve's excuses had seemed so sincere. As sincere as Wolfe's. He hadn't been able to find her, had been afraid she'd run off after Alex without him. So sincere. So plausible.

Except that whoever he'd had call Simone to convince her to leave the office had known Max was at Lincoln Park.

No, Max didn't know exactly what she'd gotten herself into. But she knew there was no one she could trust to get her out of it except herself.

And no one else she could trust to get Alex out of it, either. Because if Alex was right about his father being murdered, the sale of his father's share of Burkhartt-Dantell wouldn't end the threat to Alex, as Tomas had hoped. There would still be at least one person with reason to want Alex's disappearance to become permanent.

She had to find out what Treybold knew. Because if she couldn't find Alex, then finding the person who wanted him dead might be the only way she could keep him alive.

Chapter 15

With Sunday traffic and good fortune from the highway-patrol-avoidance gods, Max was winding her way up a lonely two-lane route into the Marin County hills barely forty-five minutes later. Yet the rolling autumn-gold fields slowly giving way to narrow ridges and steep forested valleys felt a world, and maybe a century, away from the crowded streets of San Francisco.

She eased up on the accelerator as she glanced at her odometer. She should reach the turnoff to Court Treybold's ranch in less than a mile. Steve must have been right about Treybold's making moves on Yvonne Dantell. A call to Treybold's secretary pretending to be Yvonne had garnered her detailed directions to the playboy's little love nest.

Wind and weather had faded the sign for Skyline

Ranch, but the dirt road leading from the turnoff was well graded. It led up through a sentinel row of live oaks, gradually leveling out onto a long, bare ridgetop.

As the ranch house came into view, Max revised her assessment of Treybold's "little" love nest. The curving, low-slung house crouched around a front courtyard fountain boasting a Greek revival statue of a naked Adonis carrying a water-spouting fish. Behind the house, she caught a glimpse of a swimming pool—so, she hadn't lied to Steve about that, after all—overlooking a stunning view of endless ridges and mist-draped valleys running toward the distant Pacific.

The dirt drive paralleled a long, flat tarmac track that ran most of the length of the ridge. A small plane rested at the end of the private airstrip, parked like a car beside the house. Treybold's skydiving plane.

She pulled the Spitfire up behind the only other car parked in front of the house. The ancient Honda Civic with its balding tires looked out of place against the backdrop of the ostentatious fountain. Not exactly in keeping with Treybold's flamboyant style.

In fact… Max's eyes narrowed as she climbed out of her car. It looked a lot like the old Honda Civic Lionel had bought from his uncle for eight hundred dollars two years before.

She peered through the side window. A suspicious McDonald's bag lay crumpled on the front passenger's seat, but it was the I Brake For Pinnipeds bumper sticker plastered across the glove compartment that clinched it.

Simone had said Lionel was checking out a lead connected to Alex's air travels. Max frowned at the small plane beside the house. She couldn't imagine a connection.

Then again, she couldn't imagine Court Treybold inviting a wild-haired stranger in a junkyard reject car in for a cup of afternoon tea, but he apparently had.

Max followed the brick path around the fountain to the front door. The doorbell sounded like a rustle of wind chimes. The frosted windows around the door obscured the interior, but she couldn't detect any movement. Max pushed the button again and held it a bit longer.

Perhaps Treybold and Lionel had taken their chat out by the pool. Max followed the path back around the side of the house, passing the plane with a wary glance. She could easily imagine jumping out of it, but only before it took off.

A gust of wind struck her as she turned the back corner of the house, plastering loose hair across her cheeks. Beyond the far side of the house, past the garage, below the end of the rounded ridgetop, the roof of another building, probably a barn, blended into the surrounding trees. Closer by, the kidney-shaped pool sparkled in the sun, and a smaller hot tub sat behind a redwood screen nearby. But pool, hot tub and stone patio were all deserted.

The rear of the house opened up above the valley view, with floor-to-ceiling windows overlooking the patio. Max strode up under the roof overhang to the French doors.

A high-ceilinged living room spread out before her, a huge stone fireplace competing with a gigantic plasma television. The wood floor of the living room zigzagged into the tile of the open kitchen to the left. The pale green tile showed a dark stain near its border with the wood floor.

Both rooms appeared empty, though a half-filled glass of amber liquid sat on the black countertop between them, and… Max's gaze drifted back to the tile, pulled toward the irregular stain. Dark, too viscous for a spilled drink. Goose bumps prickled down her arms.

The French doors opened easily to Max's touch. The brush of her running-shoe soles on the kitchen tile sounded loud in the silent house.

She crouched beside the stain. The edges had dried a dark, blackish brown and the faint scent of iron caught in her throat.

She stilled her body, her breathing, her sudden urge to run. She was frozen beside a smeared pool of blood in the middle of an open room in front of a huge bank of windows in an empty house in the middle of nowhere. And she hadn't thought her day could get any worse.

Maybe Treybold had dropped a whiskey glass and cut himself. Maybe Lionel had gone for a swim and cut his foot on a rock returning to the house. Maybe one was driving the other to the hospital in Santa Rosa in Treybold's Lexus.

And maybe her father had just stepped out for an eleven-year coffee break.

She rose to her feet, as quiet as the house.

She forced herself silently across the tile, eyes and ears alert for any indication she had company.

She found the telephone on the opposite side of the

kitchen counter facing the front foyer. It dangled by its cord, ripped from the wall and smashed with enough force to stave in the wood paneling behind it.

Max breathed shallowly through her mouth, keeping the sound silent. There could be an undamaged telephone in an office or one of the bedrooms. But she had her cell phone in her briefcase in her car. She just might learn to appreciate the obnoxious things, after all, if she could reach the car.

Keeping low, she crossed through the living room. The window at the end of the curved space opened just opposite where she'd parked the Spitfire.

The window rose easily, though the faint hush of its movement grated on her ears. Nothing stirred across the ridgetop except the dried grasses shifting golden in the breeze. A gunman could easily be hiding in the trees past the drive, but she'd have to take that chance.

She launched herself through the window, a perfect landing and a second lunge taking her right up to the car. She wasted only a moment on catching her breath before yanking open the driver's door. She thrust herself across the seat to grab for the case she'd tucked into the passenger seat well.

Her stomach lurched. The case was gone. She jerked back out of the car, her breathing a little noisier now. Unless her briefcase had developed wings, she wasn't alone. And whoever her unseen watcher was, he didn't want her calling the sheriff.

Max didn't like the idea of running away, but she could drive for help.

She scanned the Spitfire's undercarriage. No burning gasoline cans, but the passenger-side tires had been slashed. She glanced toward Lionel's Civic and saw similar damage to his tires.

She wasn't going anywhere.

But the saboteur hadn't come after her yet. Because confronting her directly was too dangerous? Or because without a phone or a car, he thought she was helpless?

Anger crept up her spine, entwining with the fear. She might be at her unseen enemy's mercy, but she didn't have to play his game.

She rose deliberately to her feet. Forget the window. She stalked to the front door, head high, though her senses were tensed for peripheral movement or a telltale sound.

The door closing behind her didn't ease her sense of exposure, but she kept moving. The kitchen drawers yielded a wickedly sharp carving knife, a cigarette lighter and a small, heavy flashlight on a keychain she could hook to her jeans. Not exactly an arsenal, but she'd once fought off three artifact smugglers in Thailand with less.

Okay, one of them had been eighty-five and one had a broken arm at the time, but that cast had been a nasty weapon.

Now she had to figure out what she was up against. And find Lionel.

The master bedroom suite off the living room was obviously Court Treybold's bachelor lair—wet bar, silk sheets, hot tub and all. She saw no signs of recent female occupancy.

The small office facing the airstrip looked tidy and

rarely used. No convenient .45 in the desk drawer. The one crumpled paper in the waste basket proved to be an overdue property tax notice for the ranch.

Max blinked at the amount. But she didn't think Treybold had committed suicide in the kitchen over a tax bill.

The opposite wing of the house held three more en suite bedrooms, each with its own spectacular view, ready for guests. But no current guests were evident, either in the form of neglected luggage or as bodies in the bathtub.

Max checked the bedside telephone in the final, nautical-themed bedroom, just to be thorough. Its innards had been punctured by a knife or screwdriver, the same as in the other two bedrooms.

She was about to turn away, when the drape of the bed covers caught her eye. The anchor-patterned duvet had been pulled up over the pile of goose-down pillows, but the pillows weren't quite straight, and the marine blue sheets dangled down the side of the bed instead of tucking under the mattress.

Max pulled back the edge of the duvet. Her pulse jumped in her throat. Whoever had slept in this bed most recently hadn't left only mussed sheets behind. He'd also left his pajamas, partially stuffed under the pillows instead of repacked in his bag. Max pulled out the faded gray T-shirt and the flannel wolf-print shorts. Unless they'd shrunk drastically in the wash, Treybold had never fit in these.

But they were just about perfect for a tall, skinny twelve-year-old boy.

* * *

Alex.

No wonder Treybold wouldn't answer Wolfe's phone calls. But why would he be hiding Alex Dantell? Why not take him home to Yvonne? Unless he thought Alex wouldn't be safe. Could Alex have found evidence that his father was murdered, after all?

An image of the bloodstain on the kitchen tile flashed through Max's mind, and nausea roiled her stomach. She was too late.

No.

She was a step behind. A long step. But if Alex was dead, and Treybold, and Lionel, why would the perpetrator still be hanging around Skyline Ranch?

If Alex was still at liberty, and frightened, he was resourceful enough to have stolen her cell phone and sabotaged her car.

Or perhaps he was hiding terrified in the woods, being stalked by a cold-blooded killer.

Either way, she wasn't doing Alex—or Lionel—any good sitting alone in Treybold's empty house.

She went out the same living room window she'd used before. Her car offered the only cover between the house and the trees. She barely paused behind it before dashing across the drive and plunging into the sparse tree line. The spreading live oaks quickly gave way to tangled madrone and oak thickets, which gave more cover but slowed her sprint to a walk.

As the terrain broke into uneven gullies below the ridgetop, she slowed even more, wary of loose stones and rattlesnakes.

The afternoon wind, brisk on its course from the distant ocean, covered the noise of her passage. At the same time, anyone might be hiding within a few yards of her and she wouldn't know it until she stepped on him.

She caught herself flashing a grim smile as she clambered up a gully and crept under the dusty leaves of a sharp-twigged bush. She might have found herself the hunted in this scenario, but now that she was out of the false security of the house, she was also the hunter again, a role in which she felt much more comfortable.

Ahead of her slouched the old ranch barn. Treybold Senior had probably kept a few horses to suit his movie-mogul ranch theme, but the weathered barn, though still sturdy enough, was surrounded by high grasses and encroaching shrubs, suggesting years of disuse.

Perfect.

Subduing her urgency for haste, she began her crawl to the barn. Dust and grass pollen tickled her nose and a cricket whirred away from her with a noise like a jumping helicopter, but otherwise nothing stirred but the breeze.

She reached the side of the barn and rose to her feet, taking a quick look around the front of the building. The sliding barn door stood partially open. Such a warm invitation, but she thought she'd pass it up. Two windows graced her side of the barn, both shoulder height. The first one she tried was tightly shut, but the second opened with a protesting lurch.

Grasping her pilfered carving knife between her teeth—not as easy as pirates made it look—Max levered herself through, tumbling to a crouch on the straw-dusted floor. The barn interior stretched away in shadowy obscurity. But the open door to her right let in an arrow of sunlight that showed a recent disturbance in the dust from the barn entrance to the nearby stalls.

She heard nothing, not even the rustle of mice in the hayloft above. But some warning awareness prickled along her spine. The faint scent of horses lingered in the still air, the remains of musty straw, maybe the musk of a long-ago skunk who had sought refuge from a storm.

And something else. A reminder of the bloodstain on the ranch house tile.

Holding her knife in a light grip, she padded forward. The scuff marks through the doorway were speckled scarlet. She turned toward the stalls. Each of the five stood open. Each gaped empty except for the one in the middle.

Cold iron pooled in Max's gut. She knew. If she never looked, she could pretend she didn't. But she couldn't turn away.

She unclipped the flashlight from her jeans, held it tightly in her left hand, the knife in her right. She knew she could not fight what waited in that stall, yet she moved forward soundlessly, weight balanced, tense for the attack.

Only as she neared the door to the dim enclosure did she flick on the flashlight. Dust danced in the beam; mouse pellets and faded straw were scuffed aside on the floor.

Max forced the light into the stall. She saw blood spattered on the dirt and on the stall wall. Then she saw the feet, dark leather driving moccasins dangling inches above the floor.

With a strangled growl, she jerked the flashlight up, past the gaping hole in the dead man's chest, past what must have been his heart, tacked to the center of his rib cage with a dagger.

Up to his face and his blank, surprised green eyes.

Chapter 16

Not Lionel.

Maybe she would despise herself later, that her first reaction was relief. But she shook with it for a second, anyway, even as she forced herself to look at the face again, to pick Court Treybold's high cheekbones and George Clooney squint out of the corpse's slack features.

The knife. There was the feather of Maat, obscured by blood from the heart that had been weighed and found wanting by a psychopathic assassin.

Max turned away and stumbled from the stall, gagging on the sight and the smell and her fear for Lionel and Alex. She gritted her teeth, forcing herself to breathe.

She had seen death before. Even violent death. Not all of her searches had ended with a living "find" as her search for Atchison Dantell had. She'd seen the results of a fatal plane crash. Found a victim of hypothermia. A drowned man.

Tragic. Absurd. Most of them easily preventable.

But none had left her with this taste of rage and disgust at her own species.

"Max? Max Riley?"

The urgent whisper whirled her toward the barn door, her heart beating wildly.

Sun backlit the slender young woman crouching there, firing her copper-colored hair while hiding her face. But Max could make out her dark eyes, wide with fear, her lower lip caught anxiously in her teeth.

"Are you Max Riley?" the woman asked, glancing outside, then back to Max. "Your friend, Lionel, said you would come."

"Lionel?" Max stepped forward, and the woman twitched back in fear. Max lowered her voice and her knife, stuffing the shaft of the slender flashlight into the back pocket of her jeans. "You've seen Lionel? Is he all right?"

"He's injured." The woman slipped into the barn, apparently deciding Max posed less of a threat than whatever lurked outside. "His leg. He needs a doctor, but I think he is all right for now."

"Where is he?"

The woman shrank into herself as Max approached, but didn't run. "He sent me to come find you, to take you to where we are hiding. Please, hurry. We must be gone before *he* finds us."

"*He?*"

But the woman darted out the barn door. Max followed, cursing the unnecessary exposure. The woman could run, Max had to admit, her long legs, limber in black stretch pants, carrying her in a quick, panicked burst across the clearing and into the trees.

Max dove into the brush just a few feet behind, her breath sounding harsh from adrenaline and exertion. But the woman gave her no time to pause. She grabbed Max's arm with a slim hand and pulled her on into the woods.

"What happened?" Max asked. "Have you seen a boy? A tall, skinny boy?"

"You mean Alex?" The woman glanced back, almond eyes questioning Max behind a wispy veil of metallic copper hair.

Something jerked in Max's memory, a feeling of déjà vu. "You know Alex?"

"I am Mr. Treybold's housekeeper here at Skyline Ranch," the woman said, pulling Max down the hill, away from the house and the barn. "Alex and his father have been Mr. Treybold's guests before, but it has been just Alex this weekend. When *he* came for Mr. Treybold, Mr. Lionel helped me to get Alex out of the house and into hiding."

"Is there anyone else?" Max wanted the woman to turn again, to get a better view of her face. Or was it something about her voice? But now they were scrambling through a gully, and she had to watch her feet over the rocks.

"No one. My husband went to town for some things Mr. Treybold requested. After I take you to Lionel and Alex, I will go down to the road to wait for him there. He will call for help for us."

That slight hesitancy. Almost a shyness.

"No! Wait!" There was nothing hesitant about the hand that jerked her away from the opening between two gnarled oaks ahead. "Cliff."

Max stepped forward more cautiously. Just past the trees, the hill fell away suddenly, a steep drop of forty or fifty feet into another rocky, tree-lined gully.

"This way." The woman pulled her to the right. "There's a place I know. Almost a cave. *He* won't find us there."

As she ducked under the tree limbs ahead, Max caught the shape of her face again, the skin darkening in the shadow. If her hair were darkened, too, a deep, rich black...

"There." The woman pointed ahead. "Just down around that rock."

Max turned to look, though her mind still struggled with the odd familiarity of this stranger beside her. A soft voice, calling her name. Talking of a friend....

Alaska. The Anchorage Airport. A dark-haired woman had come up to her with a message from a non-existent friend that he would hunt Max down later.

The same woman? What could Court Treybold's housekeeper have been doing in Alaska? And what possible reason would she have had to accost Max in the airport? Had Treybold been there—had he put her up to it as a joke?

An outrageous show of arrogance. Too brazen for Treybold's sly, suggestive style.

Another memory flashed at her. A black-clad figure in a black hood. Running with strong, lithe legs. Slender for a man. Watching her, teeth flashing in silent, audacious laughter.

Something tugged at her jeans, pulling her from memory.

She spun, but nowhere near fast enough. The heavy end of the flashlight struck with deadly accuracy behind her ear, and the world went black.

Chapter 17

"Miss Riley? Miss Riley, can you hear me?"

She could hear, dimly, through the pounding in her head, though she couldn't see. She smelled dirt, tasted dirt and blood. She hurt, but she wasn't sure where. Her body had no orientation in the blackness.

A hand brushed her shoulder, and she whirled to grab it—or tried to. Her body came back to her in a rush, the throbbing behind her ear, the wrenching in her shoulder, the ropes digging into her wrists and ankles.

"Are you all right?" the anxious whisper asked. "Can you open your eyes?"

Oookay. She hadn't gone blind, after all. The shallow embankment studded with rocks and tree roots in front of her limited her view. Above, twining oaks and brush dimmed the sunlight. But she could definitely see.

She twisted her neck, wincing at the pain. A face blurred into view, tousled blond hair framing anxious blue eyes.

"Miss Riley?"

"Alex?"

"Is your head all right? Are you hurt anywhere else? Don't worry, you're going to be okay."

Max blinked away her blurred vision, choking down surprised laughter. She'd been trying to find and rescue Alex Dantell for almost a week, and *he* was the one telling *her* she'd be okay.

She tried to turn toward him, but her wrists had been hog-tied to her ankles. "Are *you* all right? Can you untie me?"

"I'm tied up, too. I tried to untie Mr. Horn, but my fingers are kind of numb. I couldn't reach the knots very good."

Craning her neck and aching shoulder, she saw Alex kneeling beside her, hog-tied like she was.

"Lionel's here? Is he all right?"

"He got shot in the leg. I think the bleeding's stopped. He was in a lot of pain. She did something to make him sleep. She said he wasn't going to die."

She. Max's memory swirled. Something had happened. She'd been unconscious. Hit on the head. Her mind strained backward. Treybold's ranch. Treybold in the barn. Running through the woods. A woman with her. *Alaska.*

"Anubis."

"You know her?"

"We've met." She almost laughed again, but the dirt and blood stifled it. A slender, shy, obliging woman who could fight like a viper. *Not a bad alter ego for an international assassin.* "Where did she go?"

"I don't know. She left a few minutes ago. She said she had some things to take care of. When she told Mr. Horn he could call her Anubis, he said somebody hired her to kidnap me. Why? Why did she kidnap you and Mr. Horn, too?"

Why aren't we all dead? "I'm not sure. But I think it would be best if we got out of here before she comes back."

"I've got a Swiss Army knife in my backpack, but Anubis hung it up on that tree limb over there, and I can't reach it. I tried to cut my ropes against a rock, but it was too dull. I just scraped my knuckles. If your fingers aren't as numb as mine, maybe you could untie me."

She did laugh, finally, the movement making her head throb.

"What's funny?"

"I should have known you'd have a plan." She glanced up into his thin, earnest face, hovering on the edge of adolescence. "You're a sharp kid, you know that? A lot smarter than most of the adults I've searched for. And tougher, too."

Color tinged his cheekbones. "Dad taught me a lot of survival techniques."

"He'd be proud of you, Alex. Let me see if I can get up like you."

If she could roll onto her chest, she ought to be able to hitch her knees up under her. She rocked sideways for momentum, a rock jabbing into her hip.

Not a rock! She wrenched herself onto her stomach,

ignoring the dead leaves and twigs digging into her forehead as she squirmed her legs up under her and rocked herself back onto her knees.

She finally got a good look at Alex. He wore dirt on his face from the same maneuver she'd just made, and his baggy cargo pants sported a fresh tear above one knee, but he appeared as steady and resilient as his voice had sounded.

At the other end of their sheltered alcove lay another form. *Lionel.*

He faced away from her, hands tied behind his back. His ankles were unbound, but it obviously made no difference. His left thigh had been padded with a boy's T-shirt and wrapped with slashed shirtsleeves, but she could still see the blood.

For a horrible moment, she thought he was already dead, but then she saw his chest move.

"She made him drink some of Mr. Treybold's whiskey," Alex said. "And she did some kind of acupressure thing she said would ease the pain, and he fell asleep."

"We'll wait to wake him up." What then? They could drag him out into the woods, but how far? No sense worrying that far ahead. She couldn't even drag herself into the woods yet.

She examined the ropes around Alex's wrists. Good, lightweight nylon climbing rope. *Perfect.* "Alex, can you reach into my back pocket?"

"I can try."

Awkwardly, they scooted closer, until their shoulders and ankles bumped together. Alex's shoulder actually hit closer to her tricep and his feet knocked her ankles, but when he flexed his rope as far as it would go, he had no trouble digging his fingers into her back jeans pocket.

"A lighter!" he crowed, pulling out the small, engraved silver box she'd pilfered from Treybold's kitchen.

"Can you light it? Without burning yourself?"

"It feels like it's one of those where you just push a button. Dad had one. I think I got it!"

Twisting her chin over her shoulder, Max saw that he did have it. The yellow flame flickered perilously close to his thin wrists.

"Stay steady," she said. "You just hold still. Let me do the moving. If I can get these ropes in place…"

Without either of them having a good view of what they were doing, it sounded difficult enough, trying to get the ropes over the flame without setting herself or Alex on fire. She burned her wrist and two fingers, and Alex dropped the lighter twice, but just as she thought the whole enterprise might be hopeless, she felt the tension between her wrists and ankles slip.

The stench of burning nylon choked her nostrils, and heat burned along her palms. She jerked her body forward and her legs back. Her chest slammed into the ground, knocking air from her lungs, and a rock dug into her cheek.

But her running shoes smacked into the ground behind her.

"*Yes!*" Alex's whisper rang with victory.

Flexibility, Max could hear Tomas lecturing. *Flexibility is as important as strength.*

Jeans were nowhere near as flexible as spandex, but she managed to work her legs through the loop of her arms, much to the relief of her shoulders. "Okay, let's see what we can do."

Even with her fingers stiff from loss of circulation, untying Anubis's knots took mere minutes. Though each minute stretched into a terrifying race against Anubis's return.

"We did it." Alex's grin transformed his earnest face, making his blue eyes shine.

Max stifled the uncharacteristic urge to grab the boy in a bear hug, raising her hand for a high five instead. "We did. Now we have to get out of here. We'll have to try to reach the highway, see if we can flag down some help."

She crawled across the alcove to lean over Lionel's body. His unruly hair streaked across a frighteningly pale face, though she felt his breathing as she rested a hand on his ribs.

"Lionel?"

He shifted beneath her hand and groaned. "Max?"

"It's me. We're going to get you out of here."

Alex scooted up beside her as she untied Lionel's wrists. "We could call for help."

She shook her head. "Anubis destroyed the house telephones and took the bag with my—"

Alex lifted up a tiny silver cell phone he'd dug out of a pocket of his cargo pants, grinning at her expression. "She smashed mine, too, but I snuck Mr. Horn's out of his pants pocket when she had me help bandage his leg. She tied me up, after, though, so I never got a chance to use it."

Max stared at him. "I'm glad we're finally on the same side."

"No 911." The husky voice hardly sounded like Lionel. His eyes focused unsteadily on hers. "She has a police scanner."

"Tomas." She dialed as quickly as her numb fingers allowed. He could mobilize help as fast as the sheriff's department. But not if she couldn't reach him. No answer at his home, his cell or Pieces of Time.

Max's stomach clenched. Could he be angry enough with her to be screening out her calls?

"Simone?" Lionel suggested. But Simone had apparently followed orders to take the afternoon off, and Max couldn't reach her, either.

"Don't leave the phone on. Between calls," Lionel said. "Don't know if the battery… Charger's in the car."

Max glanced at the tiny silver display. That last little lightning bolt looked pretty lonely. *Of course.*

"We could call Mom," Alex said. "Mr. Treybold said she hired private detectives."

Yes, she could call Steve. Should call Steve. He'd been hired to keep Alex safe. He'd unforgivably broken her trust by breaking into her office, but he'd done it out of his desperation to bring this case to a successful resolution.

Or so he'd said. He'd also lied about not knowing Max had gone to Lincoln Park. Who had told him that? Only Simone and Wolfe had known where she was, and Simone hadn't told him.

No, not Wolfe. Not that she trusted Wolfe any more than she'd trust his wild namesake with a newborn lamb, but the very male friction between him and Steve hadn't been merely professional. She couldn't see him volunteering the time of day to Steve Spencer, much less her location.

Besides, Simone and Wolfe had *not* been the only ones to know her lunch plans. Wolfe had shared those with Constantine, when he'd arranged his interview with the man.

Steve. Wolfe. Like choosing between a spider and a snake.

There were reasons she worked alone. Good reasons that had nothing to do with her being a control freak. But she couldn't get Alex and Lionel to safety without help.

She had always trusted her instincts, but if she chose wrongly this time… She punched the numbers, not realizing she held her breath until he answered.

"Who's this?"

She breathed in, her heart pounding with relief and trepidation. With urgency. And with simple reaction to the sound of his voice.

"You said to ring if I needed help."

"Riley?" He sounded almost as surprised as amused. "I never thought you'd actually admit you needed help, even if you did… Wait." Disgust crept into his tone. "You're only calling because I forgot to give you Treybold's phone number."

"Treybold's dead."

He took only a second to process that, all amusement gone. "How?"

When, what, where, why… Ever the reporter.

"Anubis, the assassin." She didn't need to elaborate in front of Alex. "I'm at Treybold's ranch. I'm with Alex Dantell. He's not hurt, but Lionel's been shot."

"Bloody hell. How bad?"

"He's lost a lot of blood. I don't think we can move

him far. Anubis has gone off somewhere, but she'll
be back soon—"

"*She?*"

"Surprised me, too." The understatement of the year.
"Lionel says she has a police scanner. I haven't called
the sheriff's department. I don't know if they could stop
her, anyway. What we need is transportation."

She could hear him breathing through clenched teeth.
"*Dammit*. Hold on, Riley. I'm on my way."

"Wait. Call Tomas first." She gave him Tomas's
numbers. "He's got contacts. He'll know what to do.
Anubis is deadly, Wolfe. If you come, you'll only get
yourself killed. Tell Tomas we're in the woods, west of
the house and the barn. Tell him not to trust anyone he
doesn't recognize."

The cell phone started beeping in her ear. "Batteries.
I have to go."

"Help is coming," Wolfe said. "You hear me, Riley?"

"I hear you." The phone went dead.

She shut the phone and clenched it tight in her palm.
Help is coming. If she'd made the right choice. If Wolfe
wasn't calling Constantine right that moment, telling
him to warn Anubis that they'd escaped. If…

"This is going to be perfect." Alex brushed fallen oak
leaves over the circle of rope lying centered in the path
to the shallow alcove. "She's sure going to be surprised."

If it works, I'll be surprised, too. But Max didn't say
that. She checked the tension of the rope holding the
slender alder they'd chosen in a longbow curve. Pull the
quick release knot, and the alder would shoot into the

air, tightening the noose on the ground around the feet of anyone standing there.

In theory.

But trying to move Lionel had only started his leg bleeding again, and tough as Alex was, he could never take half of Lionel's weight on a stretcher.

"Leave me here," Lionel said again, struggling up onto his elbows where he lay. "I can pull the release rope on that thing. You two run for the road. You can bring back help."

"Great plan," Max said. "Unless we run right into Anubis's arms. I'm going with my plan. We immobilize Anubis, which will protect Tomas when he comes, as well as us."

"If anything happens, it's my fault," Lionel said. "You'd run if it weren't for me."

"And probably regret it." Max ducked into the alcove, clutching the end of the rope, to sit beside Lionel and Alex. She'd keep her ears open for Anubis's return while they talked, hoping the murmur of voices would lure the assassin into complacency about the state of her captives. "I'd rather wait for her here, where we know right where she'll be."

"Dad always said that splitting up when you get lost just means more work for the search party," Alex said.

Lionel's face twisted as much in disgust as pain. "We're not lost."

"And we want to keep it that way." Max managed a smug smile around the tension tightening her throat.

"How much chance do you really think that thing has of trapping Anubis?"

"A better chance than Alex and I have of outrunning her." At first, she'd been relieved that Lionel was awake and talking. Now she was beginning to think she should ask Anubis about those acupressure techniques Alex had mentioned. "And a much better chance than we have of outrunning her bullets."

"She wouldn't use bullets," Alex said. "She threw the gun over the cliff. She said guns are for cowards."

Max snorted. "That didn't stop her from shooting Lionel."

"Oh." Alex's eyes widened. "You don't know. Anubis didn't shoot Mr. Horn, Miss Riley."

Max turned to stare at Lionel.

He shook his head. "It's true enough. That bast—" He glanced at Alex, choked back the word. "Treybold shot me."

Max could only blink. Sure, Lionel could be annoying at times, but… "Why would Court Treybold shoot you?"

Lionel grimaced. "It sure surprised the heck out of me. When I got here, I told him I was your assistant—"

"Did you tell him you were here without my knowledge?" Max asked. "And just why *were* you here, anyway? Simone thought you were looking into Alex's flight reservations."

Lionel's pale face brightened. "I was. I finally got into Alex's online reservations account. He used his birthday as his password."

"Not in order!"

Lionel tsked. "Same numbers. Anyway, when I went back over his flights, I saw that his itinerary back from

Alaska didn't end in San Francisco. He also booked an airport shuttle up to Santa Rosa. Even more interesting, he didn't use his own credit card for the flight *up* to Alaska, either."

Max took a wild guess. "He used Court Treybold's."

"He was Dad's best friend, next to Mr. Kirygin," Alex said. "I knew the police could find out if I used my own credit card, so I called Mr. Treybold."

Even knowing how Treybold had died couldn't placate Max's temper. "So he helped a twelve-year-old kid run away to Alaska? He knew where you were the whole time and never said a word to your poor mother? He let you go by *yourself?*"

"I told him I was going to stay with Mr. Constantine," Alex said. "I knew he liked Mr. Constantine better than Mr. Kirygin, so he'd let me go."

Max turned to Lionel. "So you found out that Treybold was helping Alex, and figured Alex might be hiding out with him."

"And it wasn't that hard to find out Treybold had property up here near Santa Rosa."

"And it never occurred to you mention this to me, *your boss,* because…?"

Max was glad to note that Lionel had enough blood left to blush.

"I thought I could just check out the lead for you," he started, but then stopped and bit his lip. "I thought I could make up for letting Anubis get away up in Alaska. I thought I could prove to you that I could pull my weight."

He slapped his hand in the dirt next to his injured leg.

"But you were right. I just screwed up again. But I never expected Treybold to *shoot* me."

He shook his head in amazement. "I told him I knew he'd been helping Alex, and I thought Alex was staying here at the ranch with him. He'd had a lot to drink, and he started talking crazy, about how everything was going to hell and it wasn't his fault and he wasn't going to let himself get screwed over.

"He poured himself another drink, and his hand was shaking like he was frightened."

"Frightened?" Max asked. "Of what?"

Lionel grimaced. "I might have said something about child endangerment or kidnapping. But I said I was sure it could all be worked out, as long as we got Alex back to his mother. But he wasn't listening to me. He just started muttering about how he wasn't going to let some piss—"

Lionel checked his language once more. "Some kid and some pencil-necked geek ruin his life. And then he stalks off into his bedroom and comes back with a gun. Didn't say why. Just raised it up and pointed it at my chest. He'd have killed me if it wasn't for Alex."

"When Mr. Horn pulled up, Mr. Treybold told me to go stay in my room," Alex broke in. "But I could hear them arguing. I didn't want anyone to get into trouble because of me. I was going to go back home after I came here to talk to Mr. Treybold, anyway. I came out into the living room, and I saw Mr. Treybold point his gun at Mr. Horn."

"He yelled just as Treybold pulled the trigger," Lionel said. "The bullet hit my leg instead of my heart. I yelled for Alex to run. Treybold didn't look scared anymore.

Just really pissed. He kicked me in the leg, and I guess I passed out from the pain."

"I ran out the front door," Alex said. "That's when she found me, Anubis. She waved me over into the woods. She said she was an undercover agent. She said my mom had called in the FBI, and she was there to keep me safe."

For a moment he looked like the scared little kid everyone had been searching for, not the resourceful youth who had evaded them all.

"She brought me into the woods and told me to wait while she went to get help. She was gone so long, I thought maybe Mr. Treybold had shot her, too, but when she came back she brought Mr. Horn."

"I don't remember much about that, either," Lionel said.

"I helped her get him to this place," Alex continued. "She said Mr. Treybold was dead. And then she tied us up." His fists bunched in frustration. "I should have known she wasn't an FBI agent. I should have made her show me her ID."

"She fooled me, too," Max reminded him.

Alex's fists relaxed as he thought about that. "I guess that means she's pretty good," he decided.

Max couldn't fight down a smile. She really liked this kid. She returned her attention to the alcove entrance, ears straining in the afternoon breeze for any hint of Anubis's return.

"Why do you think she's keeping us here?" Alex asked, voice subdued as he glanced up into the brush surrounding them.

The question of the hour. "I don't know for sure, but I don't think we want to find out."

Although if Anubis wanted them dead, they would be. She obviously hadn't felt any qualms about murdering Treybold. Which lessened the chances of Treybold having hired her—it was hard to collect payment from a dead employer. But what had possessed the suave, slyly meddling playboy she had met aboard the *Persephone* to try to kill Lionel?

"What did you talk with Mr. Treybold about?" she asked Alex. "Did he…" It seemed a cruel question to ask a twelve-year-old. "Did he believe your father had been murdered?"

Alex shrugged uncertainly. "He said he did. He said it was a good idea for me to go get Dad's journal, that there might be some evidence we could use. But after I got back, he kept saying we had to proceed carefully and probably Dad just killed himself like the police thought.

"It's not true." His glare dared them to object. "But I haven't found any clues in the journal like I thought I would. It's mostly about how Dad survived in Alaska and personal stuff. But I think Mr. Treybold got kind of mad about what Dad wrote about him."

"Like what?" Lionel asked. "Hey, the guy shot me. I'm happy to hear the dirt."

Alex glanced down at his hands, obviously uncomfortable remembering Treybold's anger. "Dad was kind of mad because he'd told Mr. Treybold some of the stuff he was thinking he might want to do with the company, with Burkhartt-Dantell. And he meant it to be private, but he thought Mr. Treybold had told Mr. Mittard. I guess Mr. Treybold told Dad he didn't, but Dad called him a weaselly liar in his journal."

Max could understand why Treybold might not want such accusations to become common knowledge, but that didn't explain—

Abruptly, her whole body tensed, and she was up crouching on the balls of her feet before she even had a chance to process the noise that had alerted her.

Or, rather, lack of noise. It might have been just a shift in the wind, but the rustle of unseen creatures in the dense underbrush, the rattle of birds shaking the drying leaves of the oaks, had suddenly stilled.

"Keep talking," she mouthed at Lionel and Alex, gathering the snare rope in her hand.

"Are you sure you're all right, Mr. Horn?" Alex asked, his voice only slightly too loud to be natural. "She'll have to untie you when she gets back, so you can have some water."

Lionel groaned, the pain sounding all too real, though the hyperbole was pure Lionel. "She's never coming back. She's left us to die. All they'll ever find of us is our desiccated bones—"

Pure instinct whirled Max around, and the lightning kick from the figure dropping out of the trees missed her head, striking her shoulder instead. The blow numbed her arm, and she dropped the rope as she spun toward the ground.

Not again.

Chapter 18

Her leg came up—blind instinct—and she felt her foot connect with the assassin's elbow. The slice of a knife caught briefly in the denim of her jeans. She felt the burn, but her leg still worked.

Too fast, too strong. Max remembered Alaska. The fear that had paralyzed her. Anubis's silent laughter.

She made it to her feet somehow, spinning away from Anubis's next slash. The closeness of the alcove fenced her in, trapping her within Anubis's reach.

A smile curved the other woman's mouth, as if she could taste Max's fear. Her dark eyes glittered beneath copper bangs as her knife whipped back and forth like a cobra's head.

"Stay back." Anubis's iron voice held none of the soft shyness of Treybold's supposed housekeeper as she snapped her warning to Alex, who had jumped to his feet beside Lionel. "Miss Riley and I have unfinished business."

"Do as she says," Max ordered. But for the briefest of seconds, her eyes locked on Alex's and flicked toward the ground near his feet. She prayed he understood.

That moment of inattention was all Anubis needed to spring her attack, her knife swift and deadly as any cobra strike. Yet Max had already flinched away, the knife hissing past her close and sharp enough to snick off a feather of hair.

Max gasped, a panicked sob in the close quarters. She shot out a desperate, flailing fist, which Anubis easily avoided, but which caused her to step right into the heel Max aimed at her shin.

The assassin's amusement slipped into fury, her own vicious spin-kick catching Max on the hip, forcing her stumbling back toward the alcove entrance.

Too fast, too strong. And Anubis knew Max knew it. Her feet and fists flew, wicked, bruising, as she drove Max back. Max narrowly blocked, dodged, evaded each crushing blow that would knock her to the ground at the mercy of Anubis's knife. Any second, the assassin would overpower her or slip beneath her defenses.

Any second, as Max backed away, stumbling, skidding, in her desperate retreat....

And stopped, meeting a ferociously brutal backhand blow with a forearm block that rattled both their bones, knocking Anubis back a single, critical step.

The assassin might have laughed at the ease with which she blocked Max's tentative counterattack.

Except, even as she settled her stance for the next blow, her eyes widened at the warning snap of whipping branches.

Her reflexes were sharper than Max could believe.

But not quite fast enough.

The rope snare struck up from its covering of leaves, hissing as it tightened around Anubis's ankles, jerking her off her feet.

Even half upside-down, only the backs of her shoulders to the ground, the assassin was fast and dangerous as a snake, but freed from the pretext of terror, Max could move swiftly, as well. Her foot caught Anubis's wrist, sending the knife spinning back into the alcove before the assassin could cut herself free.

"Rope!" she shouted.

Alex tossed a length of it to her, even as he scooped up the knife.

Max met Anubis's gaze, the assassin's fury almost a physical force from her narrowed eyes.

"We can do this the easy way," Max told her. She hefted the rope. "Or I can kill you. I don't have time for games."

The other woman's gaze flicked to where Lionel lay, then back to Max's face. Shrugging, she lifted both arms over her head. Max roped them, tightening the loop with a decisive jerk before hooking the end of the rope over another tree limb. She left just enough of the assassin's shoulder blades against the ground to prevent the circulation to her hands being completely cut off. Probably. Then she tied off the rope.

For a moment, stoic detachment masked their captive's face. Then her head dropped back, spilling copper-colored hair across the leaves, and she laughed, a deep, throaty sound.

"You are not an exceptional fighter," she said, studying Max. "But you fight smart. I would rather be bested by someone with a brain." She shifted her gaze to Alex. "Like the boy. I am glad he is with someone who will see him safely home."

"An assassin who's glad to see her prey escape?" Lionel managed to struggle up to a sitting position. "I find that hard to believe."

"I was never hired to kill the boy." Her voice snapped like a snake strike. "I do not kill innocents."

"Sure," Max agreed, gathering the end of the snare rope and moving to her captive's feet. "You only kill bad guys."

Anubis's eyes darkened, and the ropes rippled with her shrug. "Warlords, drug lords, arms dealers, corrupt politicians. The world is no worse off without them."

"And you're the one to judge them." Max knew she was rising to Anubis's bait, but she kept her focus on the precarious task of binding the assassin's ankles more securely. "You're not just your average, run-of-the-mill killer for hire, after all. You're the god who weighs human hearts."

"The men I kill have no hearts."

"Court Treybold will be glad to hear it."

"Treybold." The assassin spat the name, then laughed again. "You should be thanking me for taking care of Treybold. What would you have done, knowing he meant to kill your friend?"

"Thrown him in jail, for starters." Max wrapped an extra length of rope around her captive's ankles.

Anubis's eyes widened mockingly. "You think you

can afford to be so naive? Such a wealthy man, shooting a wild-haired intruder, would never see the inside of a jail. And even if he received a slap on the wrist, who would have exacted justice from him then for Atchison Dantell's death?"

"You're lying." Alex's protest was more shocked than angry. "Mr. Treybold didn't kill my father."

But Max had already concluded that Treybold harbored some secret that had driven him to help Alex. To encourage Alex to go to Alaska, a place where the boy might disappear without any connection to his father's playboy buddy. And when Alex had not disappeared, that same secret had caused Treybold to hide the boy at his ranch, where he could control any information the boy had unearthed.

Whatever the secret, Lionel's arrival had somehow threatened Treybold, had thrown him into a drunken panic that Max doubted would have ended with only Lionel's death.

She might not agree with Anubis's methods, but she suspected the assassin had saved Alex's life, as well as Lionel's.

On the other hand...

"Treybold didn't have the ingenuity, or the stomach to muscle Atchison Dantell into a staged suicide." Contempt filled Max's voice. "He hired you to do it."

Red stained Anubis's warm-toned cheekbones. "That fool didn't have the resources to hire me."

Alex stepped forward, and Max suddenly realized he still held Anubis's knife, the red feather of Maat dark as blood in the afternoon shadows of the trees. His hand shook, but his voice didn't. "*Quit lying.* Who hired you to kill my father? Mr. Treybold never would."

Anubis's gaze met and held Alex's. "No one hired me until after your father was already dead. I did not kill your father." Her mouth moved in a grimace of disgust. "And, no, neither did that idiot Treybold, if you can believe the claims of a man about to die. But he was there."

Alex's hand shifted, the trembling tip of the knife pointing at Anubis's throat. Max began to edge toward the boy.

"I told you not to lie," he said. "My father didn't kill himself."

"I never said he did." The assassin's composure didn't falter. "Your friend Mr. Treybold claimed they only meant to frighten your father that night. To convince him to renounce his plans for the company and to agree to sell out his share."

"They couldn't have scared Dad," Alex objected.

Anubis's smile was cruel. "Apparently not, even after they showed him the letter they planned to use as his suicide note, written in his own hand. Even after they knotted the noose around his neck."

"That's enough," Max snapped. "He's only twelve years old."

"That didn't protect him from finding his father's body," Anubis said, her eyes never leaving Alex's. "Or from becoming a target of kidnapping and murder."

"Tell me what happened," Alex demanded, his face taut with suppressed emotion.

"Your father never gave in." The smile slipped, showing something that might even have been pity.

"Treybold swore they never meant to kill him, but hangman is no game for amateurs. Treybold thought he could play with the big boys. But they don't appreciate second thoughts. They play for keeps."

"Who's they? Who was with Mr. Treybold? How do you know all this?"

Max could have cried at the anger and grief twisting Alex's voice, the darkness filling his blue eyes. She could have ground the knife into Anubis's throat herself. But that wouldn't change Atch Dantell's death.

"Who was there with Mr. Treybold?" Alex persisted, jabbing the knife forward. "Who helped him? Was it you? Who hired you?"

But Anubis's smile returned as she shook her head. "I have told you I was not there. I cannot tell you any more. It would interfere with collecting my own debts."

"You *will* tell me!"

Max was moving even before Alex's hand drew back. She threw one arm around his chest and grabbed his right elbow from behind, dragging him bodily away from the assassin. The top of his head only reached her chin, but he was as wiry strong as an alley cat, and as hard to hold.

"No!" she barked, trying to break through his grieving rage. "That's not the way."

"Let me go!"

"Alex, listen to me. Violence is her solution. Not yours."

He stilled, panting. Or maybe it was sobbing. "She knows who killed my dad. She knows who wanted to kidnap me."

"I know." She turned him toward her. "Killing her

won't bring your dad back. And you'll never get the answers you want from her that way. Give me the knife."

He took a ragged breath, not sobbing, after all, though tears streaked his face. He put the knife in Max's hand.

"He'll never get the answers he wants from me, anyway," Anubis said. "But I thank you for the assistance."

"I wasn't doing it for you."

Max turned her back on the assassin, guiding Alex back into the alcove to sit beside Lionel. Lionel had slid back down onto his elbows, and though he tried to flash her a cocky grin, his face had gone from pale to gray.

"Don't mind the jackal," he stage whispered to Alex, jerking his head in Anubis's direction. "She's just pissed off. It's probably not great for an infamous assassin's reputation for her to get outsmarted by a middle school kid, a reporter and a computer geek."

Alex managed a wan grin. "Whoever *did* hire her is going to freak."

Which might just trip that person up. But the thought didn't distract Max from her primary goal, which remained getting Alex safely home to his mother. And Lionel to a hospital.

She had serious doubts about Lionel walking all the way to the house, even with her and Alex helping. And she didn't relish the idea of leaving Anubis alone. She suspected a few ropes wouldn't hold the assassin long.

"Help is coming," she said, forcing confidence into her voice. "But we need to help them find us."

"A fire?" Alex suggested, pulling Treybold's lighter out of his pocket.

Max shot a glance at the dry leaves and brush surrounding them, and Alex grimaced, tucking the lighter away.

Then his face brightened. "Wait, I know!"

He scooted over to the tree limb where his battered backpack hung. He tugged it down and dug through the outer pockets. With a cry of triumph, he lifted a small piece of orange plastic into the air.

"A whistle." Max matched his grin. "Perfect."

Alex lifted it to his lips and blew with all the power of twelve-year-old lungs. Beeeep, beeeep, beeeep. Beep, beep, beep. Beeeep, beeeep, beeeep.

"O-S-O?" Anubis asked sardonically.

But the intent of the message must have gone out loud and clear, because another voice rang out from up the hill.

"Riley? Bloody hell, Magdalena, is that you?"

The hair on Max's arms rose in reaction to the sound of Wolfe's voice, her knees suddenly weak from relief of a fear she hadn't allowed herself to feel. That he wouldn't come. That he wouldn't be able to find them. That help would come too late for Lionel.

But when Alex raised his whistle, she touched a light hand to his arm. "Give me sixty seconds, then blow again."

With Anubis's knife tucked into her belt, she climbed the embankment, pulling herself up by roots and white oak saplings, wriggling her way through the overhanging brush.

She heard Anubis's laughter.

"Never trust your friends. Enemies are more reliable.

I told you she was smart. Is she just leaving you to the wolves, little boy?"

Alex blew his whistle, drowning her out, and Max hurried on through the trees, moving up and out from the alcove.

Trust? Max had thought Treybold might be in danger, but never that he might be dangerous. She had followed an assassin into the woods and allowed herself to be knocked unconscious with her own flashlight. *Three strikes and you're out.*

Trust was one thing, stupidity another.

Wolfe hadn't come alone. She could hear them now, two distinct sets of footsteps and breathing and cursing the terrain. Her heart jumped. *Tomas.* But her mind warned, *Maybe.*

They had found the narrow path near the cliff edge that Anubis had led her along. They'd pass below her current position on the hill any moment. Single file.

She planned just to watch them pass, make a positive ID, but the first man pushing his way through the bushes below her was neither Wolfe nor Tomas. His thick dark hair brushed the top of a mahogany silk shirt that was going to be a total loss after this trek through the woods. The second man boasted no hair at all on his bullet-shaped head, and the fire-breathing mermaid on his bare arm appeared more impervious to the snagging branches than his boss's silk.

Steve and Spike?

The slightest touch on her shoulder spun her around, knife in hand, the blade tip pausing just at the junction of Davis Wolfe's throat.

He raised one sandy eyebrow. "Is this how you always greet the cavalry?"

"I told you it was too dangerous for you to come," she reminded him, her voice as low a whisper as his. "I told you Anubis was out here."

"Why do you think I let pretty boy and his pit bull go first?"

When had Wolfe's devilish grin started having that unwanted effect on her stomach? And dammit, she couldn't help grinning back. But her knife hand didn't waver.

"If I'd wanted Spencer Investigations up here, I would have called them," she said. "I didn't realize you and Steve were such good buddies."

Wolfe shook his head, impressively ignoring the blade half an inch from his throat. "Don't blame them on me. They got here the same time we did. They said Treybold's housekeeper called them. She told them Alex was here."

Treybold probably did have a housekeeper, but Max doubted she'd been anywhere near the Skyline Ranch that weekend.

But why would Anubis call Spencer Investigations? Max pulled back her knife. "We?"

"I managed to reach your friend Mr. Gregory."

"Tomas?" Max glanced around them. "Where—"

But then she heard a faint shout from the direction of the alcove. It was Lionel's voice, sounding much too glad to have just seen Steve Spencer.

Max shook her head, grinning despite herself. "Good old Tomas. Sneaking in the back."

"Hey! How about good old Wolfe?"

Max's retort died in her throat as she met his gaze, her eyes caught by the slanting play of afternoon shadow across his hazel eyes. For a moment his stare seemed as unfathomable as a wolf's indeed, as elemental as the trees around him, and much more dangerous.

"We found Treybold." His eyes betrayed nothing, but his voice ground lower. "I'm bloody glad to see you in one piece."

He raised his hand to her cheek, and the touch fluttered through Max's body. She raised her hand in response. Had she forgotten the knife in her hand, meant to touch her fingers to his jaw, the shadow of afternoon bristle there? Or had she planned to bring the knife between them, to keep him at a distance?

Wolfe reached his free hand to gently push the blade aside. He ran his thumb across hers, brushing the red enamel feather on the knife's handle. His eyes gleamed wickedly. "You can take on a hired assassin, but you're afraid of me?"

Absolutely. "What are you after, Wolfe?"

His brows met as he considered that. "I'm not sure. Just this, for now, I think."

His fingers tilted her chin, and he bent to brush his lips against hers. He smelled like trees and soap and sweat. He tasted like sunlight and shadows and mint gum. She tasted again. Spearmint.

Her free hand found his jaw and rested there, light as his fingers on her cheek. Light, indeed. Light that shimmered between them, running up her fingertips and through her veins, pooling warmth around her heart.

Despite the whisper of Wolfe's lips against hers, this was no gentle kiss. It held all the animal wildness she'd seen in his eyes, that she felt in her blood. A promise. A claiming.

They broke the kiss, and Max's eyes flickered open to meet Wolfe's, just inches away.

His voice was low and warm against her skin. "You're welcome."

She laughed. She couldn't help it. "For *kissing* me?"

"For coming to your rescue."

"We were doing a pretty good job of rescuing ourselves. But we'd be grateful for a ride."

"Ah, yes." Something like embarrassment flickered across his face. "A ride...."

"Miss Riley!" Alex's voice came muffled through the brush. "Your friends are here. You can come back."

Max scrambled down to the clearer area near the cliff edge. Wolfe dropped softly beside her.

"Where did you learn to sneak up on people like that?" she asked, leading him back toward the alcove.

"Boy Scouts."

"Right." She hadn't noticed before how much there was to Davis Wolfe beyond his cynical, wryly amused persona. Decisive action. Wilderness skills. She felt fairly certain he currently had a gun tucked into the pocket of his khaki jacket.

Dangerous, indeed. But she felt inexplicably secure having him at her back.

For the first time since seeing the bloodstain on Court Treybold's kitchen floor, Max began to think the afternoon might not end so badly, after all.

It ended pretty badly for Treybold. The thought of what Anubis had done to the man twisted in her stomach. But if she had watched Treybold try to murder Lionel, she might have killed him herself. She was glad she hadn't had to make that call.

"*Shit!* You *bitch!*"

The thud of flesh hitting flesh came from just ahead. Footsteps scuffled leaves. Alex's voice rose in a high shout.

"Stop!" Spike's voice, almost unrecognizable in pain and anger.

Max yanked Anubis's knife from her waistband just as the assassin herself burst out of the bushes a few yards ahead. In a brief second of stretched time, Max saw the blood staining the woman's cheek from a cut lip, saw the grimace of raw rage, saw the red indentations around her wrists where the ropes had been.

Max braced herself for the attack, but the assassin slowed for the briefest instant. As their eyes locked, Max saw her again as she first had, a slender, shy young woman. Her dark eyes flashed with anger, fear and something that might have been a mute plea.

But a faint echo of her mocking smile chased the moment away. "Never trust your friends."

The bushes shook again, and Anubis dodged right, her hand grabbing an alder trunk as if she meant to swing around Max and Wolfe over the very edge of the cliff.

But her shoulder jerked as a gunshot exploded the afternoon quiet.

Max saw the woman's fingers slip on the pale bark. Instinctively, she lunged forward, dropping the knife to grab for Anubis's arm. But a second bullet's impact jerked the woman from her reach.

Max heard her own voice shouting, the words raw in her throat as she watched the assassin who'd taken a jackal god's name fall from her sight. She grabbed the tree Anubis had failed to catch and leaned out over the cliff, searching for a jutting ledge that might have caught her fall.

But the cliff at her feet dropped without relief. Fifty feet below, the brush at the bottom of the rock-strewn gully had swallowed the assassin's body.

Chapter 19

The tree beside her shook as the bullet-headed Spike grabbed it to follow her gaze, his SIG-Sauer still at the ready in his other hand.

"What the hell was that?" Max jerked him back from the cliff by his tattooed arm, adrenaline overcompensating so she almost threw him on his butt. She might have followed up with more, but Wolfe's hand on her shoulder held her back. "You killed her!"

Spike stared at her, rolling the arm she'd yanked. "The bitch tried to twist off my nuts. Then she ran. What was I supposed to do, let her get away?"

Max stared back, fighting the urge to lunge for his throat, though she couldn't have said why Anubis's death should taste so bitter. "Why did you untie her in the first place?"

"You think any of the rest of you had a chance of dragging her back to the house?" He shrugged, showing off the muscles in his shoulders. "Hell, you're the one who said we were dealing with some kind of international assassin. She would have hunted us all down. I did you a favor."

"Spike." Steve Spencer pushed through the brush behind him. He tapped the man's right arm, and Spike stuffed the 9mm back into the waistband of his jeans. "We've got a stretcher set up. Come give us a hand."

"Let me take a look at Lionel first," Wolfe said, brushing past Max as he pulled a first aid kit from his jacket. Not a gun, then. After seeing Spike in action, Max was glad. "Let's make sure his leg is stabilized before we move him."

He and Spike ducked through the trees toward the alcove.

Steve turned to Max, the hard business in his blue eyes shading into his boyish grin. "I knew you were up to something. I *knew* it. And you actually had me feeling like a heel for breaking into your office." He shook his head in grudging respect. "Mad Max Riley has done it again."

Max held her shaking limbs and shredded emotions steady through sheer willpower. "Your partner just shot an unarmed woman. Did you notice that?"

He shifted an unconcerned shoulder. "She kidnapped Alex Dantell and cut out Court Treybold's heart. I'm not going to lose any sleep over it."

His brow furrowed as he studied her expression. "Hey, are you all right? Alex said you two went at it pretty hard."

He stepped toward her, his voice dropping. "If anything had happened to you." He shook his head. "Let's just say sleep would not have been the only thing I lost."

He lifted his hand to brush her hair off her cheek, but Max stepped back out of his reach.

"I'm fine," she said.

"You're going to punish me for earlier at your office, aren't you?" He crossed his arms. "Even though you're the one who came up here looking for Alex without telling me?"

She could explain that she hadn't expected to find Alex with Treybold. But she doubted he would believe her. And she didn't have the energy to try.

"I've got to get Lionel to the hospital," she said. "He's lost a lot of blood. Can we lie him flat in your car?"

Steve's gaze dropped from hers as he rubbed a hand over his jaw. "Right. The car…."

"They're bringing Mr. Horn out." Alex scrambled up from the alcove to stand beside Max. "Mr. Gregory said I should lead them up the best path back to the house."

Max managed a smile for him, as she gestured him past. "You're the man for the job. We'll follow you."

Spike came out through the brush first, gripping the uneven ends of two long branches that bore Lionel on a sling of jackets and Alex's spare clothes. Wolfe carried the other end of the stretcher, shouldering aside the bushes above the patient. He'd secured the bandaging on Lionel's leg, Max noted, and elevated it on a padding of T-shirts. Tomas followed, carrying a coil of Anubis's climbing rope and Alex's backpack.

Max and Steve each grabbed a side of the stretcher to help wrestle it up the hill. Out of the deeper shadows of the alcove, Lionel's face looked even paler.

"Don't you think this is milking your little gunshot wound too hard?" She forced the joke around the constriction in her throat. "You walked down here with only Anubis for help."

"Don't know how I did that," Lionel admitted, giving her a wan smile that fractured as the stretcher jostled through a shallow gully. "Davis says he thinks the bullet's lodged in my femur."

Max shot Wolfe an incredulous glance. "And you know this from watching too many reruns of *ER?*"

"A little field medic training comes in handy on war zone assignments." Wolfe nodded at Lionel's leg. "He really shouldn't have been able to walk as far as he did."

Lionel managed a shrug. "I guess thinking Treybold was coming after me to finish the job was a powerful motivator."

"This way," Alex called from ahead. "The bushes thin out up here. I think we're almost to the barn."

As the ground evened out, giving the stretcher bearers better footing, Max dropped back to keep pace beside Tomas.

His customary calm couldn't hide the relief in his eyes. "You're all right?"

"Scrapes and bruises." She tried a smile. "Anubis was a better fighter, but not as devious as the guy who taught me."

Tomas shook his head. "I thought we might be too late. Despite Wolfe's insane driving."

"I wasn't sure you'd come," Max admitted. "When I couldn't reach you, I was afraid you were screening out my calls."

"Because I said I couldn't help you?"

She nodded.

"I didn't mean I wouldn't try. However hopeless I might think the cause." A smile twitched at the corner of his mouth, though it didn't hide the pain in his eyes at her doubt. "You really thought I had abandoned you?"

"Of course not." *Not anymore.* She slipped her arm through his, and to her surprise, he squeezed it close as they started up the hill after the others. "I didn't think you'd knowingly leave me at the mercy of a heart-dissecting assassin. I just thought you might be avoiding me."

His smile twitched again. "As it happens, I wasn't thinking about you at all. I was with Dimitri Antonov, trying to convince the Burkhartt-Dantell board to delay selling Atchison Dantell's share of the company until they'd fully considered Dimitri's backers' offer."

She'd forgotten about the media group and the power players trying to control it. "Do you think Dimitri has a chance?"

Tomas's face hardened. "They held the vote. They will sell to Darius Constantine and his associates."

She discovered she wasn't too tired to feel outrage. "*Constantine?* How could they even hold the vote? Court Treybold, for one, obviously wasn't there."

"Toby Mittard held his proxy. For Constantine."

Alex had read in his father's journal of Treybold's betrayal. Anubis had claimed the man participated in

Atch's death. Max didn't know why she should be so surprised.

Alex was leading them around the barn clearing, but she could see the building through the trees. Grimly, she shoved the memory of Treybold's body from her mind. Betrayal had caught up with him.

"The sale isn't final yet, is it?" she asked, dropping Tomas's arm to scramble up toward the top of the ridge. "Once we get Constantine arrested for hiring Anubis to kidnap Alex—"

"Constantine *did* hire her?" Tomas's voice was sharp. "She told you that?"

"She refused to say who hired her," Max admitted. "But it sure wasn't Treybold. It had to be Constantine—"

"But you have no proof." His voice was heavy. "And Anubis will not be confessing anything to anyone, thanks to our friend Spike."

"Then I'll *find* proof." The words gritted through Max's clenched teeth.

"Darius Constantine is a—"

"Dangerous man," Max finished for him.

"A clever, cautious, deadly man."

"And I don't stand a chance against him." Max gave Tomas a look. "And you won't be able to help me bring him down."

Her mentor didn't smile. "Sometimes I wish your father had packed you off to boarding school when you were six."

"Or that I'd stuck with ballet lessons?"

"I was thinking more along the lines of your taking holy orders." He glanced at her. "But I could probably get sent to hell for wishing you on the nuns."

"I won't do anything stupid," Max promised. "At least not today. I just want to get Lionel to the hospital, Alex home and me into a hot bath."

Unfortunately, the logistics would probably put off the bath long past the time when her aching body would bruise up from the pounding Anubis had given her.

"I suppose Steve will want to take Alex in his car." The thought disturbed every competitive fiber in her body—and her protective instincts, as well. "How much room does Wolfe have in his?"

"About the cars—"

"Miss Riley!" Alex appeared just above them, at the top of the ridge. "You'll never believe it."

"Believe what?"

He shook his head, hands on his hips, as they climbed up beside him. "They can't get us out of here. Anubis ruined their tires, too."

"They're putting us on." But one glance at Tomas's face told her otherwise.

"Iron spikes," Wolfe explained as they caught up with the stretcher bearers. "She must have planted them in the driveway after you arrived."

"That's probably what she was doing after she left us tied up in the woods," Max said. Why had Anubis lured Steve and Spike up to Skyline Ranch? To get them off Alex's trail once and for all? "*Both* cars?"

"If Spencer hadn't been tailgating me," Wolfe said, grunting as he shifted his grip on the stretcher, "he might have noticed me cursing and waving him back."

"If you hadn't been driving like such a maniac," Steve returned, "and cut us off at the turnoff—"

"Is there any way we can put together four good tires, or at least four spares?" Max interrupted.

Wolfe shook his head. "She slashed Lionel's spare and the one for the Porsche in Treybold's garage, and yours is just flat."

Steve pulled a sleek silver cell phone from his back pocket. "It's all right. We'll just call for an ambulance."

But Max didn't like the look in Wolfe's eyes when he glanced down at the stretcher. Lionel's face was twisted in pain, but he seemed barely conscious enough to notice it.

"It will take an ambulance over half an hour to get here from Santa Rosa," Max said.

"If the traffic's not too bad on 101." Wolfe met her gaze. "He's hung on this long. He's tougher than he looks."

Max's stomach lurched. They'd made it. They'd freed themselves. Help had arrived. A few flat tires were *not* going to kill Lionel. "There's got to be something else we can do."

"There is." Tomas met their skeptical looks with a raised brow. "There's still one vehicle parked on this ridge with good tires."

Chapter 20

"Maybe we could just roll down to the bottom of the foothills on flat tires," Max suggested, trying not to cringe as Tomas wrestled open the rear door to Court Treybold's plane. She'd thought facing Anubis had been frightening. "We don't even know if this thing flies."

"Treybold's kept it in top condition," Tomas assured her, steadying the stretcher as Spike and Steve hefted Lionel into the body of the plane.

"I got to ride in it once, when Dad and Mr. Treybold went skydiving one time," Alex assured her. "It's a really cool plane. And this is perfect. Like a sort of miracle. We can get Mr. Horn medical attention even faster than if we drove."

If they got there at all. Max had survived the bug-smashers in Alaska. This was simply tempting fate.

"You can stay here and wait for the sheriff," Wolfe murmured as he moved to stand beside her. "I'll make sure Lionel gets to the hospital."

"I'm not afraid of flying," Max snapped. And she wasn't leaving Lionel's side. "It's not phobic to point out that Tomas has never flown this plane before."

"I didn't say it was." But when he started humming Don McLean's "American Pie," she punched his arm.

Despite Wolfe's joking, Max said a prayer as she climbed into the back of the sleek plane. It was bigger than Pete Scalisi's Cessna, but still a little cramped with Lionel, Spike, Steve and Wolfe crowded into the back with her, and Tomas and Alex up front in the pilot's and co-pilot's seats.

Since Alex had insisted on Max accompanying him, Max hadn't pointed out that someone should stay to meet the sheriff's investigators when they arrived. The logical choice to remain would have been Spike. He seemed to consider his shooting of Anubis simple self-defense, but she wouldn't have been comfortable leaving him alone with the evidence, in case the sheriff's department wondered otherwise.

"Anyone else want one of these?" Spike asked, holding up a square cloth package it took Max a moment to identify. One of Treybold's parachutes. "There's four of them."

As if the idea of jumping out of a crashing airplane wearing a contraption she didn't even know how to use would make Max feel any better. "Tomas will get us safely to Santa Rosa."

"Hey, Gregory," Spike called as the engines began to rev. "You ever flown this model plane before?"

"No."

Spike grinned and shrugged into the parachute.

The airplane shook and rattled along the airstrip. Max closed her eyes, pretending not to imagine what would happen if they'd overweighed the plane, if Tomas misjudged the length of the airstrip, if…

The plane lurched into the air. Max could have sworn it dipped again, but that might only have been her stomach. No one screamed, so she figured they'd made it into the air.

"It shouldn't be a long flight," Tomas shouted back to them. "I'll radio the Charles M. Schulz Sonoma County Airport in Santa Rosa to let them know we have a medical emergency."

Someone jostled Max's arm, and she opened her eyes to find Steve Spencer settling down beside her. He jerked his head toward the front of the plane.

"You know we're going to have to take the boy back to San Francisco, to his mother, whether he wants to stay with you and Lionel or not."

Max coolly met his gaze without expression. "He's welcome to stay with me until Yvonne can come get him if that's what he wants."

"Look, it's cute he's got a crush on you, but we're the ones Yvonne hired to get him home safe. You've got to tell him to come with us."

Max hadn't planned to have this confrontation in the plane, but it did take her mind off the thin skin of plastic between her rear end and a thousand feet of empty air.

She glanced toward the front of the airplane, but Alex was too focused on the scenery and Tomas's explanation of the controls to notice what they were saying, even if he could have heard them.

"That kid has just been rescued from a kidnapping," she reminded Steve. "I'm not making him go anywhere with anyone he doesn't know."

"Dammit, Max. You said your only interest in this case was to make sure the boy got home safely. He's safe now. If you want me to believe this isn't just some kind of ego trip—"

"I don't care what you believe," she barked back. "Alex had *better* be safe now. If anything happens to him while he's in your care, you'll wish it was Anubis after you instead of me. That goes for your boss, too, and you can feel free to pass that along to him."

"Him?" Steve's confused innocence was too vehement, even for the noisy confines of the plane. "You mean Yvonne."

"I mean Darius Constantine." She didn't need the flicker in his eyes to tell her she was right, but it made her stomach roll in disappointment, anyway.

"I don't know what you're—"

"Only four people knew where I was having lunch today," she said. "And you didn't hear it from me, Simone or Wolfe."

He put up a hand in defense. "If I'd known where you were, I wouldn't have needed to break into your—"

"Save it. You knew, and that's how you tricked Simone into leaving." She could feel Wolfe and Spike staring at her now, but she kept her focus on Steve. "And up in Alaska, you knew all about the security at Constantine's lodge, a lot more than if you'd just met the man. I should have realized it then. And I should have figured out why you weren't worried about Anubis attacking Constantine—you knew she was working for him."

"Hey, wait a minute!" The disingenuous grin he'd been attempting faded into anger. "Look, okay, yeah, I've been in contact with Darius Constantine. You know why?"

"Because he's been paying you for information!"

"That's right." His confession shocked her into silence. "He's been paying Spencer Investigations' entire operating expenses on this case. Because Yvonne Dantell's money is all tied up in her husband's estate, and she couldn't afford us. So one of her husband's friends is footing the bill. You know why?"

The question was a challenge. He answered it himself. "Because Yvonne asked him to. And you know why I didn't tell you? Because Constantine said he didn't want anyone to know, and it was *none of your business*."

Max stared into his eyes, the anger deepening the blue to a clear sapphire. Could she have been wrong about him? "You really didn't know Constantine had hired Anubis?"

He threw up his hands. "Haven't you heard a word I said? Constantine hired me to get Alex home safely. Why would he do that if he'd hired someone to kidnap the boy?"

"Backup," Max said. Tomas's lectures about Constantine's cunning and ruthlessness must have gotten to her, because it made perfect sense. "In case Anubis failed."

Steve shook his head in disgust. "You've obviously got something against the man. I admit his whole old-world aristocrat act is a bit much, but he was just doing a favor for an old friend's family."

Max didn't believe that. But it was possible that Steve did. Constantine could have used Steve as his eyes and ears in the search for Alex and then passed the information along to Anubis without Steve being any the wiser.

Either way, Constantine had what he wanted—control of Atchison Dantell's share of the Burkhartt-Dantell Media Group. He had nothing more to gain from kidnapping Alex. Whether Steve was a plant or a pawn, Alex should be perfectly safe returning to San Francisco with him.

It still didn't feel right. Maybe it was simply her competitive nature, as Steve had suggested. Or maybe it was just the rolling in her stomach from the plane ride.

But she couldn't shake the unsettling feeling that there was something...something prodding at the edge of her consciousness, warning her to be wary.

Something that Anubis had said about Treybold. *No.* Something Lionel had said.

Max forced her expression to remain calm. "Maybe you're right. But I don't understand why Court Treybold called you to tell you that Alex had gone to Alaska to see Constantine."

"Treybold?" He squinted at her. "Treybold never contacted me."

"He called Constantine then, and Constantine called you when Alex never showed up."

Steve shook his head. "Treybold never told us anything. We had no idea he'd had any contact with the boy. Not until his housekeeper called this afternoon. Or Anubis, I guess. Pretending to be his housekeeper."

His confusion, so earnestly genuine and such an out-and-out lie, fed cold steel into Max's indignation. "*Someone* told you Alex was in Alaska."

But he didn't seem to hear the anger in her voice. "No one told me. *You* certainly didn't. We found the charge for his plane ticket on his credit card records."

Max glanced down at Lionel to find him staring up at her, awake, for now, and clear-eyed. He gave a tiny nod, though his eyes warned caution.

Max ignored the warning. She was tired of lies, tired of betrayal. *Never trust your friends.*

"You can drop the bull, Spencer. Alex thought his mom would have the FBI looking for him. He was too smart to use his own credit card. Treybold bought that ticket for him."

"No." He couldn't let go of the lie. "That's not right. I'm telling you, Treybold had nothing to do with it. Spike found that ticket charged to Alex Dantell's credit—"

Steve broke off. The split second of doubt in his eyes convinced Max more than anything he could have said. She followed his gaze as it turned to his partner.

The big man crouching beside Wolfe on the other side of Lionel's stretcher shrugged lazily, making the fanged mermaid on his upper arm writhe. "So, all right. That pussy Treybold called and told me where the kid was headed. He was scared he could get in trouble for helping the brat out, made me swear I wouldn't tell where I got the intel. It didn't seem like a big deal to say I got it off the kid's card."

A simple, plausible explanation that didn't quite match the muscles still rippling beneath Spike's tattoo. An expla-

nation that didn't quite jibe with the fact that Steve
hadn't received the information on Alex's whereabouts
until a full day after Anubis had been tipped off and
arrived in Alaska, until after Constantine had time to
realize that Alex had lied to Treybold about his destination.

"Why did Court Treybold call you?" Wolfe asked
from his position by Lionel's legs. Max could barely
hear him over the engine noise, but Spike answered im-
mediately, ready for the question.

"He was calling Yvonne Dantell. Got me instead. I
convinced him we shouldn't get her hopes up until Steve
actually brought the kid home."

And why would Treybold entrust such important
information to a man he didn't know rather than to
Alex's mother?

Never trust your friends. Max had thought Anubis
meant to impart one last cynical warning. Uncharacter-
istically empty final words for an infamous assassin.
Unless they weren't a warning. An ironic comment
would have been much more Anubis's style.

Never trust your friends. Because if you *were* an
infamous assassin, your friends certainly wouldn't want
you taken into custody, where you might start thinking
that turning state's evidence sounded better than the
electric chair.

Never trust your friends. Because they might decide
you were expendable and just happen to set you free
long enough to shoot you in the back.

"You knew Treybold already." Max hardly realized
she'd risen to her feet until her head hit the curved

ceiling of the plane. "He wasn't calling Yvonne. He didn't *want* Alex returned to his mother, at least not until he was sure the police were going to rule Atchison Dantell's death a suicide."

That is, if she could believe what Anubis had told her. Looking into Spike's hostile eyes, she thought she did.

"Treybold had to make sure Alex's murder claims weren't going to be taken seriously."

"So Treybold *did* believe Atch Dantell was murdered." Wolfe didn't sound surprised to have his earlier suspicions confirmed. His hazel eyes narrowed as he considered Max's words. "And you think Treybold guessed who'd killed him?"

"He didn't have to guess. Treybold killed Atch Dantell."

"Bloody hell."

Her words shocked Wolfe and Steve. Lionel, of course, had heard the story from Anubis. Spike laughed.

"You're saying you think that pansy-assed playboy killed somebody?" He shook his head, his teeth flashing in a cold smile. "Now I know where you got that nickname, Mad Max."

"He didn't do it by himself. He took some muscle along to scare Atch into selling his share of the company, and things got out of hand." And maybe Anubis had told the truth that the muscle wasn't her.

"What happened, Spike?" The sharp ice of Max's voice sliced through the plane noise. "Did your coercion just go too far, like Treybold claimed? Or did you start that little charade in Atch's garage fully intending to murder him?"

"Riley." Wolfe raised a warning hand as Spike's

shaved head reddened with anger. "Spencer Investigations is headquartered in L.A. Yvonne Dantell didn't even call them until after Atch's death."

"But we were in San Francisco already." Steve stirred beside Max. "We were finishing up a separate matter for Mr. Constantine. He's used Spencer Investigations on several occasions in the past and appreciated our skills and our discretion. That's why he thought to hire us when Yvonne Dantell asked him for help finding her son."

"I don't think discretion was what he appreciated most about Spike," Max said, but the bewilderment in Steve's eyes as he stared at his partner flattened her sarcasm.

"You don't believe the bullshit she's slinging, right?" Spike objected, hunching to his feet. "Come on. She's got no proof of anything."

"You lied to me about the kid's credit card." Steve's voice shook with something other than the plane's vibrations. "Give me a reason to believe you're not lying about the rest. Tell me where you were the night Atchison Dantell died. Tell me you never had any contact with Court Treybold before he called about the plane ticket."

Spike was shaking his head. "You know, that bitch assassin had one thing right. Don't trust your friends. Thanks for the vote of confidence, man."

Then he smiled. "Good thing I'm not the trusting soul she was. Not as squeamish, either. If she'd let the geek die and finished off the girl wonder here when she had the chance, she'd still be alive. But no, I gotta clean up her mess."

Max had forgotten his SIG-Sauer. In the confines of

the small plane, it looked even bigger than she remembered as he casually swung it in an arc designed to hold them all in place.

"Spike, this is crazy." Steve held his hands stiffly out to his sides as his partner swung the barrel of the gun at his chest. "Whatever you've done, you can't make it better this way. You can't shoot us all before we take you down."

"Stevie." Spike's mouth drooped in mournful disbelief. "Man, we're partners. Well, you own the business and make the real money, but I'm just the dumb muscle, so what do I care? I'd never shoot you."

He shook his head. "What kind of monster do you think I am? I wasn't planning on shooting any of you...."

His left hand steadied his aim as he turned toward the front of the plane.

"No!"

Max's horrified shout spun Tomas and Alex around in their seats. Even as he turned, Tomas was assessing the situation, rising to knock Alex out of the line of fire.

Against the roar of the engines and the blood pounding in Max's head, the report of Spike's P226 sounded like a champagne cork popping. But the liquid staining Tomas's chest as he fell was red.

"No!" Max screamed again, but Spike's gun jerked swiftly to aim at her head. Then Wolfe's. Then Steve's.

He grinned again, his eyes so wide she could see the whites. "Shit! So much for not shooting anyone. I was aiming for the instrument panel. I guess taking out the pilot will just have to do."

She couldn't hear his laughter, but it shook everything but his gun arm as he reached behind him with his free hand for the catch to the main compartment door. Wind roared in as the door slid aside, whipping at Max's hair, billowing the jacket draped over Lionel below her.

"Happy landing!"

She lip-read as much as heard Spike's parting words as he laughed again and leapt from the plane.

Chapter 21

Sere brown hills, scattered oaks, ragged blue sky. They shivered in Max's vision as the eager, clutching wind reached through the gaping hole to snatch at her clothing as though it meant to wrench her outside. In nightmares, the sucking terror of the fall would pull her down while she desperately struggled to wake.

Glancing out of the plane at the ground rushing past far below, she could hardly remember why the nightmares had frightened her when so much worse could happen.

She stumbled the few steps to where Tomas had collapsed beside the pilot's seat. Alex was tugging on his shoulder, trying to turn him on his back. Max levered her arms beneath him and lifted, adrenaline making up for her poor angle as she pulled him back toward the belly of the plane, laying him flat.

The bullet had entered his chest, the blood seeping out through the lemon cotton of his shirt. *Low, right, not his heart.* But a 9mm.

Not Tomas. Oh, please, not Tomas. He's all I have left.

His chest rose raggedly beneath her hand. She saw his lips move, but could not hear what he said.

As she shrugged out of her jacket to try to stanch the bleeding, the wind in the plane abruptly ceased. She looked up to see Wolfe and Steve securing the door. Wolfe turned back toward the plane cockpit, dropping opposite Max beside Tomas.

"The controls, dammit!" Steve shouted, crowding Wolfe as though he might trample over both him and Tomas.

"It's on autopilot," Alex shouted back, his voice high with tension. "Mr. Gregory had it set. We're not going to crash."

Not until the fuel runs out. Max kept that comment to herself as she held Tomas's hand while Wolfe slashed away his shirt with a Leatherman knife. She could see the pain in her mentor's eyes, even as his fingers tightened in hers.

"How far are we from the Santa Rosa airport?" Steve asked. He crouched over Tomas's face. "How far?"

"Mr. Gregory said about twenty minutes," Alex replied as Max shoved Steve's shoulder, pushing him away. "That was about ten minutes ago. I think."

"We've got to contact the tower." Steve crowded forward again.

Max turned on him. "Can you fly this thing?"

He stared at her. "No."

"Then back off!" She looked across Tomas at Wolfe, but he shook his head.

"Land Rovers, yes. Airplanes, no."

"Max!" Lionel gestured her toward his improvised stretcher. She managed to scoot close without releasing Tomas's hand.

"Get me up into the cockpit."

She could barely hear him, and a sheen of sweat dampened his pale forehead, but she merely gritted her teeth and nodded. Moving him could start his leg bleeding again, but none of them were going to survive if the plane crashed.

"Steve!"

The investigator had finally quit hovering over Wolfe to move to the rear of the plane. When he glanced back at her shout, Max saw he was pawing through the stack of parachutes.

Four of them, Spike had said. He'd taken one, but maybe they could still get Alex off the plane. Could they double up? She didn't know how much weight one parachute would take, but—

Steve heaved one to the floor. "The bastard slashed them all."

"Help me get Lionel into the cockpit." Max forced her voice to stay calm. They couldn't afford to waste time on anger. "We're going to have to carry him."

Steve stared down at Lionel, as if only then remembering he was there. "The computer geek?"

"He can get us down. He's a licensed pilot."

Steve moved forward to take one of Lionel's arms while Max hooked the other around her neck. Wolfe gave her a quick nod, grasping Tomas under his shoulders while Alex tried to help with his feet.

As the plane shook under their shifting movements, the autopilot valiantly keeping them steady, they awkwardly moved the two wounded men, shifting Tomas to the stretcher and Lionel toward the cockpit.

As Max tried to maneuver Lionel into the pilot's seat, he shook his head, pushing against the seat back.

"Copilot. The brakes are on the rudder pedals on the pilot's side."

Max stared at him. "Brakes are good."

Lionel gestured at his leg. "I can't land the plane like this. But I can tell you how to do it."

The blood loss must have made him delirious. *He's lost his mind.* But someone else could do it....

She glanced back to the body of the plane. Wolfe crouched over Tomas's body, his face set in grim determination as he struggled to stop the blood flow and keep Tomas alive. Alex huddled beside him, face set just as bravely, but barely looking even twelve.

And then there was Steve Spencer, who'd regained a dogged composure of his own—and whose partner had gotten them into this predicament in the first place.

"Over there," she told Steve, directing him to put Lionel into the copilot's chair before throwing herself into the pilot's seat.

Plexiglas surrounded her with a panoramic view of the land below. Flatter now, it stretched ahead in fenced pastures and farms and the outlying pockets of the valley towns.

Max's stomach dropped, and for a moment the scene before her wavered, fading into darkness.

"You can do it." Lionel's upbeat confidence annoyed her back to consciousness. "No scarier than driving a car."

Max's gaze dropped to the incomprehensible array of instruments in front of her. "Right."

"At least, not the way you drive."

She couldn't return his grin, but she took a deep breath and gingerly grabbed the handles of the… "What is this thing?"

"The yoke. That controls the altitude. The foot pedals control the rudder. You'll use them to turn."

"This is insane." Steve leaned over Max's shoulder, staring at the terrain in front of them. "A total amateur can't just land a plane."

"Back off!" Max and Lionel shouted in unison.

"Just relax," Lionel added, reaching over to touch Max's hand on the yoke. "The autopilot is taking us where we want to go. I'll call the tower and let them know we have an emergency situation, ask if they can reroute all other traffic until we land."

And make sure there's a fire truck on hand, as well as an ambulance, Max thought, forcing herself to focus on the view ahead as she listened to Lionel calmly report to the airport controllers on Treybold's radio. By the time he finished, she could watch the ground and hold the yoke without the sensation she might pass out any second.

"Pretend it's a flight simulator," Lionel said. "A video game."

"I hate video games!"

As Lionel reached over and did something to the controls, the yoke came alive in Max's hand.

Breathe. Don't clutch. Focus. Calm and smooth.

"That's right, little adjustments, just like driving a car. Try a right turn. Slow and easy."

The tool is merely the extension of your own will.

She could hear Tomas's voice in her head as clearly as Lionel's in her ear, settling her pulse, steeling her nerves as the plane shifted easily beneath her feet. Right turn. Left. Straighten attitude. Hold altitude. Watch the horizon.

Breathe.

She knew Wolfe fought for Tomas's life behind her. When Alex came forward to see what she was doing, she didn't have to look back to feel Steve take his arm and gently sit the boy beside him. She could see cars below, busy speeding to two-dimensional destinations, unaware of what was happening overhead.

She knew Lionel struggled just to sit upright, to keep his voice steady as he spoke with the airport tower and with her.

But she focused only on the airplane around her, on the clear, calm instructions from Lionel, on the airfield she'd more than half believed they'd never reach that finally came into view up ahead.

As Lionel guided her in lining up for the landing, she realized Steve had been right. This was insane. It was one thing to keep a plane flying through the air. That was what airplanes were designed to do. Taking one down to ground level and balancing it on three tiny wheels without ripping it apart in a violent somersault or careering off the end of the runway into a ditch was something completely different.

She was going to kill them all in a furious ball of fire.

"You're doing great. Now ease off on the throttle."

Ave Maria…

"Keep the nose up. That's right. You've got it."

Ora pro nobis, nunc et in hora mortis nostrae…

"Steady! Steady!"

The yoke nearly jerked out of her hand as the plane bounced on the asphalt. A wing dipped, trying to wrench the nose from her control. She wrestled it back as the wheels bounced again.

"Brakes!"

And again. And again. And…

"Whoo-hoo!"

Lionel's shout nearly brought her out of her skin as the plane skidded and jerked, all three tires firmly on the ground and slowing to an almost manageable roll.

"You did it!" Alex crowed, grabbing the seat back behind her to look out the windshield.

"You did it," Steve echoed, sounding equally thrilled, but much more surprised. "There's the ambulance waiting for us. You can roll right up to it."

Even as she brought the plane to a jerking stop and cut the engines, the EMTs were running to meet them. She heard Steve opening the rear door, heard Wolfe's voice as he explained Tomas's condition.

But it took her a long moment to release her fingers from the yoke. She turned to meet Lionel's gaze.

He grinned at her, though with the adrenaline fading, he was sagging in his seat. "You did it."

"We did it," she corrected.

His grin widened. "Does this mean you'll reconsider never letting me come on another search with you as long as I live?"

"I might." She knew she'd regret it. She already did. There were good reasons she worked alone. But she wouldn't be alive to work again at all without each of the people on that plane. "Next time, you drive."

Even the presence of her favorite orchids on every flat surface couldn't mask the faint beeping of the heart monitor, the leftover smell of boiled greens and bland gravy, the sealed window overlooking concrete and Dumpsters. Max might have found the room depressing if it hadn't been so much better than the ICU up in Santa Rosa. She had broken down and wept in that windowless, cheerless cubicle the first time she'd been allowed to visit Tomas after the operation to repair the damage Spike's bullet had done to his lung.

Fortunately, he'd been unconscious at the time. But even now, after watching him pick at his unpalatable lunch and filling him in on her latest e-mail from Alex Dantell—he'd convinced his mom to let him take karate lessons, but he was still grounded for life—Max had to fight back tears when she thought how close she'd come to losing Tomas. He still looked shockingly fragile, leaning back in the adjustable hospital bed.

"I'm sorry." She'd struggled for days with how to say the words, but they came almost without thinking.

Tomas's eyes fluttered open, his gaze meeting hers with a sharpness that belied his pallor. "Sorry?"

"This is my fault. You told me I was in over my head. That I didn't know what I was doing. That someone was going to get hurt." She found it suddenly difficult to swallow. "I never thought it would be you and Lionel. I'm so sorry."

He reached up to the bed rail to rest his hand on hers. "I told you that you didn't have a chance of thwarting a man as powerful as Darius Constantine."

"And I didn't. He got what he wanted." The sale of Atch Dantell's share of Burkhartt-Dantell was already complete.

Tomas raised an eyebrow. "Perhaps he did. But so did you. Alex is safely home with his mother. The police are conducting a manhunt for Spike and have reopened the investigation into Atchison Dantell's death. And Constantine's arsenal has been reduced by one very deadly assassin."

"I wish I could be sure of that." The Marin County Sheriff's Department had found bloodstains on the rocks where Anubis had fallen, but had been unable to locate her body. The official determination had been scattering of the remains by coyotes or wild dogs, but Max wished they'd found a body.

Tomas's pale eyes darkened as they searched hers. "Magdalena, I think I am the one who owes you an apology."

"For what? Trying to warn me?"

"No." The faintest hint of a smile crossed his face. "No, for trying to protect you from who you are. Your father raised you to be a strong, honorable person. I did my best to teach you the skills you would need to be a survivor. What right do I have to complain when I discover we succeeded?"

Max stared into his face, not quite sure she'd heard his praise, not sure at all that she deserved it.

"I've spent the past eleven years trying to protect you, but I've been warned I won't be able to do that anymore."

The tears finally stung Max's eyes. "The doctors say you'll recover just fine. It will take time and you'll have to do your physical therapy, but I can help with—"

He squeezed her hand. "I mean you have warned me. I have no right to challenge your decisions about your life. I will always offer what help I can give, but only if you ask."

A smile pulled at Max's mouth. "Even when you don't agree with my decisions?"

"I'm not dying. You won't get any deathbed concessions."

She did smile then. "Fair enough. As long as you don't expect any deathbed promises."

"Not unless this hospital food kills me."

She left Tomas's side with a promise to bring him some of Signora Molinari's lasagna for dinner. Simone was waiting for her in the hall.

Max glanced at her watch. "I thought I was supposed to meet you in Lionel's room. Is he all right?"

Simone rolled her eyes. "If you count threatening to check himself out of the hospital against doctor's orders all right, he's just fine. I told him he was more agreeable unconscious."

Considering that Simone had spent even more time

than Max at Lionel's hospital bedside, Max could only hide her smile.

Simone's heels clicked a rapid beat on the linoleum as they headed for the elevators. "You haven't been checking your messages again, have you?" She didn't bother to wait for Max's answer. "I know you're still angry, but I told him you were here. He said it was important—"

"Who did?"

But as the elevator doors opened, Max saw for herself. The hint of Steve Spencer's boyish grin, his *GQ* hair, his lime-colored silk shirt, all looked even more appealing juxtaposed against the sterile blandness of the hospital corridor.

"I'll meet you down in the lobby," Simone said, smoothly stepping past Steve into the elevator.

Barring an undignified dodge and sprint, Max guessed she'd have to wait for the next elevator. But she didn't have to like it. She crossed her arms over her chest.

"I came to apologize." Steve reached inside his smooth black jacket and offered Max a single pink rose. "I know you like orchids, but they didn't have any in the hospital shop. I had to buy a whole horrible bouquet of dying mums just to get the rose."

Max didn't want to smile. "You should have stopped while you were ahead." She took the rose, holding it to her nose. "So what are you apologizing for? Lying to me? Breaking and entering? Trying to seduce and use me?"

"For my partner turning out to be a homicidal sociopath and nearly killing us all. For breaking and entering. And I feel just as terrible about lying to you as you feel about lying to me."

He had her there, and he obviously knew it.

"And as for trying to seduce you…" His smile turned distinctly less innocent. "I'm only sorry I didn't succeed. I'm hoping I can make that up to you one of these days."

"Are they predicting a cold spell in hell?" But she could tell her words didn't have the sting she intended when he only grinned. She never was very good at holding a grudge.

"I also came to say goodbye. I've wrapped up the Dantell case, helped Yvonne to install some new security measures at her house, and I'm catching a plane back to L.A. this afternoon."

"And you've received your payment from Darius Constantine?"

"He wasn't too happy about my having an alleged murderer on my staff, but we came to an accommodation."

Max stepped around him to punch the elevator button.

"Look, I don't know why you won't give the man a chance. He was genuinely glad to see Alex returned home safely. You've got no proof he ever intended anything else."

Max shook her head. "You really think *Spike* masterminded the plot to kill Atch Dantell and take over his share of the company?"

Steve opened his mouth, then sighed. "I didn't come here to argue. I just wanted to see you before I left. And to make you a proposition."

Max managed more iciness this time. "Even purgatory is predicting steamy weather."

"A business proposition." He tilted his head to catch

her eye. "As it happens, I seem to be short a partner. I'd like you to come to L.A. and work with me."

That surprised her out of her temper. "I'm not a private investigator. I'm a reporter."

"You run Quest Research."

"Research being the operative word. People finance me to find things that are lost, not stolen." Most of the time. "More Robert Ballard than Sam Spade."

Steve grunted. "I think you'd give old Sam a run for his money. You've got the instincts. Let me take you to lunch at Zuni Café and make you an offer."

He was serious. Max remembered her thoughts in Alaska, about how they could be a good team. She'd wondered at the time if she could be a good team player. She didn't like relying on other people, didn't like watching anyone else get hurt.

After almost losing Lionel and Tomas, she liked it even less. But she had to admit, she had liked the feeling up at Treybold's ranch that she had someone to watch her back. That there were people she *could* rely on. If she had to.

The problem was, those people were Alex and Lionel and Wolfe and Tomas. Not Steve Spencer.

The elevator hushed open, and Steve followed her in.

"I like what I'm doing, writing for the *Sentinel* and my freelance work," she said. "And I like San Francisco. I'm not an L.A. kind of girl."

"It wouldn't have to be full-time." His boyish grin wasn't just a put-on, it had real charm behind it. "You could try it on a part-time basis, see what you think. Give the City of Angels a chance to grow on you. Maybe me, too."

A new challenge. A sexy boss. A new city and a new start. A boss who was a really good kisser. A place where she wasn't responsible for anyone else's safety. A boss who…didn't mind working for Darius Constantine.

"You're tempted."

She shook her head. "I belong where I am. I like the freedom to choose what I want to do, maybe even make a difference every now and then. And I have people who are counting on me."

She gave him the hint of a smile. "Maybe I can hire you freelance if I ever need some research from L.A."

"If you think you can afford me." He gave a wry smile of his own. "Business brings me to San Francisco from time to time. And when the police catch Spike, I'll have to come up for the trial. Maybe I can call in that rain check for dinner and try to change your mind."

"Maybe."

The elevator door slid open, and they stepped out into the hospital lobby.

"I'll see you around. That's a promise, Mad Max Riley."

She watched him stride for the wide front doors, his Italian leather shoes snapping smartly against the gleaming floor. Her heart wasn't sorry to see him go. She'd meant what she said about belonging where she was. Not just in her work, but with Tomas, Lionel, Simone…her *family*.

But her libido might just be a little miffed.

"Good riddance."

She turned at the laconic comment to find Davis Wolfe standing beside her, his permanently wind-ruffled hair and rumpled oxford shirt with the sleeves rolled up a striking contrast to Steve's designer chic.

"What are you doing here? I'm going to kill Simone." She glanced around, but saw no sign of her secretary's nutmeg hair in the small, high-ceilinged lobby. "Where *is* Simone?"

"I told her to go home." Wolfe placed a hand on Max's elbow, the blunt fingers warm on her skin, and started her toward the door.

"And she *left?*"

They stepped out into a gray afternoon, the high fog lending a chill to the city breeze.

"I told her we had work to do." Wolfe turned her toward the parking lot. "Grant Fowler's been breathing down my neck over that collaborative feature we promised him."

"That he forced us to promise him." The *Sentinel* had already published the facts of Court Treybold's death and his implication in Atchison Dantell's murder, as well as Wolfe's two-part series on the Dantell legacy at the Burkhartt-Dantell Media Group and the changes the company might experience under its new board.

"Fowler's salivating at the idea of getting an eyewitness, in-depth account of the events at Treybold's ranch from his two best reporters."

"His best reporters?" Max had to smile. Grant was laying it on thick.

"At least until Leticia Moon uncovers another scandal at City Hall or Chick Prentiss shoots next year's summer swim fashion preview spread."

Wolfe paused beside a '67 Buick Skylark and opened the door. "I brought my laptop. We can go to your office."

Max sighed as she slid into the car. "I could be eating oysters and Tuscan bread salad at Zuni's right now."

Wolfe cocked an eyebrow at her. "How could that possibly compare to a working lunch over take-out Chinese? Lemon chicken. On me."

"You really know how to treat a girl."

He grinned, the green in his hazel eyes flashing with wicked promise, and Max's whole body remembered that Steve Spencer was not the only one who had given her a kiss worth remembering that week. "Trust me, Riley. You're worth it."

* * * * *

Vaughn Monroe hesitated, unsure for a second, hugging the brick wall and peering into the darkness beyond. The smell of spring dampened the night air. A whip-poor-will's trill was cut off midnote with crickets playing beyond the mowed grass. Traffic far down in the valley hummed past while her heart beat shallow and fast.

Had she killed him? Or should she have tried harder?

The run uphill had been rough, guided only by the moon glowing overhead and the vapor arc lamp in the opening between buildings hunkered down in the stillness, obsidian slabs casting more shadows.

She'd trained for this, anticipated the drill inside and out. But knowing and doing were worlds apart. How many had he said? Five total? She'd counted four down. One to go.

Not bad for a deb. Take that, Stone, and stuff it up your backside.

She crouched lower, not wasting much effort on celebrating. Yet. Not while he could still be out there somewhere, waiting.

Overextended muscles cramped in her lower stomach, mimicking those in clenched fingers cradling the modified Walther PPK. She ignored everything except the space before her. She hadn't come here to fail. This time, she was going to win. Two hundred yards and she was home free. Another quick scan as she swallowed hard.

She should have made sure she'd taken him out back at the creek. Maybe it'd been enough. But the man was like Lazarus—killing him meant nothing.

She stepped forward, heard the brush of her crepe-soled boots against the gravel.

Damn!

She froze, breath stalling in her lungs, muscles quaking, sweat trickling along her lower back.

He was there. She knew it.

Waiting. Watching. Anticipating.

He wanted to stop her.

Tough. Let him want.

Nothing.

When pinpricks circled her vision, she gave in, gulping a ragged fistful of cool air. Only then did she move forward into the shadows.

Wall to her left, steel building to the right. Objective at four o'clock.

Where would she hide if she were him?

Straight in front of her. Downwind. Easier to hear movement. He'd stay south of the objective, where the darkness deepened between two buildings.

She smiled, stood and crept forward. Ten feet. Eight. *Almost there. Stay focused, no time to get cocky.* Five.

A whisper of cloth against cloth. That was all.

Too late.

She whirled. The slam of a shoulder careened along her rib cage, twisting her, rolling, her back punched against packed gravel. She couldn't inhale, couldn't move.

A knee slammed to her chest. Hand to her throat. Pressing.

He had her. And there wasn't a damn thing she could do about it.

"You're dead," he whispered, leaning so close his breath warmed her face. "Mission failed."

Lights blazed on all around them. The exercise was finished. She swallowed the defeat clogging her throat, telling herself it was physical pain but knowing she was lying.

She noted only his eyes, inches from hers.

Death promised less pain than they did.

This wasn't over. Not by a long shot.

SPECIAL EDITION™

Bound by fate, a shattered family renews
their ties—and finds a legacy of love.

Family
BUSINESS

HER
BEST-KEPT
SECRET

by Brenda Harlen

Jenny Anderson had always known
she was adopted. But a fling-turned-serious
with Hanson Media Group attorney
Richard Warren brought her closer than ever
to the truth about her past. In his arms,
would she finally find the love she's
always dreamed of?

Available in May 2006
wherever Silhouette books are sold.

BOMBSHELL™

COMING NEXT MONTH

#89 THE SPY WITH THE SILVER LINING—Wendy Rosnau
Spy Games

Chic superspy Casmir Balasi had played the game too well this time—getting love-struck master criminal Yuri Petrov to propose on bended knee…and fall into her trap. But when he escaped prison and vowed to enforce the "'til death do us part" clause of their sham marriage, all Casmir had for protection was her arrogant if irresistible bodyguard. Would her protector's secret agenda lead her into the hands of the enemy? Or into his arms?

#90 LOOK-ALIKE—Meredith Fletcher
Athena Force

Agent Elle St. John's loyalty to Russia clashed with her twin sister Sam's to America, but they were on the same team when it came to finding the truth behind their spy parents' deaths. Scouring Europe for clues—and fighting her attraction to the shadowy German helping her—Elle soon discovered a web of deceit entwining her parents, an Athena Academy blackmailer and security secrets from both twins' homelands.

#91 NO SAFE PLACE—Judy Fitzwater

When her estranged husband's dead body turned up—not once, but twice!—Elizabeth Larocca knew his dangerous secret life had caught up with him…and was about to catch up with her. So she took her grown daughter and ran. But her husband's associates were after her, men whose offers of help came across more as threats. Trusting no one, Elizabeth's only hope was to solve her husband's murder—and maybe prevent her own….

#92 INVISIBLE RECRUIT—Mary Buckham
IR-5

Jet-setter Vaughn Monroe needed a change. Why not try spying on for size? After all, her daddy was the CIA director. But it was tough joining the IR Agency, a group of covert women operatives, because her instructor mistook the debutante for dilettante. She proved him wrong—using connections to access a sinister private auction in India that other agencies couldn't infiltrate. Now, the fate of millions rested on Vaughn's next move….